Murder Cuts
the Mustard

Books by Jessica Ellicott

MURDER IN AN ENGLISH VILLAGE

MURDER FLIES THE COOP

MURDER CUTS THE MUSTARD

Published by Kensington Publishing Corporation

Murder Cuts the Mustard

Jessica Ellicott

KENSINGTON BOOKS
www.kensingtonbooks.com

KENSINGTON BOOKS are published by

Kensington Publishing Corp.
119 West 40th Street
New York, NY 10018

Library of Congress Card Catalogue Number: 2019944525

Kensington and the K logo Reg. U.S. Pat. & TM Off.

ISBN-13: 978-1-4967-1054-3
ISBN-10: 1-4967-1054-1
First Kensington Hardcover Edition: November 2019

eISBN-13: 978-1-4967-1055-0 (ebook)
eISBN-10: 1-4967-1055-X (ebook)

10 9 8 7 6 5 4 3 2 1

Printed in the United States of America

Murder Cuts the Mustard

Chapter 1

Edwina stood with her hand hovering above the door handle of the motorcar.

"Are you quite certain this is a good idea, Beryl?" she asked.

"There is no one I would trust more with my prized possession than you," Beryl said. "Besides, what's the worst that can happen?" She yanked open the passenger side door and slid across the smooth black leather seat. Edwina reluctantly eased open the driver's side door and leaned her head inside.

"I imagine that I could run us into a tree, crumple the bonnet, and permanently incapacitate us both," Edwina said. Her stomach roiled at the thought of causing an accident. The news would be all over the village by teatime.

"We are only taking it round the drive, Ed. There is very little trouble you can get us into if we confine your lesson to off the road," Beryl said, patting the seat beside her encouragingly. "Besides, imagine how smart you will look in a new driving cap."

That decided things. There were many things in life Edwina loved, but very near the top of the list was a reason to purchase a fetching new hat. Edwina tipped her head to the side, imagining a trip to the milliner. She hoisted herself gingerly behind the wheel.

"Now, you remember what we discussed during our practice run?" Beryl asked. "Keep your eyes sharp and both hands on the wheel."

"I can't help but believe there is a good deal more to it than that," Edwina said.

Beryl leaned over and patted her arm. "That's really all you need to think about for your first run round the drive."

Edwina nodded and adjusted her perfectly ordinary hat on her head. She grasped the steering wheel with two gloved hands. Within moments, and with only a few choking, sputtering false starts, Edwina managed to start the car and to begin creeping along the drive.

"I think I might be getting the hang of it," Edwina said, her voice quivering with excitement.

"Give it a little more gas," Beryl said. "Or, as you would say, petrol." Obediently, Edwina pressed a bit more firmly down upon the accelerator and moved the motorcar along the drive at a speed approximating that of a pedestrian stroll.

"How's this?" Edwina asked.

"You need to give it more gas, or it's going to stall out," Beryl said.

Edwina most assuredly did not want to go through the ordeal of getting the motorcar started up again. She stomped on the accelerator, and the car lurched forward violently. Beryl began shouting something about the clutch and perhaps the gearbox, but Edwina's attention was firmly fixed on a red squirrel that had appeared in the drive a few feet in front of her.

She felt her normally impeccable posture stiffen to a painful degree. Her head and neck seemed to have lost the ability to turn. The animal stopped and stood stock-still in the middle of the drive then reared up on its hind legs to face her. She wrenched the wheel and swerved away from the creature, careening the motorcar off the drive and into a handsome stand of beeches, for which her house was named.

The motorcar shuddered to a stop. Edwina heard a hissing noise issuing forth from somewhere under the bonnet. Through clouds of steam she watched as the squirrel raced up the side of one of the beeches and paused halfway up to chatter a vehement scolding at her. She could not bring herself to face Beryl.

She knew she had not been ready to drive any motorcar and had been even less prepared to learn on Beryl's pride and joy. She had suggested that if learning to drive were really so important, she ought to take lessons from the driving instructor at the local garage, but Beryl had insisted on providing both the vehicle and the lessons herself.

"As first lessons go, I think you did rather well," Beryl said.

"How can you say that?" Edwina asked. "Your motorcar is ruined." She turned with a heavy heart to face her friend. Beryl simply shook her head and waved one of her hands dismissively.

"I did far more damage to it crashing into the pillar at the end of the drive the day I first arrived at the Beeches last autumn. If necessary the Blackburns will have it put to rights," Beryl said.

Edwina had no desire for news of her reckless driving to make the rounds in the village. While she wished Michael and Norah Blackburn every success with their garage and driving school business, she did not relish the notion of serving as an example of why it was unwise to attempt to learn the art of motoring without their assistance.

"Must we tell them how the damage occurred?" Edwina asked. She valued honesty as much as the next person, but there were times when it did not seem necessary to tell all one knew. And Beryl was always willing to stretch the truth if it pleased her to do so.

"We shall say that urgent business called me into the house and I forgot to set the hand brake, which caused the old bus to roll into the trees whilst my back was turned," Beryl said magnanimously. "Why don't you head back into the house and fix yourself a cup of tea. I'll check the old bus over and join you soon."

Edwina nodded and extracted herself from behind the wheel. As relieved as she was to follow Beryl's suggestion, she could not help but feel her friend had hurried her away. She couldn't help but wonder if Beryl was more distressed than she wished to appear. Despite her misgivings, she hurried as quickly as her quaking legs would carry her to the back door leading into the scullery.

Beryl scrambled out of the automobile and held her breath as Edwina made a beeline for the house. After assuring that her automobile had sustained no real damage, she allowed herself to turn her full attention to the potting shed situated at the edge of the garden. Just before Edwina had yanked on the wheel, Beryl had unexpectedly spotted a figure through the shed's window. Mercifully, Edwina had been far too concerned with preserving the local wildlife to notice any irregularities herself.

The door of the shed opened, and Edwina's disreputable and elderly jobbing gardener emerged. It was not one of his scheduled days to tend out on the Beeches. Simpkins, a man never interested in doing more work than he could absolutely get away with, was unlikely to be at his place of employment for any wholesome reason.

Unless her eyes were deceiving her, it appeared that not only was Simpkins at the Beeches on the wrong date, but he was swathed in altogether the wrong sort of gear for the job. Beryl cast a glance over her shoulder, and after assuring herself that Edwina was not looking out the window, she took a few steps in his direction. Even at a distance there was no doubt about it. The man was clad in a dressing gown. She did not want to entertain a guess as to what purpose had urged him to wander out of sight around the back of the shed.

As far as she was concerned, Edwina was altogether too inclined to be hard on Simpkins. While she loved her friend, she knew that Edwina struggled with class consciousness and the role a gardener was expected to play. Simpkins seemed to delight in thwarting his employer at every possible turn. He appeared at mealtimes, eager to stick his hobnailed boots beneath her dining room table. He disagreed with her on the subject of all gardening matters, and he made a habit of interrupting when guests came to call. All in all, their relationship was a contentious one.

Beryl, on the other hand, found Simpkins to be a tonic. They shared a love of all manner of racing, card games, and high-proof spirits. He had even been instrumental in helping them to set up in business and in solving their first cases. She had done all that was in her power to shield Simpkins from Edwina's wrath whenever possible. Beryl was not eager for him to be dismissed for appearing in the garden in a state of undress.

There was only one thing for it. She would have to inform Simpkins that he had been discovered and encourage him to make himself scarce. Then she would make sure to keep Edwina occupied at the front side of the house whilst he did so. She crossed the lawn and met the elderly man as he made his way back to the front of the shed. He gave her a gap-toothed grin and raised a gnarled paw in the direction of the automobile.

"I knew you shouldn't have insisted on teaching Miss Edwina to drive," he said. "With you as her instructor, it was bound to end in tears."

"So is your history of employment with her if she finds you lurking about the property, not as dressed as you ought to be," Beryl said, trying to keep the irritation out of her voice. If there was one person in the world she felt qualified to speak on the finer points of piloting any form of conveyance, it was she. After all, Beryl was a celebrated adventuress who held a number of both land-speed and airspeed records. Simpkins's assertion was preposterous. "If you do not wish to explain what you are doing here on your day off, wearing nothing but a bathrobe, you had best do a flit."

"I was just on my way to the pub, anyway. I expect you plan to be there yourself, don't you?" he asked, casting a glance towards the house.

"I wouldn't miss it. Why don't you hurry on ahead and save me a seat. As soon as I make sure Edwina has suffered no lasting effects from our adventure, I will join you."

"I'll have them put the first round on your tab," Simpkins said with a wink before slipping back into the shed.

"Are you sure you will be all right if I leave you on your own?" Beryl asked. "I'll be gone for some time."

"I will be fine. Although, I'm still not sure it's quite nice for you to spend the afternoon at the pub," Edwina said.

"Nonsense," Beryl said. "Think of it not so much as spending time at the pub as participating in what will prove to be a historic event."

"And how do you figure that?" Edwina asked.

Edwina was not one for the pub. In fact, Beryl had just barely introduced her to the value of strong drink in the face of a crisis. She was pleased to see that her friend had proven an apt pupil on the subject of gin fizzes. But gin fizzes or no gin fizzes, Edwina was not willing to hobnob with the locals in the pub. She much preferred to imbibe in the privacy of her own home or that of those she considered her equals.

"It's the first time the results of the Derby Stakes are being broadcast on the wireless," Beryl said. "Even you have to admit that that's quite an extraordinary event and worthy of attendance."

Edwina picked up her knitting from the side table next to her favourite spot on the sofa in the parlour. Beryl marveled at the amount of knitted output Edwina could produce in any given week. For a woman with only one pair of hands, one pair of feet, and one head, she seemed to be constantly creating hats, mittens, and socks for someone. Beryl squinted at the soft woolly item emerging on Edwina's rapidly clicking needles. It appeared to be some sort of tiny pair of trousers. Beryl could not imagine spending her time in such a way.

"I prefer the wireless to be used for more wholesome pursuits, like the agricultural report or the upcoming weather," Edwina said. "I shudder to think what Marconi would think of his magnificent invention being used for such unsavory purposes."

"Having met Mr. Marconi, I assure you he would most definitely approve," Beryl said. Her travels had taken her far and wide, and she had met many interesting and famous people along the way. She didn't usually like to boast, but occasionally, she could not resist needling Edwina ever so slightly. After all, her friend was as interested as the next person in celebrities, even if she was loath to admit it.

"I expect there will be no changing your mind," Edwina said.

"None whatsoever. Are you quite certain you won't join me?" Beryl asked.

Edwina looked up from her hands and gave Beryl a withering glance. "Driving around the grounds earlier was quite enough excitement for me for one day," Edwina said. "I'm quite sure an outing to the pub to get the latest on a horse race would be the end of me. It would certainly be the end of my reputation."

"Suit yourself. But you will be glad I went if I find out that I won," Beryl said. "I rather hope the wager that I laid brings in a tidy sum."

"I thought you weren't interested in races in which you are not a contestant," Edwina said. "Besides, can't you listen to the results of the race here?" Edwina pointed her empty knitting needle at the new wireless set Beryl had purchased from the winnings of her last bet. Edwina conveniently forgot about how strenuously she disapproved of gambling when it came time to listen to something on the wireless.

"It's just a very small flutter," Beryl said. "Besides, I want to keep my hand in with Chester White. You never know when a bookie's information will come in handy."

With that, Beryl headed out of the parlour and along the corridor. As she picked up her handbag from the hall table, she was quite certain she heard the opening music to one of Edwina's own secret vices. Despite her genteel exterior and vigorous protestations to the contrary, Edwina possessed a thirst for adventure, at least so far as it extended to the realm of fiction. Many was the time Beryl had paused at the door to the parlour and eavesdropped on Edwina as she sat close by to the wireless set, listening to lurid radio programs. She smiled to herself as she let herself out the door and closed it behind her a little more loudly than was absolutely necessary. Why should Edwina not enjoy herself too?

Beryl pushed open the door of the Dove and Duck and looked around. The pub was unusually busy, and the atmosphere buzzed with excitement. Beryl squeezed through the crowd, not an easy thing to do with a figure as statuesque as her own, and stepped up to the bar. Bill Nevins, the publican and a somber man with a mustache like a push broom, gave her the nod and asked for her order.

"A largish whisky, please, Bill," Beryl said as she glanced about, looking to see if her favourite table was available. She was not at all surprised to see Simpkins in possession of it. He could frequently be found at the pub and had taken to occupying the table she preferred. Beryl was not sure if he liked being seen with a celebrity or if he thought her a soft touch where paying for drinks was concerned. It was even possible he enjoyed her company as much as she did his.

She hoped to catch his eye to offer him another round, but his head was tipped towards another man, who was also seated at the table. The second man was significantly younger, with dark hair and a slightly disheveled appearance. Even from a distance, the conversation between the two did not look to be a pleasant one. She called for the publican again and ordered a second whisky for Simpkins. She could not imagine the old reprobate would deign to refuse it.

Bill nodded, poured out a generous measure, and slid the glasses along the bar without a word. If Beryl had to guess, she would say the popularity of the Dove and Duck had a great deal to do with the owner's ability to keep quiet about all that he saw. In the months she'd spent in Walmsley Parva, she'd barely heard more than a sentence at a time pass the man's lips. Although it was possible he had a great deal to say but that the sound of his voice rarely made it past the barrier of his facial hair.

She started a tab and made her way towards a table near the edge of the room. Beryl always liked to sit where she could keep her back to the wall and her eye on the exit. One never knew when hostilities would break out in an unfamiliar environment. Not that the pub was unfamiliar, mind you, but it was a habit of long practice, and she did not feel comfortable giving it up.

Her travels across the globe had taught her that the most powerful position in the room was a place where one could watch everyone else. As she traversed the smoky low-ceiling space, patrons seated at several tables closer to the center of the room invited her to join them, but she shook her head firmly and continued on. As she approached, Simpkins abruptly shoved back his chair and towered over the second man. He made a fist and shook it in the other man's face.

"Say that again and you won't live to say it a second time," Simpkins shouted.

The voices in the pub fell silent as heads turned to stare at Simpkins. Beryl could feel the anger pulsing between the two men like a live thing. The second man grabbed his pint of beer and stood. He shrugged and gave a little laugh before turning slightly to make sure he could be overheard.

"You must be going soft in the head if you think you could inflict any damage on me. Stick to what you know, old man," he said, pointing at Simpkins's nearly empty glass. He turned his back and strode across the room to the bar.

"Who the devil was that?" Beryl asked, handing Simpkins the drink she had brought him before taking a seat.

"No one," Simpkins said. He lowered himself into his chair and sent a blistering scowl towards the younger man's back.

"Come now, Simpkins, from what little I heard of your conversation, I assume that you at least know his name," Beryl said.

"More's the pity," Simpkins said. "Aye, you could say that he and I have an acquaintance of long standing." Simpkins leaned back in his chair and took a long tug on his whisky.

"I confess, Simpkins, I'm surprised to hear you speak of anyone derisively. You're usually such an affable fellow," Beryl said. "Do tell."

"I'm very sorry to say that man is my brother-in-law Hector Lomax," Simpkins said.

"That's Hector?" Beryl said. She had heard of Hector Lomax from other people in the village. She even knew that Hector and Simpkins shared a cottage on the outskirts of Walmsley Parva. But what she did not know was that they had had a falling-out.

"I thought you were quite close to your wife's brother," Beryl said. "Has something happened to cause a rift?"

"You could say that," Simpkins said.

Before she could ask for the cause of the familial discord, the publican called for everyone to quiet down. He turned up the wireless, and the results of the Derby were dutifully read aloud.

"Have you made a killing?" Beryl asked Simpkins when the results were in.

"I believe I've made a tidy sum, but I am content to wait here until some people have cleared off before I collect my winnings," Simpkins said. He lifted a knobby finger towards a table in front of them, where Chester White, the local bookie, held court at the center of the room. Men of all types clambered around Chester's table. Chester sat facing the door, with a well-worn leather ledger spread out before him. One by one, men approached the table to check on their winnings. With no concern for the queue, Hector muscled his way to the head of the line. The pub seemed to hold its collective breath as Chester ran his finger down a column in his ledger.

"Better luck next time, Hector," Chester said.

"I followed your advice, and look where it got me," Hector said.

"You know I never hand out advice, at least not where betting is concerned," Chester said. "Your bets are your own responsibility."

"I don't know how you live with yourself, taking money from an honest workingman like me," Hector said.

"No one is forcing you to place a bet," Chester said. "Everyone here knows how this works, and with the number of bets you place, you know better than most." Chester leaned back and looked behind Hector. He motioned for the next person in line to step up to the table. A bearded man with a limp, whom Beryl knew to be Frank Prentice, moved up next to Hector. Hector turned to him and gave him a sour look.

"Everyone also knows you aren't exactly an honest workingman either," the bearded man said.

"What's that supposed to mean?" Hector asked.

"It means exactly what it sounds like. You aren't above spreading lies to get what you want," the man said.

Beryl thought she detected a slight wobble in Frank's gait. Not that she was surprised. Frank was known to have trouble with drink. It was an all-too-common state of affairs and one she attributed to memories of the Great War. Frank was said to drink up the grocery money, but she had never heard he was at all violent. She had made a point of asking around about him after having formed an unexpected attachment to his young son Jack, the paperboy. If she had caught wind of Frank laying a hand on that likable child, she would have made quick work of sorting him out one way or another.

Although she could not blame him for seeking solace in the bottom of a bottle, as so many others had done in the years since the war began, there was no denying that men like Frank were just the sort the temperance movement had used as examples to convince Congress to pass the Eighteenth Amendment, enacting Prohibition. And while Frank was English rather than American, it was not stretching the facts to say men just like him back home were Beryl's reason for seeking sanctuary in Great Britain until what she considered America's collective madness was repealed.

Frank reached out and placed a hand on Hector's back. In the blink of an eye, Hector batted away Frank's hand and sent him sprawling onto the floor. All the men in the line took a step back and looked away from Frank except for one. She saw several different men elbowing each other or furtively lifting a finger and pointing in Hector's direction as a bald man with round cheeks leaned over and helped Frank to his feet with one powerful tug of his hand.

"Up to your old tricks, then, are you, Hector?" the bald man said. "Knocking a man down without warning." He crossed his bulging arms over his broad chest and glared at Hector.

"Do you want to have a go at me too?" Hector said. "We can take it outside as soon as you say."

"I've a mind to finish my drink, but I may just take you up on that once I've collected my winnings. Unlike you, I know how to back a winner." The bald man turned his back on Hector and bent over Chester's ledger.

Beryl kept her eyes moving over the scene in front of her. There was something in the room she didn't like. She had met more men like Hector than she cared to remember, and they brought trouble with them wherever they went as surely as Edwina brought her knitting.

Sure enough Hector reached for a chair. He managed to lift it as high as his waist before Bill, the publican, made it out from behind the bar.

"Out," he shouted. "And you too." He raised a finger and pointed it at Frank and the bald man.

Hector turned and gave Simpkins a smile before heading out the door. Frank followed on his heels, and the bald man trailed after once he had concluded his business with the bookie. Even Simpkins seemed to have lost interest in his drink. To Beryl's absolute astonishment, he shoved away his half-filled glass, stood, and shuffled out the door without stopping to collect his winnings.

She would not have believed it unless she had seen it with her own eyes. But there was no sense in letting good whisky go to waste. She finished off the contents of his glass. After all, considering the winner of the Derby, she had cause to celebrate.

Chapter 2

Beryl, as was her habit, was still asleep when Edwina heard the relentless pounding on the front door. Ever since Beryl had moved into the house several months earlier, Edwina had come to value her own lifelong habit of rising early. Back in the autumn she had been desperate for some company, her loneliness a burden almost as crushing as her financial woes.

But even though she found Beryl's companionship the most agreeable she had enjoyed in all her years, she still valued a small measure of solitude on a daily basis. Beryl never made plans before midmorning if she could help it and often lolled about in her dressing gown until the middle of the afternoon if she had no pressing engagements.

As a result, Edwina had developed a morning routine that balanced her need for companionship with her desire to do as she saw fit without input from anyone else. Edwina needed at least a few hours each day when she wasn't attempting to ward of some outlandish suggestion or another. While it was true that life with Beryl had proven exhilarating, there was only so much excitement a body could take without a few restorative moments to potter about the garden, read the newspapers, or even simply stare up at the ceiling.

She had just settled in to read the *Walmsley Parva Echo* at the kitchen table, with two slices of hot buttered toast and a cup of tea, when Crumpet sprang from his basket, dashed out of the kitchen and down the front hallway. Edwina gave her plate of toast a longing glance, then followed her little terrier to the sound of the knocking. She smoothed her hair and cast a quick glance in the hall tree mirror as she passed.

Edwina believed in being prepared for whatever the day might hold, and to her that meant properly dressing before leaving one's bedroom. Although it was just before eight in the morning, she felt sufficiently presentable to receive a visitor despite the earliness of the hour. Edwina pursed her lips. It was simply not done to pay calls at this time of day. Whatever would her mother have said?

She coaxed Crumpet away from the door and pulled it open with a firm tug. Although her financial position had improved since Beryl's arrival, she still did not have the necessary capital to make improvements to her beloved ancestral home. The doors that opened under protest, the patches of damp creeping along the ceilings, and the puffs of smoke backing out of the chimney continued to plague her. But perhaps one day she and Beryl would have sufficient clientele from the proceeds of their private enquiry agency to warrant spending the money on the long overdue repairs.

Although it could rightly be said that Edwina would not have welcomed any visitors so early in the day, she was even more displeased to see Constable Gibbs standing on her front step, an official scowl stamped upon her face. Her heart hammered in her chest as she considered the possibility that the constable wished to question her over the incident with the motorcar. Had she committed a crime by motoring around the property without being in possession of a driver registration?

"I know he's here, so don't bother denying it," Constable Gibbs said. She took a step forward, as though she would enter the Beeches without an invitation. Without thinking of the way it would appear, Edwina placed one of her small hands on the doorjamb and created a barrier. Really, she thought to herself, Beryl's shocking influence was having an effect on her.

"To whom are you referring?" Edwina asked.

Clearly, the constable was not there to discuss illegal piloting of the motorcar. Suddenly, an even more horrifying thought flitted through her mind. She had not seen Beryl return from the pub the evening before. Was it possible that Beryl had not come home unaccompanied? Was there any possibility that the snoring Edwina had heard coming from Beryl's bedroom had not belonged to her friend?

While she did not like to entertain such spurious notions, the truth was that Beryl was not the most conventional of women. And her interest in and attraction for the opposite sex were legendary. Her string of ex-husbands alone brought a blush to Edwina's cheeks whenever she considered the sheer number of them. It simply did not do to consider it.

"Simpkins, of course." Constable Gibbs adjusted her uniform cap and deepened her scowl. "I need to speak to him immediately."

Edwina swallowed dryly. As much as her upbringing did not allow her to approve of entertaining assorted gentlemen in one's bedchamber, the idea that the man in question might be her own employee did not bear thinking about. For a moment, Constable Gibbs's face seemed to fade out of focus, and the world went a bit swimmy. Edwina heard the blood swishing in her ears and felt her stomach grow cold.

A thing like this would be impossible to live down. She could just hear Prudence Rathbone, the local postmistress and sweetshop owner, crowing about Beryl's escapades to every person in Walmsley Parva who came in to purchase a postage stamp or a pound of Turkish Delight. There was nothing for it. She would have to sell up and immigrate to New Zealand. Crumpet, sensibly, commenced to growl. His resolve snapped Edwina from her dark thoughts.

"Simpkins? Here? I assure you that you are mistaken," Edwina said. She stood up a little straighter and looked Constable Gibbs directly in the eye. Surely, her suspicions about Beryl and Simpkins represented a brief flight of unbridled and sordid imagination. She really did need to stop reading so many crime novels. It made her unduly suspicious of everyone.

"I have it on good authority that Simpkins has been living here," Constable Gibbs said.

At that, Edwina felt herself well and truly rally. Beryl might have committed indiscretions and even shown an occasional lack of judgment. She might have even returned home from the pub the night before slightly squiffy, but she certainly would not have moved Simpkins into the Beeches without at least talking it over with Edwina first.

"Whose authority is it that you have it on exactly?" Edwina said. "Simpkins is a jobbing gardener, as well you know. He does not live here on the property, as the gardeners did in my grandfather's day. Besides, today is not his day to work, not that he does much work, anyway."

"Half the village informed me that he has been living in your potting shed for the past several days," Constable Gibbs said. Edwina was so stunned that she took a step backwards, as if to ward off the police officer's words. Constable Gibbs took this as an invitation and shouldered past Edwina and proceeded down along the hall. Crumpet commenced to bark ferociously once more. He advanced upon Constable Gibbs and clamped down loyally on the back of her sensible leather boot.

Suddenly, Beryl appeared at the top of the stairs. Her dressing gown flowed out behind her, and an eye mask perched on her forehead. Edwina looked up and felt inordinately pleased to find Beryl was alone.

"What is all the ruckus?" Beryl said. "I had rather a long night of it and have yet to catch my forty winks."

Beryl often claimed never to suffer the ill effects of over-indulgence, but Edwina did not agree. While she had yet to notice Beryl complaining of a headache or a sensitivity to noise after an evening bent on merrymaking, she could say without equivocation that excess drink made Beryl snore.

"Constable Gibbs claims that Simpkins has been living in the potting shed. Did you know about this?" Edwina asked. She felt her hands sneaking up to her hips, a vulgar stance but an effective one. From the way Beryl snapped her mouth shut, Edwina realized with discomfort that there was truth to the constable's claim. "You did know, didn't you?"

Beryl nodded unapologetically as she sauntered down the stairs. "I knew I had seen him rather less dressed than he ought to have been yesterday morning, when we were having our driving lesson. I knew it would upset you terribly, so I didn't point it out," Beryl said.

"You'd best call off your dog before I'm forced to have him put down as a vicious creature," Constable Gibbs said, shaking her leg with considerable force.

Edwina swooped forward and gathered up Crumpet into her arms. With her head held high, and without a backward glance either for the police officer or for her friend, she led the way through the kitchen and out the scullery door. The morning dew soaked her shoes as she crossed the velvety green lawn. The charming twitter of songbirds refused to gladden her heart as she approached her potting shed.

It had been on her mind for some time to relieve Simpkins of his duties. Not that it would be much of a relief, considering he was hardly burdened by them. The man spent far more time with his hobnailed boots stretched out under her kitchen table, guzzling countless cups of tea, than he did pruning roses or double digging the vegetable beds. This was one outrage too far.

She reached out and depressed the latch on the potting shed

door, flung it forward, and stepped inside. There, curled up on a bedroll consisting of burlap sacks and a grubby counterpane, lay her elderly gardener. A shaft of light passed through the door, over her shoulder, and onto Simpkins's stubble-covered face. He blinked twice, then creaked up into a seated position. Edwina was horrified to discover, as the counterpane slid away from his torso, that Simpkins did not bother himself with pajamas.

"Please make yourself presentable. Then join me in the garden. Constable Gibbs requires a word," Edwina said, then withdrew from the shed and pulled the door firmly shut behind her.

It seemed an effort to remember to breathe. She was not sure with whom she felt most angry. The constable, for bringing her news of public humiliation; Beryl, for keeping secrets from her; or Simpkins himself, for abusing her trust in such a flagrant manner. Crumpet let out a slight squeak, and she realized that she had been squeezing him rather too tightly. Refusing to make eye contact with either of the other two women, she bent forward and gently placed her dog on the crazy paving path in front of her. She felt rather than saw Beryl attempting to attract her attention. She kept her eyes firmly fixed on a prized Fothergilla bush that was putting on a quantity of new growth.

Behind her she heard the door of the potting shed opening once more. She spun around to face her errant employee. Before she could open her mouth to question his presence, Constable Gibbs stepped forward and shook her beefy finger in his face.

"Albert Simpkins, I am here to question you in the murder of your brother-in-law Hector Lomax," she said.

Chapter 3

Beryl had had an uneasy feeling something like that might happen. After all, the scene in the Dove and Duck the evening before had not boded well. And while she was not entirely shocked to hear that Hector had come to a very bad end, from the look on his face, it was clear that Simpkins was stunned.

"Hector's dead?" he said in a quavering voice. His usually tanned complexion had instantly gone the color of cold breakfast porridge. And although Edwina had built up quite a head of steam, and rightly so, even she seemed to have deflated visibly.

"Bashed over the head and found in the churchyard, dead as a doornail," Constable Gibbs said. "What I want to know is, where were you when it happened?" The constable pulled a notepad from her uniform jacket pocket and pried a pencil from behind her ear. Beryl could not help but note the similarity between the constable's writing implements and the ones that Edwina had taken to using for their investigations. It seemed they were having an influence on the constable, whether she herself realized it or not.

"Why would you want to know where I was?" Simpkins said.

"Because you are the prime suspect in his murder," Constable Gibbs said. "You don't deny that you have been on the outs with him of late, do you?"

"Hector and I have never rubbed along all that well. Everyone knows that," Simpkins said. "But I certainly wouldn't have wished him to end up coming to harm." The old man sagged back against the doorjamb of the potting shed, as if he needed its sturdy frame to support him. Beryl wondered if he was headed for a collapse. But in her experience, old geezers tended to weather storms much better than the newer models. After all, they'd seen so many of them before.

"Not getting along is one thing. You were witnessed shouting at him and threatening him with physical violence not long before he was murdered," Constable Gibbs said.

Beryl felt her heart sink. She knew the scene in the pub had attracted a great deal of attention.

"Are you talking about our row at the Dove and Duck yesterday evening?" Simpkins asked. "We always spoke to each other like that."

"Not in my family, we don't. And when someone ends up dead within hours of a public display of animosity, a thing like that has to be taken seriously," Constable Gibbs said.

"You surely can't believe that Simpkins had anything to do with his brother-in-law's death," Edwina said.

Beryl was glad to see Edwina had recovered some of her voice. Simpkins glanced over at her, and Beryl noticed he straightened away from the doorjamb. While Edwina was someone who was very conscious of social norms and one's place in society, she was also exceptionally loyal. Simpkins spending the night in her shed without her leave was one thing. Besmirching his reputation and accusing him of murder were entirely another. If Beryl had to choose one person to have her back in a fight, it would be her mild-mannered, diminutive friend.

"I don't have to explain myself to any of you," Constable

Gibbs said. "Albert Simpkins, I ask you again, please describe your movements after leaving the pub last night." She held her pencil above the pad of paper as she waited for him to speak.

Simpkins looked over at Edwina as if to ask what he should do.

"Unless you have something to hide, Simpkins, and I'm sure you don't, it would be best to tell the constable what she wants to know and to send her on her way," Edwina said.

He nodded and cleared his throat. Beryl watched as his prominent Adam's apple bobbed beneath the greying stubble on his neck. If he had been camping out in the potting shed, it explained why his appearance had become even scruffier of late. She doubted very much he had brought his shaving kit with him.

"It's true that I left the pub rather earlier than I had planned last night," Simpkins said. "I was just too riled up by seeing Hector to want to stay."

"Witnesses describe an argument between the two of you, and they also reported that you left the pub not long after Hector."

"I did leave right after Hector did, but I didn't see him again," Simpkins said.

"We only have your word for that, though, don't we?" Constable Gibbs said. "Witnesses also said that you left the pub without bothering to collect your winnings. That doesn't sound like you, now does it?"

"I wasn't worried about Chester refusing to give them to me another day," Simpkins said. "And I just had my pay packet from Miss Edwina, so I wasn't feeling a pinch in my pocket."

"But you did follow him out of the pub, didn't you?" Constable Gibbs said.

"He left the pub, and then I left the pub. That doesn't mean I followed him. I already told you I didn't see him again," Simpkins said.

"Where exactly did you go?" Constable Gibbs said.

"I walked up the high street, then along the lane that heads for the Beeches. I'm sure somebody saw me. It was light out-side still, and there were plenty of people about," Simpkins said.

"Just the fact that they saw you does not mean that you didn't double back and cosh him over the head," the constable said. "I think I'm going to take you down to the station for a more formal questioning."

Simpkins sagged back against the doorframe once more. Edwina stepped closer to him and faced the constable.

"Hector Lomax has been a thorn in the side of the entire village for years. He's a lazy, no-good lout, and frankly, I'm surprised that no one has done away with him before now," Edwina said. "Do your witnesses have anything to say about him bothering anyone else in the pub that night?"

"They ought to," Beryl said. "He argued with a bald man, with Chester White, and even with Frank Prentice."

"Have you questioned any of them yet?" Edwina asked.

"Simpkins was first on my list," Constable Gibbs said. "As soon as the murder was reported, I headed here straightaway."

"And what made you decide that Simpkins was the first one to question?" Edwina said.

"Well, for one, the vicar was the one who reported the body. When he telephoned the station, he said that he saw Simpkins arguing with his brother-in-law in the pub and that the quarrel had turned violent," the constable said.

"Was there anything else?" Edwina said. "After all, as Beryl said, there were several people heard arguing with Hector not long before you say he died."

"Simpkins is likely to inherit the property where he lived with Hector upon Hector's death. If that's not a decent motive for murder, I don't know what is," the constable said.

Edwina looked over at Simpkins. "Simpkins, why have you taken up residence in my potting shed?" she asked.

"It's like this, miss. Hector and I had a disagreement over some property," he said.

The constable scribbled furiously in her notebook.

"Just as I suspected. A property dispute," she said. Beryl noted a touch of glee in the constable's voice.

"The property had been in the family for several generations. After Hector's older brother died, Hector seemed determined to let the place fall to wrack and ruin," Simpkins said. "It just broke my heart to see it that way. The old place had meant so much to my Bess and the rest of the family." Beryl thought she saw moisture gathering in the old man's eyes. He was a sentimental old cuss, there was no denying it.

"So that's why you killed him? So that you could run the property your own way?" Constable Gibbs said. "Seems like an open-and-shut case to me." To emphasize her point, the constable snapped her notebook shut and jammed her pencil back behind her ear.

"I did nothing of the sort. I told Hector he was lazy and always looking for an easy way out of any manner of work. I told him if he didn't know how to run the property, he could always ask me for help. After all, if there's one thing I know how to do, it is to make plants grow," Simpkins said.

Beryl couldn't swear to it, but she thought she heard Edwina stifle a guffaw.

"So you claim that you were offering assistance to your brother-in-law when you threatened him with violence at the pub," Constable Gibbs said.

"No. I offered him assistance over the course of the past several weeks, as I watched the plants on the property languish. At the pub I couldn't stand the sight of him, because he wouldn't take me up on my offer or listen to any advice before it was too late. If he kept on the way he was going, this year's harvest would be lost," Simpkins said. He shrugged his bony shoulders, as if to ask what anyone could do when confronted with such an overwhelming display of stubborn stupidity.

"Is that why you turned up here and took up residence in the potting shed?" Edwina asked.

Simpkins nodded slowly. If she had to guess, Beryl would have said that Edwina was coaching him. While the two of them had a contentious relationship, it was one of long standing, and she had noticed that they were able to read each other's moods almost like family.

"That's right, miss. I just couldn't stand to be Johnny-on-the-spot anymore. Watching those poor plants cry out to me was doing me in. I tossed a few things in a rucksack and came here, seeking shelter, two nights ago," Simpkins said.

"So you admit that it was a bad enough argument to drive you from your comfortable home," Constable Gibbs said.

Beryl wondered how Simpkins was going to refute that. Constable Gibbs had been known to arrest suspects on far less evidence than what she had in this case.

"Simpkins, how would you say the conditions in the potting shed compare with those at the cottage you share with Hector?" Edwina said.

"Well, not to cast a bad light on your hospitality, miss, but I can't say it stacks up all that well. After all, at the cottage I have a large bed with a soft mattress. In there, I bedded down on top of some burlap grain sacks." Simpkins glanced over his shoulder at the shed behind him.

"Don't you have rheumatism?" Edwina said. Beryl knew that Edwina did not believe the old man had rheumatism but that he simply used it as an excuse to work at a slower pace. She wondered where her friend was going with this line of questioning.

"Dreadful, 'tis," Simpkins said. "The hard floor did me no good whatsoever. You notice how long it took me to come out the door this morning. That's on account of the stiffness in my joints and how difficult it was to get up off the ground."

Beryl noticed a deep raspberry-colored flush crawling up the back of Edwina's neck. She was quite certain that her friend had seen more of Simpkins in the potting shed than she could ever forget. Edwina only flushed when she found a situation deeply uncomfortable. It was one of the ways that Beryl knew how strong Edwina's hand of cards was when they were playing bridge. It was a certain enough tell that she had not encouraged her friend to learn to play poker. Any cardsharp worth the name would gobble Edwina up within a couple of hands.

"I don't see how you could possibly think that Simpkins here could be responsible," Edwina said, turning to Constable Gibbs.

"And what makes you so sure of that?" Constable Gibbs said.

"If Simpkins had bashed Hector over the head and killed him, he would have known that there would be no reason to keep him from heading back to the cottage and sleeping in his own comfortable bed for the night," Edwina said. "I suggest that you go and interview your other suspects and leave Simpkins alone until you have better evidence to stand on."

"This doesn't prove anything," Constable Gibbs said. "If I don't find that someone else has a stronger motive or a weaker alibi, I'll be back for you." With that, she hurried down the garden path and around the side of the Beeches.

Beryl realized she was holding her breath, waiting for Edwina to give Simpkins a piece of her mind. She exhaled slowly and attempted to turn the conversation in a less unnerving direction.

"What an invigorating way to start the day," Beryl said. "I don't suppose there's any truth to the constable's accusation, now is there?"

"Of course there isn't," Edwina said. "Simpkins, I suggest you pack up your things and then come into the house for some breakfast. Unless I miss my guess, it's going to be quite a long day. We've put the constable off for now, but it won't be long before she returns with more impertinent questions. I shan't wish to face them on an empty stomach, and I don't suppose the two of you will either."

"You haven't got a bit of bacon on the go, have you?" Simpkins said.

Beryl knew what he was driving at. There was nothing like a full English breakfast, complete with bacon, eggs, and grilled tomatoes, to sop up a night of excessive drinking. While Simpkins had lighted out of the pub far earlier than she would have expected, Beryl doubted that had slowed his tippling. Many was the occasion Beryl had shared a flask with Simpkins in the potting shed when Edwina was not paying any attention. She expected he had gone straight to the shed and set about making up for lost time.

"Toast and eggs will have to do. We have to get you back to your cottage and get you cleaned up," Edwina said.

Chapter 4

Edwina looked with remorse at her cold toast, with its extortionately priced butter scraped across its surface now congealed into miniature hillocks. She collected her plate and took it back into the garden and tossed its contents out for the birds. If she was going to go to the bother of making breakfast for Simpkins, she certainly could do with a fresh plate for herself.

Simpkins sat stunned at the kitchen table, his customary hobnailed boots shedding great clods of cut grass on the stone-flag floor beneath his feet. Beryl, knowing how little use she was in the kitchen, sat beside him and now and again patted his hand. Edwina set about making breakfast. Pulling crockery down from the cupboards and setting the kettle to boil gave her mind the freedom to sort through what had just taken place.

Hector Lomax was not someone with whom she would have chosen to associate. His reputation was that of a braggart and a man who, if hired for a job, was inclined to loaf. Rumors around the village had it that he had indeed allowed the family farm to go to wrack and ruin just as soon as his brother was in the ground.

It was widely viewed as a terrible shame. The Lomax farm had been in the family for several generations. They had taken advantage of the thriving small-fruit market that was such a part of the Kentish countryside. Fields had been planted out to berries and currant bushes. They had even tried their hands at a few acres of grapevines. The elder Lomaxes had built their business up from a small market garden to a sizable concern that supplied fruits to the preserves manufacturers.

With Kent's relative nearness to London and to reliable transport by train, the fertile lands all around the district were valued for their produce. By the time Hector's older brother, Donald, had taken over, the business was thriving. Even during the war years, somehow they managed to keep it going.

But Hector had not shared his brother, Donald's passion for the family business or hard work. He had only shown a passion for other people's wives. And for gaming and strong drink. His mismanagement and lack of attention to the everyday responsibilities of a farm had been much talked about by the residents of Walmsley Parva. Edwina would not have been surprised if the ghost of one of his forefathers had risen up out of its grave and coshed the arrogant laggard over the back of his head with an otherworldly shovel.

Still, it did no good to say such things to Simpkins. By all accounts, Simpkins's late wife, Bess, had adored her younger brother despite his faults and had insisted on remaining in her childhood home even after her marriage in order to keep an eye on him. Once Bess had died, Simpkins had continued to rattle around the cottage with Bess's two brothers. Donald's demise the year before had left no one to serve as a buffer between the two other men.

Simpkins had never claimed to share his wife's affection for Hector and, indeed, had often mentioned that he found it difficult to tolerate the younger man. Still, from the look on his face, it had clearly come as a shock to hear that Hector had been murdered. Well, of course it had. Edwina felt quite shocked herself.

Edwina cracked six eggs into a cast-iron skillet sizzling with a dollop of bacon fat. She flipped them expertly and then liberally salted and peppered them before sliding them onto three plates. She pulled fresh pieces of toast from beneath the grill and slathered them with butter. This was no time to be concerned about the rationing or the housekeeping budget. Truly, Simpkins looked as though he might slide right off the chair and under the table.

Beryl got to her feet and helped to carry the plates of food to the table. From the way she tiptoed about so uncharacteristically, Edwina was quite certain Beryl was heartily ashamed of herself for not informing Edwina of Simpkins's presence in the potting shed.

Simpkins simply stared at the plate placed in front of him, his egg yolks growing firmer as they chilled. Edwina reached out and tapped on the plate in front of him.

"You must eat something," she said. "I've already wasted a plate of toast on account of Constable Gibbs's visit. I don't intend to waste any eggs this morning too."

He bobbed his chin and lifted his fork, clutching his fist around it with all the grace of a caveman. Edwina averted her eyes.

From the way Beryl kept sneaking glances at him, Edwina could see that Beryl was as concerned about Simpkins as she herself was. Beryl arched an eyebrow, and Edwina knew her friend had thought of something distracting to chat about. Her next words confirmed it. Beryl was trying to draw Simpkins away from his distressing thoughts.

"I've been thinking, Ed, about starting a new project," Beryl said. "Something entirely different and, if I do say so myself, quite timely."

Edwina hoped that Beryl's idea of something different was learning how to make her own bed. While her friend had many admirable skills, simple housekeeping duties were not amongst them. As she noticed a flush of excitement on Beryl's cheeks,

Edwina felt her hopes fade and felt a knot grow in her stomach. Every time Beryl got a new notion, it tended to make Edwina quite queasy.

"I've decided to write a book," Beryl announced.

"A book?" Edwina said. This was an entirely unexpected turn of events. Even Simpkins seemed to snap out of his malaise and turned to face her with bits of toast crumbs adhered to his stubbly chin.

"Yes, a book, which I am eminently qualified to write," Beryl said.

She took a maddeningly long sip of her coffee. Edwina could see that Beryl was trying to hide a grimace as the flavor of the brew registered on her palate. Try as she might, Edwina could not get the hang of brewing a cup of coffee. She knew she was failing at it utterly, but she did not dare risk Beryl taking over any of the culinary duties.

Her friend had nearly ruined every piece of cooking equipment she had touched. Beryl claimed that the best coffee was made over a campfire and involved a sock and an egg white. With claims like that, there was no way Edwina could take her seriously or allow her anywhere near the cooker. Still, it did hurt one's pride to see such a grimace when one's offerings were imbibed.

"It's not a cookery book, is it?" Simpkins asked. From the slightly jocular tone of his voice, Edwina realized that Simpkins was going to be right as rain before much more time had passed. That is, as long as Constable Gibbs did not actually arrest him for murder. Edwina could not bear to think how her reputation would suffer if not only her jobbing gardener was correctly rumored to have been living in her potting shed, but the fact that she had been harboring a murderer as well.

"Certainly not," Beryl said. "Although I have a few things to say about food in the book I have planned. I've decided to write a lady's guide to adventure travel." Beryl took a crashing bite of toast and chewed it with gusto.

"While I agree you know plenty on the subject of travel, I daresay you know very little about the practicalities of writing a book," Edwina said.

"How difficult can it be?" Beryl asked. "The way the world is filling up with books, it seems every Tom, Dick, Harry and their uncles are writing them. I see no reason why I shouldn't toss my hat in the ring. Do you?"

"I can think of two reasons," Edwina said.

She looked over at Simpkins, who seemed to share her skepticism. He sensibly flicked his eyes back to his plate and began dunking pieces of toast into the oozing yolks of his eggs. Watching Simpkins eat was one of the more harrowing aspects of Edwina's life. Which, she supposed, was why Beryl was more qualified to write a book on adventure travel than she would ever be.

"Which are?" Beryl asked. Edwina thought she detected the smallest hint of pique in Beryl's tone of voice. Her friend was not easily offended, but she did not like for anyone to dampen her enthusiasms. Truth be told, Edwina spent much of her time feeling like a wet blanket.

"Well, for one thing, one has to sit still and stay put long enough to write a book. You have a great deal of ability for moving about and going on adventures. Sitting still is not amongst your strengths," Edwina said.

"I'm sure I could get the hang of it. After all, I'm sitting right now, aren't I?" Beryl said. Edwina did not point out that Beryl fidgeted and shifted even as she spoke. "What's your other objection?"

"I believe in order to be someone who is capable of writing a book, you have to be the sort of person who frequently reads them," Edwina said.

"I shouldn't think that was true," Beryl said. "If you can read a book, you should very well be able to write one."

"I, for one, look forward to reading whatever you come up with," Simpkins said with guarded enthusiasm.

Edwina should have known that he would take Beryl's part in any disagreements. He so often did, as the two of them were birds of a feather in so many ways.

"I still think you ought to have some sort of experience before you set off on a project like that. How about writing a poem or a short story? Maybe an article for the newspaper," Edwina suggested.

"We had absolutely no experience in running a private enquiry agency before we set out to do that," Beryl said. "And look how successful that has become. If one waits until one is ready, one will never try anything new."

With that, Beryl wiped the last bit of egg from her plate with her piece of toast and popped it into her mouth. Then she pushed back her chair and headed off down the hall, humming a little tune under her breath.

Chapter 5

The Lomax farm must have been a pretty piece of property at one time, Beryl thought as she looked about. The low stone cottage, with its white trim, surrounded by rolling fields of plantings dotted here and there by gnarled apple and pear trees presented a bucolic picture. However, as they stopped in front of the cottage, she could see signs that the property was more run down than it first appeared. Upon closer inspection, it was easy to see that the paint was peeling from the windowsills and the doors. A few slates from the roof had come loose, and weeds choked the plantings on either side of the walkway leading to the door.

Simpkins led the way and pushed open the door with a hesitant hand. Beryl wondered at the cause of his trepidation. Did he expect Hector's ghost to be wandering the halls? Or was he more concerned that there had been some mistake and his brother-in-law had not really passed on to his eternal judgment? She looked over at Edwina, who wore a troubled look on her face. Edwina hurried after Simpkins, leaving Beryl to bring up the rear. The elderly gardener shuffled into the kitchen. Even

Beryl, with her limited housekeeping skills and even lesser amounts of house pride, was surprised at the mess.

Crockery was piled in the slate sink, and several cooking pots littered the surface of the cooker. Windrows of dust clung to the skirting boards, and one would have needed rather more courage than even Beryl felt she possessed to clear off the kitchen table sufficiently to sit down for a meal. She heard Edwina exhaling with the whistling sort of a noise that indicated extreme displeasure.

Simpkins simply stood in the center of the room with his shoulders slumped. Edwina uncharacteristically took him by the arm and carefully guided him towards the adjoining room. Beryl followed as they entered the parlour. Edwina gently pressed Simpkins onto the couch, then crossed the room and firmly tugged open the draperies. Light spilled into the low-ceilinged room, and Beryl could see that it had once been a cheerful and pleasant place to pass an evening.

It was no wonder Simpkins was so fond of spirits. It was clear the heart had gone out of his home. Beryl suspected it had happened long before Hector died. She took a seat on the couch next to Simpkins. Edwina lifted a pile of papers out of a straight-backed chair and placed them on the floor. She lowered herself gently onto the seat and cleared her throat.

"Now, Simpkins, I think it's time you told Beryl and me the truth about your argument with Hector," Edwina said.

Simpkins lifted his forlorn face and returned her stern gaze. "So you didn't believe we argued about the farm?" Simpkins asked.

"I certainly did not. Having seen the attitude with which you care for my plants, I could not imagine you having an argument with your brother-in-law over the conditions of the farm, which led to you abandoning your home. I have to assume that it was something that would cast you in an even more suspicious light with the constable, if that was the reason you gave," Edwina said.

Simpkins nodded. "That's true, miss. It is," he said. He leaned back and stuffed a weathered paw into his trouser pocket. With a grunt, he pulled something out and opened his hand to show the contents to Edwina. Beryl leaned forward to get a look at it too. There in his hand lay a glittering woman's ring.

"You fought with Hector about jewelry?" Beryl asked.

"I rowed with Hector about thieving," Simpkins said.

"Why don't you tell us about it," Edwina said.

"This was my Bess's ring. My mother gave it to me when I told her I was going to ask Bess to marry me," Simpkins said.

"Your mother must have approved of your choice of a bride," Edwina said.

"The two of them got on like beans and toast," Simpkins said. "She wanted me to give this to Bess because she said it was just as lovely as she was. As far as I was concerned, nothing was as lovely as my Bess, but I was right proud to give it to her just the same."

"Where does the theft come in?" Beryl asked.

"It might have been wrong of me, but I couldn't stand to have Bess buried with this ring. It reminded me of her and our life together. We never had much except each other, and the ring was a symbol of how much I loved her," Simpkins said. "Hector knew that."

"Did Hector steal the ring?" Edwina asked.

"I caught him at it red-handed. I always kept it on the little dressing table that Bess used in our bedroom. A couple of days ago, when I came home from working at the Beeches, I didn't see it in its usual place. I asked Hector about it, but he claimed not to have seen it," Simpkins said.

"I'll venture a guess that you didn't believe him," Beryl said.

Simpkins let out a snort. "Of course I didn't. As soon as he went to the loo, I searched his room. He had it tucked up in a pair of socks in his chest of drawers. I confronted him about it right quicklike," Simpkins said.

"What did he say for himself?" Edwina said.

Beryl was sure she saw a small tear threatening to trickle out of Simpkins's eye. "He said Bess had no use of it anymore and I was a fool for hanging on to something so valuable. He said he had planned to pawn it and use the money to keep the farm afloat," Simpkins said.

"That's dreadful," Edwina said. "I never did like that man."

A look passed between Edwina and Simpkins that Beryl could not quite interpret. It looked like acknowledgment and agreement. As much as everyone had made her feel very welcomed in Walmsley Parva, from time to time, she was silently reminded that she really was a newcomer. There seemed to be something that happened when one spent so long living in a single place. Edwina had a sense about things that Beryl simply did not. It was as though there was an unwritten code, a tapping into a collective knowledge, that the residents of Walmsley Parva shared and that she simply had not been able to access. Perhaps, she thought with a surprising pang, she never would.

"He always was a wrong'un," Simpkins said. "And a fool besides. Saving the farm would have taken more money than pawning Bess's ring could've provided. It would have been simple enough to keep things running if he had ever bothered to throw himself into the tasks at hand instead of looking for ways to cut corners and shirk his responsibilities."

Beryl could see that Edwina was keeping her lips firmly clamped shut. Many was the time Beryl had heard her friend saying the very same sorts of things about Simpkins's own slap-dash attitude towards the gardens at the Beeches. She was relieved when Edwina's mind seemed to take another tack.

"May I see the ring more closely?" Edwina said.

Simpkins gently placed it in Edwina's outstretched palm. She stood and carried it to the window. A shaft of sunlight beamed through the wavy glass and landed on the stones studding the ring. Dozens and dozens of sparkling reflections danced about the room.

"Beryl, come take a look at this."

Beryl got to her feet and joined Edwina at the window. Edwina passed the ring to her, and Beryl gave it a closer inspection. The stones were quite large, and the cut exquisite. She lifted the ring to eye level and held it up to the light. Even without a jeweler's loupe, it was possible to see that the clarity was very fine indeed. Clusters of emeralds, sapphires, and rubies surrounded a large center diamond. It was an extraordinary piece of jewelry, even more so considering it had been pulled from the depths of a workingman's pocket. It was at least as surprising that Simpkins's mother had had it simply on hand to give to her future daughter-in-law. She passed the ring back to Edwina with a raised eyebrow.

Edwina carried the treasure back to Simpkins and placed it gently on his calloused palm before sitting once more. "You say your mother gave you this ring for Bess?" Edwina asked.

Simpkins nodded.

"Do you happen to know how she came to have it?"

"I asked her that at the time, but she said it was something she just happened to have tucked away for a rainy day. A family heirloom is what she told me," Simpkins said.

"I think you may be wrong about your estimation of its value," Beryl said.

"What do you mean?" Simpkins said.

"I believe it is a very valuable piece of jewelry," Beryl said.

"Well, it's valuable to me, and I know it was to Bess, but I'm sure it's nothing more than a bit of paste," Simpkins said. "Not that my wife didn't deserve more, but we were never people of means."

"Having been the recipient of a large quantity of jewelry

over the years," Beryl said, "I assure you that ring is not made of paste."

Simpkins looked from Beryl to Edwina, a look of shock on his face. Beryl feared for the elderly gardener's heart. Two great shocks in just one morning might prove too much for any man.

"What do you think, Miss Edwina?" Simpkins asked, turning to Edwina. "A lady such as yourself would be likely to recognize a fine piece of jewelry, would she not?" Beryl had noticed that although the relationship between Edwina and Simpkins was often combative, he did seem to respect her opinion on matters he judged to be over his depth.

She wondered if that meant that Simpkins thought she was not an authority on jewelry of quality. She wondered if he thought Americans were easily fooled by chintzy glitz or if he did not think of her as a lady. She didn't suppose she could blame him for either opinion.

"I would have to agree with Beryl. I think you would be wise to keep that ring somewhere very safe. I don't know how your mother came to have it, but although I would not consider myself an expert, I would say that it's worth a great deal," Edwina said.

"If that's the case, would you be willing to do me a favor?" Simpkins asked.

"That would depend on what you require," Edwina said.

"Would you take it back to the Beeches with you and put it somewhere safe?" Simpkins said. "I can't say as I feel too secure keeping it on my person. Especially if the constable decides to arrest me."

"I would be happy to do so," Edwina said. "If you would like, I shall put it in my mother's jewelry box."

Beryl didn't say so, but she knew that there was plenty of room in the late Mrs. Davenport's jewelry box. Much of Edwina's education on the value of jewelry had been hard won during her recent economic slump.

Edwina got to her feet. Beryl joined her.

"Simpkins, I suggest you get to bed. I'm sure you slept poorly on the floor of the shed last night and have had a nasty shock. You may rest assured that we will keep your ring quite safe. Do let us know if you need anything," Edwina said.

With that, the pair of them took their leave and headed back out the door. As soon as they pulled it closed behind them, Edwina turned to Beryl.

"I've sold enough of my mother's jewelry to know that Bess Simpkins's is worth far more than anything I ever had to sell," Edwina said.

"It certainly rivals anything given to me by any of my husbands," Beryl said. "It even rivals gifts I received from men who were married to other women." The two of them exchanged a significant glance.

"I feel torn, Beryl," Edwina said.

"Because the theft of this ring gives Simpkins an even better reason to have murdered Hector?" Beryl asked.

"Exactly," Edwina said.

"You aren't suggesting that we tell that to Constable Gibbs, are you?" Beryl asked.

Edwina assumed a shocked expression. "Assuredly not," she said. "After all, what sort of private investigators would we be if we left all the detecting to Constable Gibbs?"

"Where do you think Simpkins's mother got the ring in the first place? Wasn't she a local girl here in Walmsley Parva?" Beryl asked.

"Yes, she was. From what I understand, Simpkins's family goes back for generations in the village. Perhaps they are not as well established as the Lomax family, but they definitely have deep roots here in the community," Edwina said.

"Then how can you possibly account for her having something of such value? It's the sort of a ring you would never expect to find just languishing in the bottom of someone's jewelry box," Beryl said.

"I suppose we ought to do some poking around about it, especially if it has anything to do with what happened to Hector," Edwina said.

Beryl was about to agree when she heard a man's voice shouting at them from the road. Beryl squinted at him and realized that he was the bald man she had seen the previous day at the Dove and Duck.

Chapter 6

Edwina was not surprised to discover the source of the shouting was the owner of the neighboring farm, Clifford Hammond. The morning sun glistened off his sweaty bald head, and Edwina found she would have thought him decidedly repulsive even if he had not been assailing them with angry words. This would never do. Her first thought was to climb back into the motorcar and leave him and his angry gesticulations in a billowing cloud of dust.

But first thoughts were often far more appealing than practical. If there was one thing she had learned in her short time as a private enquiry agent, it was that people often had much to reveal when they were upset. Despite the fact that every fiber in her being urged her to flee, Edwina took a step towards the angry man.

She was inordinately pleased to feel Beryl walking along beside her. There was something about being part of a team that made things seem far more manageable than they did when one was on one's own.

"As there is no one else about, I can only assume you are attempting to converse with us," Edwina said with far more vinegar in her voice than she actually felt.

Clifford Hammond was an imposing figure. His broad shoulders and thick chest, as well as his bulging arms and callused hands, made it clear that he was a man who was physically quite capable.

Edwina did not like to imagine what he might do if provoked. She spared a thought for Beryl's penchant for carrying a pistol in her pocket. She fervently hoped it would not come to a thing like that.

"Well, of course I am," Clifford Hammond said. "You don't think I'm shouting like this at the local wildlife, do you?"

"I've oftentimes been counted as some of the local wildlife," Beryl said. "I always took it as a compliment."

"From his mannerisms and tone of voice, I am sure that is not what Mr. Hammond intended," Edwina said. "If you would like to keep our attention, I suggest you control yourself and come to the point."

Mr. Hammond jutted out his jaw and crossed his beefy arms over his chest. Edwina wondered if she had provoked him unduly. She forgave herself for any lapse in judgment, as it had been a most trying morning.

"I wanted to know if the rumors were true," he said.

"Which rumors would those be?" Beryl asked.

Edwina felt her stomach roll over. She most assuredly did not wish to discuss the sleeping arrangements of her jobbing gardener with a man like Clifford Hammond. There was only so much a body could take in one day.

"About Hector Lomax. I was down in the village this morning, and scrawny old Prudence Rathbone came scurrying out of her shop just as I went by. She couldn't wait to tell me Hector had been found dead in the churchyard," Mr. Hammond said. "But with the way Prudence gossips, I wasn't sure I should believe a word she said."

Edwina felt Beryl's eyes boring into the side of her face. Word was spreading around the village, so there was no use in trying to quell the flow of information. Besides, it was not their place to do so. And Mr. Hammond might have some information about Hector's murder. After all, he was his closest neighbor and might easily have seen some of what went on at the neighboring property.

"I'm sorry to say that the rumors are true. Constable Gibbs informed Simpkins only a couple of hours ago that his brother-in-law was found dead this morning," Edwina said.

She kept her eyes trained on Clifford Hammond's face as she confirmed the rumor. Edwina prided herself on her ability to ferret out lies. A lifetime spent posing uncomfortable questions to household help, as well as countless hours volunteering with the church youth group and the village girl guides, had honed her nose for the truth to a very fine degree. At least most of the time. Clifford Hammond seemed to have no intention of keeping his feelings to himself. A wide smile spread across his weathered face, and he rubbed his broad, work-worn hands together with glee.

"That's the best news I've had in ages," Mr. Hammond said. "I hardly dared to hope it was true, but I'm sure that I can believe it if a woman of as sterling a reputation as you is saying so, Miss Davenport." Edwina thought that if the laws of gravity were not so firmly fixed, Mr. Hammond would have levitated off the ground in his delight.

"That's hardly the reaction one would expect from a man whose neighbor has been murdered," Beryl said.

"Murdered! The news just keeps getting better and better," Clifford Hammond said.

"Really, Mr. Hammond, that is quite enough," Edwina said.

"I'll tell you it's not enough," Mr. Hammond said, jabbing an index finger in the general direction of the cottage Simpkins shared with Hector. "I've every right to be overjoyed at this news. I can't think of anyone more deserving of that sort of a fate than Hector Lomax."

"I agree that Mr. Lomax did have a deservedly disreputable reputation," Edwina said. "Still, I haven't heard anyone say they wished him dead. He must have done something especially egregious for you to feel so pleased about his untimely demise."

Mr. Hammond nodded and swept his arm out in front of him, gesturing towards his rolling fields. For the first time since they arrived, Edwina took note of the Hammond property. In truth, the plants, trees, and shrubs looked no healthier than the ones on the Lomax farm. As much as Clifford Hammond was not the sort of person with whom Edwina would prefer to socialize, she had heard only praise for his abilities as a farmer. The condition of his fields surprised her.

"Hector Lomax is the reason that my farm looks like it does. Because of him, I expect the crop this year is entirely ruined," Mr. Hammond said. "Next year's, too, most likely."

"Your plants do look a bit peaked. Why would you blame Hector for what ails them?" Beryl asked.

"You do know there's a drought on, don't you?" he asked.

Both Beryl and Edwina nodded. The entire country had been suffering from an unusually dry spell. News reports filled the papers and the wireless daily with dire warnings about water conservation and potential crop failures. Edwina had taken to prioritizing water for the trees and shrubs over the bedding plants that year.

As much as she wished she could lay any present disappointment in her garden at Simpkins's feet, she knew in her heart of hearts that much of it was beyond his ability to fix. The gentle spring rains and summer showers England was known for had failed to appear, and no one quite knew what to make of it.

"Of course we do. I'm a keen gardener myself, and my own plants have been suffering," Edwina said. "But I don't find myself blaming my neighbors for the condition of my herbaceous borders."

"Then count yourself lucky. It's one thing to blame Mother Nature, as she's unlikely to laugh in your face when ill using you. The same cannot be said for Hector," he said.

"What exactly did he do?" Beryl asked.

"Come with me and I'll show you," he said.

Mr. Hammond stomped towards them, pushed past them, and walked across the nearest field on the Lomax property. With trepidation, they followed him. At least trepidation on Edwina's part. Beryl, characteristically, strode along as though nothing whatsoever worried her.

They crossed the field, and Mr. Hammond climbed over a stile that marked a gap in the hedgerow. Beryl scrambled up after him and reached out a hand to pull Edwina up behind her. They made their way down the other side, to where Mr. Hammond stood pointing at a pile of stones.

Edwina came alongside him and looked down. The stones were large and neatly chinked together to form a dam. Someone had blocked up a naturally occurring stream and had diverted the flow of water towards a series of holding tanks.

"This stream is supposed to flow across the field we just traversed and on into my own property. Most years it doesn't make any difference whatsoever," Mr. Hammond said. "But in times of drought, I have always been able to rely on this stream as a backup source of water. This year Hector got it into his head to keep it all for himself."

Clifford Hammond made a rumbling noise down in his throat, then spat out a gob of something unmentionable right into the watering tank. Edwina shuddered all the way to her toes.

"Is that legal?" Beryl asked.

"I have no sway over what a man does on his own property. I tried to appeal to his better nature and asked that he let the water flow, but he said he wouldn't do so unless I made it worth his while."

"Are you saying he tried to extort money from you?" Edwina said.

Mr. Hammond nodded. "That's exactly what I'm saying. He told me that there was no more free water, and unless I paid up, he would be keeping all of it for himself or selling it to another buyer," Mr. Hammond said.

"Well, I suppose I shouldn't be saying this, but I can understand why you would be glad to hear he will no longer be your neighbor," Edwina said.

"I'd say you had a very good reason to want him out of the way," Beryl said. "Would you mind telling us where you went last night when you left the pub?" Beryl turned on one of her winning smiles, but Edwina was surprised to see it did not have its usual effect on Mr. Hammond.

"I would mind very much. Are you accusing me of something?" Mr. Hammond crossed his arms over his chest again, and Edwina suddenly became more aware of how isolated the back field at the Lomax farm just happened to be.

"I was simply asking you a question," Beryl said.

"I can't see that it is your place to do so," he said. "If there are any questions that need to be asked, I expect the constable to be the one to ask them. I'll take my leave of you."

With that, he turned his back on the women and strode back over the field, across the stile, and onto his own property. The two investigators followed at a sedate pace. Partly to give him time to cool off and partly to speak without him overhearing.

"I should think that Clifford Hammond had at least as much of a reason to kill Hector as Simpkins did," Edwina said. "What was all that about the pub last night?"

"You remember how I mentioned to Constable Gibbs that several people argued with Hector at the pub last night?" Beryl asked.

"I do," Edwina answered.

"Clifford Hammond was one of them," Beryl said. "I happened to notice that he left not long after Hector. I wondered if he could account for his whereabouts any better than Simpkins could."

"I'm sure she won't appreciate us telling her how to do her job, but I think that's exactly the sort of thing we ought to report to Constable Gibbs, don't you?" Edwina said.

"I think it would be in Simpkins's best interest if we did. But, I daresay, we can wait until after lunch," Beryl said, linking her arm through Edwina's. "Shall we head back to the Beeches?"

Chapter 7

Beryl kept quiet on the way home. After all, Edwina really had had a rough morning. She had been absolutely shattered by the knowledge that Simpkins had been sleeping in her potting shed. Hector's murder and then the ugly confrontation with Mr. Hammond had only compounded the earlier shock. Still, Edwina's look of surprise as Beryl pulled to a stop in the driveway of the Beeches seemed unreasonable considering how careful she had been to slow down before taking the turn to enter the property.

"I'm afraid there may be more bad news," Edwina announced, inclining her head towards the front step.

Jack Prentice, the local paperboy, stood pacing back and forth on the wide stone step to the front door of the house. He held his flat cap clutched in his small hands, and even from a distance, Beryl could see that the boy quivered with agitation.

While children were not creatures for whom Beryl often had a soft spot, she had been surprised at how easily she had taken to Jack when she met him shortly after arriving in Walmsley Parva. She admired his grit and his work ethic. She had also found him to be remarkably useful on occasion. It was not a quality she attributed in general to children, and the novelty of it had been especially endearing. She slid from behind the wheel and hurried towards him, with Edwina close on her heels.

"Jack, I can't imagine that you are here to deliver the papers. What seems to be the trouble?" Beryl asked.

To her horror, he looked as though he might burst into tears. She cast a glance over her shoulder at Edwina, who had much more of a knack for dealing with children, despite the fact that her friend was uncomfortable with emotional outbursts of any kind. Fortunately, Edwina rose to the occasion.

"Come along in, Jack. I'll fix you a cup of tea and you can tell us all about it," Edwina said as she pushed open the door and purposefully moved down the hallway. Jack followed her, and Beryl gratefully brought up the rear.

After all these months Beryl still found herself astonished by the enervating quality of the suggestion of a cup of tea. She could have understood had cocktails been on offer. Not that that would have been appropriate for a boy his age. Still, she couldn't see how hooking children on something as odious as tea made any sense either. Nevertheless, she had made it a point of honor to respect local traditions no matter how bizarre and so kept her thoughts to herself.

Edwina busied herself filling the kettle and setting it on the hob. She produced a tin of biscuits, a food that Beryl would have called cookies, from somewhere secreted in the back of a cupboard and pried off the lid. She placed them on the table and indicated that Jack should take a seat and help himself. Beryl understood the depth of his distress when he shook his head and pushed the tin away.

"I haven't much money, but I need to hire you," he said. Beryl heard the trembling in his voice and felt her heart squeeze. If she had been a different sort of woman, she would have attempted to embrace him. As it was, she simply took the chair next to him.

"Hire us for what?" Beryl asked.

A ragged choking noise escaped Jack's throat. "Constable Gibbs has arrested my father," he said.

"Not to make light of the difficulty," Edwina said, "but I rather think this is not the first time that has happened, is it?" She lifted three cups down out of the cupboard and placed them on the table.

"My father has spent more than a few nights in the constable's custody for public drunkenness, it's true," Jack said. "But the constable has arrested him for Hector Lomax's murder." With that, Jack dug his ink-smudged fingers into the pocket of his worn coat. He extracted a small and pathetic handful of coins and deposited them on the scrubbed wooden table.

"Why has the constable arrested him?" Beryl asked.

"Because the vicar found him passed out in the churchyard, not far from where Hector's body was found."

"Being in the proximity of a body might cast suspicion but is not a good enough reason to make an arrest. Constable Gibbs is enthusiastic in the dispensing of her duties, but she's not a foolish woman by any means," Edwina said. "There must be something more to it than that."

Edwina spooned loose tea leaves into a Brown Betty teapot and poured steaming water over them. She carried the pot to the table and sat down.

"She said that judging by his injuries, it looked like Hector was killed by being clobbered over the back of the head with a shovel. She said there was a shovel covered in blood lying right next to my father when she found him," Jack said.

"Did she say what she thought the motive was?" Beryl asked. She had a sneaking suspicion that the constable had heard about the confrontation Hector and Frank Prentice had had in the pub.

"My father and Hector got into it again at the pub yesterday, but they've been rowing for a couple of weeks," Jack said.

"Is this about the sexton job?" Edwina asked.

Beryl never failed to be astonished by the small goings-on in

Walmsley Parva Edwina seemed to be privy to. It was as though she simply gleaned them from the air.

"My father was still angry about being dismissed from that job. He really needed the work," Jack said. His gaze landed on the small pile of coins he had placed upon the table. "It was really unfair."

"Can you tell me what happened? I don't know anything about this," Beryl said.

"I believe that the vicar acquiesced to Hector's insistence that Frank be relieved of his duties as the church sexton after a dispute about Hector's brother's grave. Is that right, Jack?" Edwina said.

"Hector said my father didn't do a good job digging the grave for his brother. He complained to the vicar and got him sacked," Jack said. "My father always thought there was more to Hector's complaints than what he told the vicar."

"Didn't your father work from time to time at the Lomax farm too?" Edwina asked.

"He did when old Mr. Lomax was alive. He helped with the planting and the weeding and the harvesting. Old Mr. Lomax said he was a good worker and that he always had a place there," Jack said.

"Did Hector relieve him of his duties there too?" Beryl asked.

"He said the farm wasn't doing well enough to justify having any help this year," Jack said. "My father said Hector had run the farm into the ground and that it was a shame that a man like him had a property and the likes of us didn't."

Edwina lifted the lid on the teapot and peered inside. Then she uncharacteristically slid the sugar bowl and small pitcher of milk over to Jack to add as he saw fit. Beryl knew that there was a social order to the serving of tea. Someone had mentioned to her that members of the lower classes were accustomed to adding milk to their tea and also to placing the milk in the cup before the tea was poured in.

It was said that the practice stemmed from both a desire to improve the flavor of the low-quality tea they were able to afford and the need to protect their even lower-quality crockery from cracking when the hot tea was added to the cups. Sure enough, Jack splashed some milk into his cup before holding it out to Edwina.

"I should think a growing boy like you would like his tea with plenty of sugar," Edwina said. "Please do fix it just as you like. Sugar is very good for the sort of shock you've had."

How like Edwina to think of things like that, Beryl thought.

"Thanks, miss," Jack said, adding five lumps of sugar to his cup. It set Beryl's teeth on edge just to imagine guzzling such a sweet slurry. Still, Jack took a sip, and Beryl was pleased to see a bit of color returned to his face.

"So what is it exactly you would like for us to do?" Beryl asked.

"I want you to find out who really killed Hector Lomax, because I'm sure my father didn't do it," Jack said.

Beryl and Edwina exchanged a glance over the top of the boy's head.

"Does your mother know you're here?" Edwina asked.

"No, she doesn't. When my father's away, and sometimes even when he's not, she relies on me as the man of the house. I'm sure it's fine that I came to hire you without consulting with her," Jack said. He squared his small shoulders and lifted his chin defiantly.

Edwina nodded slowly, as if she was not surprised. "But you don't intend to keep that information from her, do you?" Edwina asked. "We have your permission to speak with her, do we not?"

"Does that mean you will take the case?" Jack asked.

"It means we will make enquiries on your behalf. But, Jack, it's not within our power to change facts. If your father is guilty, our investigation will show that. You understand, don't you?" Edwina asked.

"My father didn't do it, and I know that the two of you will be able to prove that. I bet he'll be home by the end of the day," Jack said.

"We really appreciate your faith in us, but I don't think you should set such high expectations," Beryl said. "After all, Constable Gibbs can be quite difficult to convince once she sets her mind to something."

Jack scraped back his chair and stood. He drained his cup, then set it carefully back on the table.

"I have no doubt you'll get to the bottom of it," Jack said. "Now, how much do I owe you to get started?"

"This is the sort of case that we take on a results-only basis," Beryl said, looking over at Edwina.

Edwina gave the tiniest of nods.

"What does that mean?" Jack asked. He eyed the paltry pile of coins and bit his lower lip.

"It means that we do not charge anything unless we get the desired result," Edwina said.

"You mean you won't charge me anything if you don't get my father off the hook?" Jack said.

"That's right," Edwina said.

Jack smiled and swept the coins into his pocket. "Then I'd best get back to work. I'm going to need to sell a bunch more papers today, because I know you're going to want to collect your fee. Thanks very much, ladies." He gave them each a nod and popped his hat back upon his head before turning to the scullery door and dashing out through it.

"Oh dear," Edwina said, looking after him. "I'm afraid that boy is in for a terrible disappointment."

"It looks grim for Frank Prentice, doesn't it?" Beryl said.

"It's all too easy to believe that the town drunk had one too many and delivered a fatal blow to someone with whom he had a long-standing argument," Edwina said.

"Hector Lomax seemed to be the sort of man that many people wanted to murder. I suppose it's not a surprise that Jack's father would be amongst them," Beryl said.

"It may not be a surprise, but it certainly is a tragedy. That family's been barely clinging on to what little they have without this happening. I've heard in town that they were in danger of being turned out of the cottage they are letting because they had failed to pay for the past several months," Edwina said. "It was said that Frank losing his job at the Lomax farm started them towards ruin."

"If Hector knew how much Frank relied on his job at the farm, it seems downright cruel for him to go out of his way to get Frank fired from his job as the sexton as well," Beryl said. "Do you know of any reason why he would be so vindictive?"

"I'm afraid that's just the sort of man he always was. He seemed to take delight in causing others pain. I can't say I'm glad that he has been murdered, but just like Clifford Hammond, I can't say that I'm surprised."

"Do you think Frank's the one who did it?" Beryl asked.

"As much as I hate to think so, I think often the obvious solution is the correct one."

Chapter 8

Edwina felt her usual trepidation at the idea of taking on a new client. While she had derived a great deal of satisfaction from the fledgling private enquiry agency, which Beryl had suggested they open only a few weeks earlier, Edwina was still not certain that either of them was truly qualified to represent herself in such a way. And while she could not deny that the earnings from their last case had kept them from going into arrears with the merchants of Walmsley Parva, it was less likely that this case would do so. After all, even if they did pull off some sort of miracle and prove Jack's father to be innocent, there would be no money in it.

Not that that was the most important reason for taking the case, Edwina reminded herself sternly. She felt rather shocked and amazed that her mind could take such a mercenary bent in the face of another's tragedy. That little shadow of shame slithering through the privacy of her own mind galvanized her into action.

"I propose we start with the scene of the crime," Edwina said. "I expect the vicar will be at the church. Since that is where Hector's body was found, I suggest we have a word with him."

She began to gather up the crockery and place it haphazardly in the sink. Usually, she would take the time to wash the dishes straightaway, but as an independent businesswoman, she could not always make housekeeping her priority. Whatever would her mother have said? She didn't like to consider it and was somewhat relieved to realize she needn't care. Besides, the death duties after her mother died were one of the reasons Edwina had felt such pressure to look for a source of income. She hurried down the hall, with Beryl close at her heels. Crumpet capered along beside them, begging to be included. She took pity on him, bent down and strapped on his lead.

"I suppose this means you don't wish to take the automobile," Beryl said, looking down at Crumpet.

"He needs a walk, and so do I," Edwina said. "You know very well that the churchyard is within easy walking distance. Besides, the fresh air will do us all good."

Edwina lifted her second-best hat from the hall tree and looked in the mirror as she placed it on her head. While she had never been a classic beauty, Edwina had always been rather proud of her complexion and even now had no desire to spoil it with too much sun. She also had not any desire to behave as a modern woman when it came to hats. She was rather too fond of them for that. Beryl felt no such affinity and strode out the door bareheaded.

Despite the tragedies of the day, Edwina found herself enjoying the sights and sounds of the countryside as they walked along the lane. Birds chirped merrily up in the trees, puffy white clouds scudded across the brilliant blue sky, and Crumpet found seemingly endless pleasant scents to inspect at the base of the hedgerows. Edwina could almost forget the purpose of their errand. Although, Jack's face filled with misery flitted through her thoughts, unbidden, as they neared the imposing grey stone structure that was the church.

"I think I should take the lead here as far as any questions are concerned," Edwina said. "Vicars are, after all, far more my area of expertise than yours."

It was surprising, but it was true. Edwina happily conceded that Beryl had far more expertise with almost every variety of man than she herself had. But if there was one subspecies of the sex that Edwina was more qualified to interrogate, it was a country vicar. Something about her flamboyant friend reduced the already unprepossessing vicar, Wilfred Lowethorpe, to an even more shadowy version of himself whenever she spoke to him.

No matter how many times Edwina reminded Beryl that the best way to deal with him was to refrain from flirting and winking, her friend simply could not be convinced. It was a failing that had not endeared Beryl to the vicar's wife, a local paragon of godly good works and no-nonsense acts of charity.

Edwina had always gotten on quite well with Muriel Lowethorpe, despite some trouble she and Beryl had created at the recent May Day celebration, of which Muriel was the chairwoman. Edwina certainly did not want to test a relationship that had just gotten back on solid footing.

"I defer to your better judgment," Beryl said. "Where do you suggest we begin?"

They came to a stop right outside the lych-gate and peered into the churchyard over a low wooden fence. A movement at the far corner of the grounds caught Edwina's eye. The vicar stood stooped over a headstone, and Edwina could hear him muttering to himself. She inclined her head in his direction and, after fastening Crumpet's lead to a post, beckoned for Beryl to follow her. She would not get very far with the vicar if she allowed her dog to prance about on the graves. The vicar was, quite properly, a stickler for propriety when it came to the dead.

The vicar straightened as they approached, then took a step back when he spotted Beryl. Edwina fervently hoped her friend could control any enthusiastic bouts of winking or an inclination to elbow the vicar in the ribs.

"What brings you two ladies to the church this morning?" he asked. He cast a worried glance over his shoulder, and Edwina wondered if Muriel was within the church, polishing the brasses or arranging some flowers in front of the pulpit.

"We've been retained by Jack Prentice to look into the case against his father," Edwina said. "We felt it best to start at the beginning, so we came to see where both Hector's body and Frank Prentice were found."

The vicar bobbed his head as a sort of acknowledgment that the churchyard was indeed the place where such shenanigans had taken place. Edwina could not help but note his usually grey coloring had gone even more ashen. He lifted a bony finger and pointed to the other side of the yard, and as he did so, two bright spots of color appeared on his gaunt cheeks.

"I found Hector Lomax's body right over there. It gave me a terrible turn. At first, I thought he had simply fallen asleep. It wouldn't be the first time someone who had had too much to drink stumbled onto the grounds for a quiet nap," the vicar said.

"When did you realize that he was dead?" Edwina said.

"When I bent over and shook him by the shoulder. I must have gone about it a bit more vigorously than I had realized, because his head turned sideways, and that's when I saw the blood and the dent in his skull," he said. The scowl on his face deepened, and Edwina found herself surprised that he was not disposed to be more charitable towards a member of the community who had met with such a fate.

"Did you find Frank Prentice too?" Edwina asked.

"No, I didn't. Constable Gibbs found Frank as she was making a thorough search of the grounds for clues. I feel as though everywhere I turn, the entire property has been desecrated," the vicar said.

"What do you think happened?" Edwina asked.

"My first thought was that it had something to do with the vandalism we've been experiencing lately. I haven't liked to say anything, but now that there's been a murder, I don't suppose litter and desecrated graves are of much account," he said.

"Have you been finding a lot of vandalism at the church? That seems surprising. I would not have thought anyone would have dared," Edwina said.

Behind her Beryl let out the smallest of snorts. Edwina shot a warning glance over her shoulder. Fortunately, the vicar seemed too caught up in his own emotions to have noticed any lack of respect on Beryl's part.

"Oh yes. I haven't wanted to draw attention to the behavior, because I thought that would encourage more of it. But we have had quite a rash of vandalism over the past few weeks. Considering who I suspect was responsible, I now feel as though I should have said something to the authorities," the vicar said.

"Who is it that you suspect of being responsible?" Edwina asked.

"Well, until today I shouldn't have liked to have named names. I have always believed in not being the first to cast stones," the vicar said.

"Very admirable, I'm sure," Edwina said. "It sounds as though you regret not doing more to get to the bottom of it."

"Indeed I do. I keep asking myself if I had taken action if Hector Lomax would still be alive," the vicar said.

"Does that mean you suspect that the vandalism and the murder are connected?" Beryl said. Edwina worried that Beryl's interjection would stem the flow of information from the vicar, but she needn't have worried. Truly, she had never seen the man so worked up.

"I am very sorry to say that I believe Frank Prentice is responsible for the vandalism and for the murder," the vicar said.

"I hate to speak ill of any man, but the evidence is too strong against him."

"What evidence is that?" Beryl asked. Edwina shot her a warning glance, and Beryl gave a slight nod of her head.

"Although we have experienced a bit of vandalism off and on for some time, it has occurred more frequently ever since I unfortunately relieved Frank Prentice of his sexton duties," the vicar said.

"So you believe the fact that you let him go caused him to turn to vandalism in retribution?" Edwina said.

The vicar nodded. "That's exactly what I believe. The attacks on the headstones, the building, and the grounds have escalated ever since he lost his job here. I cannot help but conclude that he lashed out in a drunken fit at Hector and killed him," the vicar said. "Perhaps if I had shared my suspicions with Constable Gibbs earlier, she would have either warned him off or caught him red-handed and put him away for a little while."

"Do you really think that Frank would have been so angry about the loss of his job that he would make a leap from vandalism to murder?" Edwina asked.

"He's been lurking around the churchyard ever since I let him go. When I confronted him about being responsible for the vandalism, he threatened me. He said he didn't blame me for what had happened but that he was desperate for the money. He actually put his hands on me and demanded I give him what I had upon my person," the vicar said.

"He must have been very desperate indeed," Edwina said. "He has no history of violence."

"What exactly happened with Frank and Hector?" Beryl asked. "Was it enough to get Frank dismissed?"

"Hector's complaint about Frank's work was simply the last straw. Frank had been negligent in his duties for quite some time. He simply was not the same man that he once had been. I tried to be patient and show mercy, but eventually, enough was enough," the vicar said.

"What sorts of things was he failing at?" Edwina asked.

"As the sexton, he was responsible for having graves dug in time for funeral services. More often than not, I would need to go and seek him out when he didn't show up and the hour was growing late. Every time, I found him in some state of a drunken stupor. You know what he's like," the vicar said, turning to Edwina.

Indeed, Edwina did know what he was like, as did all the rest of the village. His son Jack had the unpleasant duty of collecting his father at the pub every night in an effort to ensure he found his way home. The family's financial troubles had a great deal to do with how much of their small income he drank.

"So when Hector complained about the grave not being dug in time for his brother's funeral, you decided finally to dismiss him from his duties?" Edwina said.

"I am sorry to say it was my sad duty to do so. Hector was the last in a long line of complaints, but Frank fixated on him as the sole reason he had lost his job. I think it had a great deal to do with the fact that Hector had let him go from his work on the farm as well," the vicar said. "Looking back, it might have been wiser if I had waited until another parishioner had complained before speaking to Frank. I feel quite guilty about what has happened."

"When Jack Prentice came to ask us for help, he said that his father was found with a bloody shovel next to him," Edwina said.

"It was actually a shovel that belongs to the church. In fact, it is the very one he used to dig the graves. I suppose he was trying to make some sort of a statement," the vicar said.

"Then in your mind there is no doubt that Frank is the one who committed the crime?" Beryl asked.

"I wouldn't go so far as to say absolutely no doubt, but I am willing to say that I would be more surprised to hear that it was someone else. Although, the world has changed so much since the war that I suppose nothing feels as certain as it used to," the vicar said.

"Could you show us exactly where Hector's body was found?" Edwina asked.

"Follow me," the vicar said, setting off across the lumpy ground. Even in the churchyard, evidence of the drought could be seen. Much of the grass was brown at the tips.

The vicar stopped near a forlorn grave at the edge of the hallowed ground. The headstone was for a man who had died more than a hundred years earlier. Edwina felt a wave of sadness wash over her as she looked at the weeds and brambles collecting at the base of the stone. It was clear that there was no one who still cared about this man enough to bother to tend his grave.

Considering her branch of the Davenport line was likely to die out with her, Edwina suddenly felt as though she were looking at her own future. Would anyone bother to visit her final resting place after she was gone? She doubted very much it would take one hundred years for her own headstone to look so thoroughly neglected.

"He was sprawled out right here. I thought he had simply indulged in a night of excess after hearing the results of the Derby. And look, there's some more deviltry," the vicar said, pointing at a nearby headstone.

Edwina squinted at a grave marker pleasantly nestled against a small copse of trees. Edwina and Beryl followed him to the headstone, where he clucked his tongue as he looked at a pile of ash tapped out on its top.

"I don't know what this world is coming to when folks feel free to tap out their pipes on headstones," the vicar said.

The two spots on his cheeks deepened in color. Beryl leaned over the small pile and sniffed. She walked around the back side of the headstone and stood a few feet back in amongst the trees. Edwina wondered what had gotten into her.

"It does seem quite a sacrilege," Edwina said soothingly.

"That's it exactly. The very thought of someone committing murder on hallowed ground would have been unthinkable before the war. Sometimes I find myself wondering, what the world has come to," the vicar said. "Still, there is much of God's work yet to do. You will have to excuse me."

Edwina watched as he hustled away. Muriel had appeared in the doorway to the church. She stood with her hands on her hips. Edwina wondered how much of the vicar's sudden urgency had to do with God's work and how much of it had to do with the list that Muriel likely had assigned. She turned back to Beryl.

"If one were about to murder someone, this would be a rather good place to lie in wait, don't you think?" Beryl said.

"I suppose it would, but only if you knew to expect someone," Edwina said.

"That's exactly what I was thinking. How would anyone know to wait for Hector here?" Beryl asked.

"Perhaps the pipe smoker was not waiting for Hector, or anyone else, for that matter. Perhaps he was just hoping to have a pipe in peace and didn't wish to be seen. Or perhaps he just wanted to lean against a tree while he smoked," Edwina said.

"It seems like quite a coincidence that he would pick this very spot, where Hector would be found only a few feet away."

"But we don't even know how long the ashes sat there. There's nothing to say the pipe smoker was here at the same time as Hector," Edwina said.

"They can't have sat here long. It wouldn't take much of a breeze to blow the pile away. Besides, right now it's the only clue we've got," Beryl said.

"Why did you smell it?" Edwina asked.

"Most pipe smokers are quite loyal to the tobacco that they

choose. I thought that if I could identify it, I would be able to recognize it again if we find someone else who smokes this particular type of tobacco. That might lead us to a witness, at the very least," Beryl said.

"You really are quite a good detective," Edwina said. She reached into her pocket and pulled out her notebook. She carefully ripped a piece of paper out of it and folded it into a makeshift envelope. Using a second piece of paper as a brush, she scooped the ashes into the envelope and tucked it away in her pocket. "We can always ask at the tobacco shop in the village which sort of tobacco this came from."

A broad smile broke out across Beryl's face.

"You're rather a good detective yourself," she said.

Chapter 9

Jack and his family lived in an overcrowded, ramshackle cottage well outside the village. Without the use of the automobile, it was a hot, dusty trudge. Beryl noted she was even more in need of a conditioning regime than she had previously realized. By the time they arrived at the footpath leading to the cottage, she was overheated and slightly out of breath. Perhaps Edwina had done her a favor by putting the automobile temporarily out of commission.

"I hope we are not making a nuisance of ourselves," Edwina said. "After all, it is Jack who hired us, not Mrs. Prentice."

"We shall soon find out," Beryl said.

They advanced on the front door, and Beryl proceeded to rap sharply upon it. After a moment it creaked open, and Beryl was surprised to see a small child, not more than four years old, appear in the opening. Beryl turned towards Edwina, hoping she would take the lead. Urchins were decidedly not her best audience.

"Is your mother at home?" Edwina asked.

The child nodded solemnly and opened the door wider. Edwina stepped across the threshold, and Beryl followed her. The small cottage was clean and resoundingly bare. A small wooden table with three chairs placed around it were the only pieces of furniture in the large first-floor room.

Beyond them what must have been considered the kitchen filled the back wall. A small window sat above a cracked trough. Beryl saw no evidence of an indoor pump. A small stove, which she expected did double duty for cooking and heating, sat against another wall.

At the table a faded woman of about Beryl's own age sat slumped in one of the chairs. The small child who had opened the door went to her side and tugged on her sleeve. The woman looked up, as though startled from a sleep.

"Mrs. Prentice?" Beryl asked.

The woman nodded. Everything about her oozed a sense of defeat. Her mousy-brown hair fell slackly at either side of her face. If Beryl had to guess, she was wearing the same thing she had worn for many days previously. She had no shoes on her feet, and her soles were in need of a scrub with a stiff brush.

"Your son Jack has asked us to see if we can help with the trouble your husband has found himself in."

The woman registered a flicker of surprise across her face. "Now, why would he do a thing like that?" she asked.

"Jack seems to believe that his father isn't guilty," Beryl said.

"Oh, Frank's guilty, all right," the woman said.

Beryl heard Edwina let out a small gasp. Beryl was a bit surprised herself that any wife would so confidently proclaim her husband's guilt.

"Maybe not guilty of Hector Lomax's murder, but he's certainly guilty of being a wretch."

"Do you mind if we sit?" Edwina asked.

"Suit yourself. Mind you, I can't offer you any refreshments," the woman said.

"We wouldn't think of troubling you," Edwina said. "We did want to ask you some questions, though."

"What sorts of questions? Like where was Frank last night? Did he have a temper? Do I think he could have held a grudge against Hector?" Mrs. Prentice asked.

"That's exactly the sort of thing we wanted to ask," Beryl said.

"I've already answered the same questions from Constable Gibbs," the woman said. "I don't expect I'll have any different answers for you. I am bone tired, and I hate to waste your time." She slumped even deeper into the chair.

"We want to help. Anything that you can tell us about your husband's whereabouts could help to prove his innocence," Edwina said.

"As I'm sure you know, from gossip around the village, my Frank spends more time drinking at the pub and sleeping it off somewhere besides his own bed than he does here at home with the little ones and me," Mrs. Prentice said. "I'm not sure that anything that I can tell you will make him look less guilty." She shook her head sadly and let out a long sigh.

"Do you remember when the last time you saw him was?" Beryl asked.

"He came home around noontime yesterday, saying he wanted something to eat. That's about the only reason he does come home unless I send Jack out to fetch him. I fixed him some beans on toast, and then he went back out again," she said.

"Did he say where he was going?" Edwina asked.

"He mentioned wanting to see Hector Lomax to ask for his job back," Mrs. Prentice said. "He said he was going to head back down to the pub after that. He promised me he wasn't drinking but that he was going to listen to the results of the Derby on the wireless."

"Did you believe him when he said he wasn't going out drinking?" Beryl asked.

"What kind of a fool do you take me for? Of course I didn't. We had a massive row about it, and he stormed out the door. I'm sure he used that as just another excuse to topple down into his cups," Mrs. Prentice said.

"Most people with the drink problem tend to have a lot of excuses for it," Beryl said. "I've known many men who came back from the war needing some way to forget what they saw."

Mrs. Prentice looked up at Beryl with surprise. For the first time, a bit of softness crept into her face. Beryl realized that Mrs. Prentice was far younger than she had first appeared. The war had aged so many people beyond their years, and not just the men. The people who stayed behind had shouldered a great burden too. Sometimes it was hard to remember the things that used to seem normal, after all they had gone through.

"You wouldn't know it to see him now, but my Frank was a hardworking and conscientious man before he went to France. He doesn't talk about what he saw over there, and I don't ask. I know before he took to sleeping rough, with a bottle clutched in his hands, he would cry out in his sleep. Many's the night he would wake me with his thrashing and moaning."

"It's not an unfamiliar story, although it is a tragic one," Beryl said.

"It sounds hardhearted to say it, but in some ways it's a relief the nights that Jack can't find his father to bring him home. Even with the drink, he still cries out in the night and disturbs all the household. Ever since he came back, it's as though I have another child to take care of. And to think I was so happy when he first got home and seemed to be all in one piece, unlike so many others."

"So much of the damage to our soldiers isn't easy to see on the surface, is it?" Edwina said. "Even the ones who look like they were the luckiest oftentimes feel tremendous guilt, on top of all their other difficulties."

"Perhaps that's the cause of it. Frank has seemed bent on de-stroying himself ever since he got home. He never used to have a temper, and now every little thing sets him off. I was afraid of what he might do, to tell the truth, when he announced that he was going to confront Hector. Even when he hasn't been drinking, he's become unpredictable," Mrs. Prentice said.

Beryl exchanged a glance with Edwina. Things were looking worse all the time for Frank.

"Do you know if he actually saw Hector at his own prop-erty?" Edwina asked.

"I have no idea. I hadn't seen him since he left after lunch. I was so angry, I didn't even bother to send Jack out to find him that evening. The whole house got a decent night's sleep for a change," Mrs. Prentice said.

"Do you think he might have actually killed Hector?" Ed-wina asked.

"I won't go so far as to say that. But I will say not much would surprise me anymore," Mrs. Prentice said.

Edwina longed for her bicycle. It was hot, and she felt rather far from home. How much easier it would be if Beryl had one of her own and the two of them could cycle together to some of the far-flung locations their investigations always seemed to re-quire visiting.

Besides the convenience cycling offered, she found it uplift-ing to swoop down hills and around corners. Whilst on her bi-cycle, her cares seemed to glide off behind her, and she felt the desire for such comfort. She had been deeply affected by the bleak circumstances at the Prentice home.

Edwina wondered if there was some way that the village could be more help to the soldiers who had returned with so much damage. It was a difficult thing to even consider. Scarring and amputations visible on the body of a returned soldier were hard enough to know how to acknowledge without causing insult or further injury. Traumas and difficulties to the mind and spirit were an even more delicate matter.

Beryl's words to Mrs. Prentice had given Edwina pause. She wondered if her dear friend had spoken only of the secondhand experiences of others or if she herself had reasons why she so enthusiastically imbibed cocktails in the evening. Edwina was not one to pry, but she suddenly was surprised to realize she had applied the same reticence to questioning Beryl's wartime years as she did everyone else's.

What had her friend been up to? Her position as a celebrity might have provided her many opportunities to assist various organizations in the war effort. Perhaps Beryl's offhand comments about working with and making the acquaintance of luminaries such as the king might have more basis in fact than Edwina had previously considered. She glanced at Beryl from the corner of her eye and allowed herself to imagine her friend dropping behind enemy lines or smuggling maps or secret communications from one location to another.

It was not difficult in the least to imagine Beryl breezily entering enemy headquarters and charming a high-level dignitary out of his secrets. Edwina rather thought that Beryl had much more to give in terms of storytelling than advice for lady adventurers. She probably would be better suited to writing a spy novel. She was brought back to the present by the sound of Beryl's voice.

"It certainly doesn't look very good for Frank, does it?" Beryl said a little breathlessly. Edwina suddenly thought her friend might benefit from a bit more time spent wandering the highways and byways of Walmsley Parva on foot rather than in her motorcar. She might just mention purchasing a second bicycle, should the funds miraculously appear.

"No, I suppose it doesn't. If it comes to trial, it's a good thing Mrs. Prentice cannot be forced to testify against her husband," Edwina said. "I shouldn't like to think what would become of them all if he does go to prison, or worse."

"I don't know about that, Ed. They may be better off without him," Beryl said. "After all, he's drinking up the housekeeping money and providing very little of it into the coffers in the first place."

"When you put it like that, I suppose you're right. I hate to think what we shall have to report to young Jack if we don't turn up anything more promising than we already have," Edwina said.

"I suppose the best thing we could do at this point is to go directly to the source," Beryl said.

"The source being who, pray tell?" Edwina said.

"Frank himself, of course," Beryl said. "I'm very much afraid one of us will have to go down to the police station and interview him."

"And how do you suggest we will be able to do that? After all, it isn't as though Doris Gibbs is inclined to do either of us any favors," Edwina said.

"Now, that's just the sort of attitude a private enquiry agent does not need, Ed. There's no sense in being defeatist. I always believe that where there is a will, there is a way," Beryl said. "How do you think I managed to bob about the globe with nothing more than a picnic hamper and a hot-air balloon?"

Edwina had been stirred to admiration the first few times she had heard this speech. But sadly, she had become used to Beryl's admonishments and had developed a remarkable tolerance for them. There was only one way to deal with such boasting.

"I shall be very glad to hear your report on the matter. I propose to head to the Beeches while you visit the police station by yourself," Edwina said.

"You don't wish to accompany me to see how it's done?" Beryl asked.

"I'm sure you will be more than happy to tell me about it later," Edwina said. "Besides, after all this jaunting around, I expect you would enjoy a decent meal. And while you may be adept at going on adventures with a picnic hamper, I have never known you to be someone who is capable of filling one."

Chapter 10

Beryl could not be quite sure, but she thought she had detected the slightest tone of derision in Edwina's voice. While she generally thought of Ed as receptive to her pep talks, perhaps she had been laying it on a bit thick. The fact of the matter was, Beryl was concerned. The possibility that Jack's father might be guilty of murder weighed heavily upon her heart.

Sometimes she was apt to behave a bit too breezily to counteract any feelings of heavyheartedness. Her conversation with Jack's mother about the chilling effects the war had had upon the soldiers had bothered her more than she cared to admit. It was far easier to spend energy and thought on the past when one recollected only the triumphs rather than the tragedies.

She made her way into town on foot, more sure than ever that she needed to undertake some decisive action concerning her fitness. It was beastly to greet passersby while one was out of breath. The small brick police station came as a welcome sight as she trudged up the high street. She could almost feel Prudence Rathbone's eyes boring into the back of her neck as she mounted the steps and let herself into the station. Prudence would be sure to spread the news that Beryl had been there before she even managed to get into the constable's good graces, Beryl was sure.

She stepped up to the counter and was surprised not to see Constable Gibbs glowering from the other side. In fact, there seemed to be no one manning the police station at all. Hardly daring to believe her luck, Beryl backed away from the window and headed for the corridor that led to the only cell the police station housed.

Before she had taken three steps down the passageway, a door to another room creaked open. Retired constable Lyndon Wilkes stood tucking his non-uniform shirt into his trousers. Beryl was glad she had not brought Edwina with her, after all. They had encountered former constable Wilkes at an earlier crime scene. Beryl had not enjoyed making his acquaintance but was quite sure he had enjoyed making hers. Edwina would not approve of Beryl applying her feminine wiles to the former constable's considerable weakness when it came to the fairer sex, but Beryl had no such compunctions. She turned up the flame on her already bright smile and commenced to look delighted to see him.

"Constable Wilkes, I should have realized you would be asked to assist with the goings-on," Beryl said. She stepped forward and looped her gloved hand through the constable's arm and gave it a squeeze. "Still keeping fit, I see. I seem to remember you having a great deal of strength in these hands and arms of yours when you wrapped your fingers around my ankle the last time we met."

She shamelessly batted her eyelashes at the poor man and spared a thought to any preexisting cardiac conditions he might have. Although, if he were to drop on the floor in some sort of a fit, she would be hard pressed not to step over him in order to interview Frank. Still, it might be best to modulate the effect of her charms. She had not been exaggerating the strength of his grasp. She had no intention of putting herself in a position where she would need to find her way out of a firm embrace.

"What brings you in here, missy?" Constable Wilkes said. "Doris didn't say she expected you in for questioning." Beryl noticed that although his tone was gruff, he made no effort to withdraw his arm.

She steered him ever so slightly around to face the end of the hall where the holding cell could be found. It was an easy enough thing to manage. She simply kept turning slightly to face him. He really was quite elderly. Beryl thought it likely he had become a bit duffer headed in his old age. She took a small step towards the far end of the corridor and felt him move alongside her with ease.

"I'm here to speak with the suspect, of course," Beryl said. "I'm sure you've heard from many sources how instrumental my friend and business partner, Edwina, and I have been in bringing criminals to justice in the recent past," Beryl said, bathing him in the radiance of her smile.

"Doris has mentioned your meddling now and again," Constable Wilkes said. "You say she asked you to stop by and question the suspect?"

Beryl shrugged elegantly. "If Constable Gibbs did not see fit to share such information with you herself, I'm not sure that I am authorized to do so. You know how she likes to keep things close to her vest."

"Are you sure you ought to be here? Perhaps I should try to find Doris before you go in to see him," the former constable said.

"I suppose you could do that, if you're the sort of man who needs to double-check on every little thing. I shouldn't have thought a man of your experience and wisdom would need to ask for permission. After all, it's not as though I'm trying to escort him out of the station. I'm just here to confirm a few facts in the case," Beryl said. She shrugged again and turned, as though she were about to leave.

"Not so hasty there, missy," Wilkes said. "I don't need Doris's permission to act on police business. If I did, she would not have left me in charge of the station while she was away."

He reached down to his belt and jangled a set of keys. He strode to the room at the end of the hall and fitted a heavy iron key into a sturdy lock. With a flourish, he pressed open the door and stepped out of the way for Beryl to pass through. She once again bestowed a brilliant smile on him, then stepped into the cell, where Frank Prentice lay curled up on the narrow bunk built into the wall.

"I'll take it from here, Constable Wilkes," Beryl said. "I'm sure you've already heard this man's sorry tale as many times as you've any interest in."

"That's for certain. I'll be out front when you're finished," Wilkes said. He pulled the door closed behind him, and Beryl felt a frisson of fear as she heard the tumblers of the lock click back into place. She reminded herself she was on English soil, and calmed herself with a deep breath.

"Well, Frank, you seem to be in a bit of a pickle," she said.

"You're that woman what's been in all the magazines and newspapers, aren't you?" Frank said. "The one my boy Jack goes on and on about every chance he gets." Frank sat up and swung his long legs over the side of the bunk.

"I'm an admirer of Jack's too," Beryl said. She gingerly took a seat on the edge of the bunk closest to the door. She crossed one long leg over the other and leaned back against the stone wall behind her. "As a matter of fact, Jack is the reason I am here."

"Jack sent you?" Frank asked.

"Indirectly. He has hired my partner, Edwina, and myself to prove your innocence. From the preliminary investigation we have conducted, that will prove to be a difficult thing to do," Beryl said.

"He shouldn't have wasted the money," Frank said. "It's not as though there is enough to go around as it is."

"We have no intention of taking Jack's money. But we are committed to helping to find the guilty party, whether it was you or someone else," Beryl said. "Which leads me to ask, Did you do it?"

"I don't remember. I don't remember much after leaving the pub last night. I certainly don't remember whether or not I hit Hector Lomax over the back of the head with a shovel," Frank said.

"The consensus around Walmsley Parva is that if anyone was likely to bear Hector ill will, it was you," Beryl said. "Are you sure you don't remember anything at all?"

"I remember stumbling out of the pub and feeling angry. After that things get very hazy," Frank said.

His shoulders sagged. Beryl wished Jack had a better example as he was growing into a man himself. She could see what Mrs. Prentice might have found attractive years earlier, though. Once, he must have been a fine-looking man. With his jet-black hair and bright blue eyes, he would have cut an alluring figure. Now his eyes were deeply bloodshot, and there was a bit of grey speckling his temples. Although, that might have little to do with his age. She remembered hearing stories of people during the war going entirely grey, or even white, almost overnight.

"Let's start with something simple. Do you remember going to the churchyard?" Beryl asked.

"Vaguely. Although, I can't be sure if it was last night I'm remembering or some other time."

"Do you often end up going to the churchyard after a bout of drinking?" Beryl asked.

"Let's say I spend an awful lot more time in the churchyard than I do in my own home," Frank said.

"Even though you were let go from your duties as the sexton?" Beryl said.

"What can I say, I like it there. The residents don't have a lot to say," he said. Beryl noticed the ghost of a smile playing across his lips. She saw the hint of a pair of dimples and thought once more she understood why Mrs. Prentice had once found him charming. She could even see a bit of Jack in his face.

"If you spend so much time there, perhaps you could help clear up a different mystery. Have you ever seen who's responsible for the vandalism that's been going on there?" Beryl asked.

Again, Frank smiled ever so slightly. He shook his head. "Have I seen the person that's done it? No," he said. Beryl caught a teasing note in his voice.

"That sounds like you are slicing things finely. Do you know who's been vandalizing the churchyard?" she asked.

"Is it likely to help me if I say that I do?" Frank said.

"I suppose that depends on who it is and whether or not they had been seen threatening Hector Lomax right before his death," Beryl said. "Do you know?"

"I already told you I don't remember anything that happened last night, after leaving the pub. How could I possibly tell you who had been seen with Hector just before he died?" he asked.

"Are you the one who's been vandalizing the churchyard?" Beryl said. "It wouldn't be surprising if you had. After all, few would blame you if you thought the vicar was being unfair in relieving you of your duties. He knew you needed the job and had a bunch of mouths to feed," Beryl said, hoping her appeal to his sense of outrage would bear fruit.

"So what if I was? It doesn't mean I killed Hector," he said.

"Let's say you are the one who has been damaging headstones and scrawling obscenities on the walls of the church. I suppose if you are willing to do things like that, you wouldn't stop at using a headstone as a place to tap out your pipe, now would you?" Beryl said.

"If I was the person vandalizing the churchyard, I'm sure that a little thing like that would in no way bother me," he said.

"So did you tap out a pipe on the headstone near where Hector was found?" Beryl said.

"I most assuredly did not," Frank said.

"I thought you said you couldn't remember anything after leaving the pub," Beryl said. She felt the shiver of excitement she always experienced when she thought she was making progress on an investigation. Then she remembered she did not want Frank to be guilty, and her heart sank.

"I may not remember where I was, but I most assuredly remember the fact that I don't smoke a pipe," Frank said. "I never have and don't have the money to start doing it now." He leaned back and crossed his arms over his chest.

"You're sure about that?" Beryl asked.

"Ask anyone in the village. Anyone who knows me can tell you that I have never been one to smoke a pipe. Before I joined up, I'd smoke a cigarillo now and again, but not since," Frank said. He tapped his chest with an open palm.

"Gas?" Beryl said.

"My lungs aren't any good anymore. If I want to stay above ground long enough to see my little ones grow up, I need to steer clear of smoking."

"If you want to stay alive long enough to see your children grow up, we need to find a different suspect in Hector's murder. You haven't been much help," Beryl said.

"You can't be more sorry about that than me, can you?" Frank said.

Chapter 11

Crumpet heard the door before Edwina and went tearing off down the corridor, barking. She hurried after him, wiping her wet hands on her pinafore. She had barely finished filling the sink with hot, soapy water in order to do the breakfast dishes when she heard the commotion. At this rate, she would never get a meal on the table before Beryl returned from her visit to the police station.

She pulled open the door and was surprised to see her friend Charles Jarvis standing on the front step. He was accompanied by another man, attired in a similar manner. Both gentlemen wore suits and hats. The stranger carried a gleaming leather briefcase.

"Hello, Charles," Edwina said.

"Hello, Edwina," Charles said. "I am very sorry to have disturbed you, but my friend and fellow solicitor, Arthur Pettigrew came down by train from London and was most insistent that we pay a call here at the Beeches. I hope you don't mind."

"Certainly not. Do come in."

She motioned for them to follow her and hurriedly removed

her pinafore as she walked down the hallway. She stuffed it into a large porcelain vase as she crossed the threshold into the parlour. As she caught a glimpse of herself in the mirror hung over the mantel, she reached up and patted a few stray hairs into place.

Although it was in her nature to be hospitable to guests, she vastly preferred to expect them rather than to be surprised at their arrival. She motioned to two upholstered chairs and perched at the edge of the sofa, one neat ankle crossed over the other.

"What brings you by, Charles?" Edwina said. "I'm sure you are not looking for a game of bridge at this early hour."

Charles had partnered with Edwina many times at the bridge table to modest success. In the past several weeks, however, he had played with Beryl on several occasions. Edwina had noticed his game improved considerably when matched with her friend rather than with herself.

She had always thought Charles a rather conservative and even dull player, until she had seen him partnered with Beryl. She had been surprised to consider that he had in fact been adjusting his own manner of play to meet hers.

Beryl had suggested on multiple occasions that Charles was interested in partnering with Edwina for more things than bridge. Edwina felt flustered by the notion and dismissed it out of hand every time her friend brought it up. She couldn't help but hear Beryl's words rattling around in her head as she sat patiently waiting to hear the reason for the lanky solicitor's visit.

Charles held his hat in his hands and looked uncomfortable. She noticed he shifted his weight in the chair and cleared his throat several times.

"I'm not here about bridge, and as much as I wish we were, we are not actually here to speak with you," he said.

"I am afraid Beryl is out at present," Edwina said. She wondered momentarily if even Charles had fallen prey to Beryl's considerable charms. She certainly could not blame him. He would not be the first man to do so and surely would not be the last.

"Actually, Mr. Pettigrew is here to speak with Simpkins," Charles said.

"Simpkins?" Edwina repeated. It was as though she was now running a boardinghouse, like Mrs. Plumptree over at Shady Rest.

"That's right, Miss Davenport," Mr. Pettigrew said with a deep, rumbling voice. "I urgently need to speak with Mr. Simpkins on a matter of great importance."

"I suggest you call in at his cottage. Charles, you know where it is, don't you?" she asked, making to rise to her feet.

"We already tried at the cottage. Someone left a note pinned to the door, saying he could be found in the garden at the Beeches. Which brings us to you," Charles said.

Edwina felt her cheeks begin to flame. Had she not ushered Simpkins back to his own home just a few hours earlier? Was it not enough for the people of Walmsley Parva to know he had taken up residence on her property? Would the residents of London need know it too? He must be spoken to at once. She shot to her feet.

"Then I suggest you present yourselves at the potting shed. Despite my best efforts to send him home, it seems he is determined to remain here," she said. She hoped she had managed to keep the trembling from her voice, but she rather thought she had not.

"I think it would be best if you accompanied us to deliver Mr. Pettigrew's news, Edwina," Charles said, struggling to his feet. "I really haven't the least idea of how he will take it."

Mr. Pettigrew nodded silently, his small dark eyes crinkled with concern. Really, it had been a most disconcerting day, Edwina thought as she led the pair of men to the garden and rapped sharply on the door to the potting shed.

She was embarrassed to be in the position of needing to

knock on her own shed door, but she had no intention whatsoever of encountering Simpkins in a state of undress ever again in her life and certainly not in front of a pair of gentlemen. The mere thought of it made her feel a bit faint. When there was no answer, she rapped again and called out.

"Come now, Simpkins, I know you are within. I have it on good authority that you left a prominently displayed note announcing your intention to return. There is no use pretending you are elsewhere."

She heard a shuffling, banging noise, followed by a spate of low-toned expletives, which she decided to ignore. If Charles felt there was reason she was needed, it was likely he was correct. Charles was not a man who made controversy where none need exist.

The door creaked open, and Simpkins peered out through the crack with a sheepish look on his face. Edwina placed her small hand firmly upon it and pressed it open farther. Simpkins looked no better than he had when she and Beryl left him earlier that day at his cottage. She doubted very much that he had taken a nap or even had a noon meal.

"Mr. Jarvis has brought a man to see you. He is a solicitor and has come down especially from London on urgent business that involves you in some way," she said.

She stepped to the side to make room for Mr. Pettigrew, who had placed a large, expensively shod foot in her delphinium border. She supposed he could not help a lack of horticultural sensitivity, considering his city origins. As she surreptitiously inspected the plants for signs of damage, she felt a little sorry for someone for whom the delights of the herbaceous border were so alien a thing.

"Is it correct to assume you are Albert Simpkins, only son of Orelia Judd Simpkins?" Mr. Pettigrew asked.

"That's me. But I can't for the life of me guess why you would want to know," Simpkins said. "Am I in some sort of trouble?" He turned his watery gaze first on Charles and then on Edwina. She hoped fervently that he was not.

"No, nothing of the kind," Mr. Pettigrew said. "In fact, I hope you will find what I have to impart to be extraordinarily good news."

Edwina was surprised at the tension she felt in her neck and shoulders. She noticed she was holding her breath and forced herself to exhale slowly and silently. Charles turned his head to look at her and gave her a reassuring nod. Perhaps he understood how she felt about surprises and about unexpected news.

She could not say she had survived the war years and the flu epidemic with her previous love of the unanticipated intact. She wasn't sure that anyone had. Those years had been like an extended period where the hand of fate turned the handle on a jack-in-the-box with excruciating slowness. One clung faithfully to hope, awaiting the barest scraps of news, but there simply wasn't any to be had. And then, out of nowhere, the lid flew off your world, and a burst of dread broke free and laughed in your face.

No, Edwina assuredly did not like surprises. From the guarded look on his face, neither did Simpkins. She saw his posture stiffen, and he gripped the doorjamb, as if to brace himself for whatever was coming.

"Well, best let me have it, then," he said. Edwina thought he sounded rather like a young boy about to take a few lashings from his father for some misdemeanor or other.

"I have the very great privilege of informing you that you have been left a substantial inheritance." Mr. Pettigrew paused for effect, and Edwina felt her nerves stretching even more tautly. He cleared his throat and continued. "In fact, it could be considered a fortune."

Simpkins looked at Charles and then over at Edwina, as if to ask if some sort of jest was at hand. "You're having me on, aren't you, sir?" he asked Mr. Pettigrew.

"Indeed I am entirely in earnest. I am here on behalf of the

estate of Colonel Kimberly, who has left you controlling interest in Colonel Kimberly's Condiment Company," Mr. Pettigrew said. He popped open the latches on his dispatch case and
pulled out a thick sheaf of papers, which he attempted to pass
to Simpkins. Simpkins waved his hands in front of them, as if to
ward off the documentation.

"That can't be right," Simpkins said.

"I assure you, it is correct. Colonel Kimberly himself had me
draw up this, his last will and testament, and you are named as
his primary heir. He has left almost everything, with the excep-
tion of a few small legacies, to you," Mr. Pettigrew said.

Edwina felt overcome by a wave of dizziness. In fact, she had
trouble catching her breath. Simpkins had grown decidedly
grey in complexion, and Edwina was quite certain that had she
been able to see her own face, it would have looked much the
same.

"Simpkins, have you ever heard of this Colonel Kimberly?"
she asked.

"Well, I have a bottle of his brown sauce on my kitchen table
and a pot of his rutabaga chutney in the cupboard, but beyond
that, I can't say we're well acquainted," Simpkins said.

"Then why in the world would he have left his company to
you?" Edwina asked. She turned to Mr. Pettigrew.

"I suppose it's because Mr. Simpkins was known to the
colonel in some significant way," Mr. Pettigrew said. "When he
asked me to draw up the will, Colonel Kimberly mentioned
disbursing an obligation to Mr. Simpkins's family."

"That can't be right," Edwina said. "Simpkins's parents were
residents of Walmsley Parva. Simpkins grew up here, right
along with my own mother. They had no relationship with a
London-based mustard monger."

"I assure you that the inheritance is genuine and that you,
Mr. Simpkins, will be a very wealthy man as soon as the estate
clears through the courts," Mr. Pettigrew said.

Simpkins took one last look at each of the people standing

before him, then stumbled from the potting shed and hurried as quickly as his elderly and unsteady gait would allow in the direction of the wood at the edge of the property. Edwina started to follow, but Charles laid a restraining hand on her upper arm.

"I expect it's been a bit of a shock for the poor fellow. He might just need some time to let it all sink in," Charles said. "As, I'm sure, do you. To tell the truth, Edwina, you look almost as shocked as he did."

Edwina felt ashamed of herself at the number of thoughts that had run through her head when Mr. Pettigrew mentioned Simpkins's windfall. The idea that her jobbing gardener was now a very wealthy man beggared belief. This was just one more proof that the social order had completely collapsed. It was utterly unimaginable.

As she watched Simpkins disappear between the trees, she wondered whom she was possibly going to get to help out in the garden now.

Chapter 12

Beryl walked home from the village, lost in a fog of thought. So far, things looked very black indeed for Frank. His wife did not feel she could vouch for his character or his whereabouts. He himself remembered nothing of the time in question. The only clues that pointed at other possible motivations for the crime were a bit of pipe ash and Hector's flaming disputes with other residents of the village not long before he died.

She did not wish to follow a line of enquiry that would lead away from Frank and straight back to Simpkins. The fact of the matter was she was quite fond of the elderly gardener. And while she would never admit it out loud, Edwina had a hidden soft spot for him as well.

She knew Simpkins thought the world of Edwina in return. He had said as much one night at the pub. Simpkins had undertaken the task of keeping an eye on her after her parents had both passed on. Beryl thought it was rather sweet.

She gratefully mounted the stone step to the Beeches and let herself in the front door. Beryl never ceased to be amazed by the fact that Crumpet always seemed to know if she or Simpkins was the one to enter the house. The little dog never barked at either of them. She peeled off her driving gloves and placed them on the marble shelf on the hall tree. She leaned into the mirror and squinted at her face.

Beryl was not a particularly vain woman. She took no real pleasure in her appearance. But she did realize how much of her celebrity was built on her image as both an adventurous and glamorously attractive woman.

In the months she had been living a quiet life in Walmsley Parva, she had made an effort to uphold the standards of appearance she had expected of herself throughout her life. Still, it would be rather nice to dispense with some of the frippery from time to time. Maybe when the private enquiry business had taken the nation by storm, she would allow herself to consider it.

She headed straight for the kitchen. Edwina was sure to have something wonderful awaiting her for a meal. After all, hadn't she used that as her excuse to stay at the Beeches and to leave Beryl the unpleasant task of getting past the constable and interviewing Frank? Although, truth be told, Beryl would rather face any number of constables, or even angry lions, for that matter, than stare into the abyss of a cookery book.

She swept into the room, her stomach rumbling, but Edwina was nowhere to be found. Not only that, there were no signs of cooking. The sink was half filled with water, and a few tenacious bubbles of washing soap clung to the sides of the sink, but nothing else indicated Edwina had been present.

Beryl backtracked to the parlour and peeked inside. Edwina's chair was empty. Finally, she called out for her friend and heard a faint response coming from the library. Beryl knew that the library was Edwina's favourite room in the house. Edwina had had a spot of difficulty there back in the autumn and had unfortunately given the room a bit of a miss in the intervening months. Beryl wondered what could have happened to send her friend scurrying for the comfort of that space.

She thrust open the door and stepped inside. Edwina was sprawled—yes, sprawled—in a wingback chair nestled alongside a long window overlooking the garden. Her feet, still shod, sat propped up on the ottoman. They fell sideways like a duck's. Beryl had never seen Edwina, even at repose, without her ankles crossed in a ladylike fashion. A book lay abandoned on the floor, and Edwina's gaze remained firmly fixed on the wall opposite her even after Beryl called her name. Something was well and truly up.

"Has something happened with the case?" Beryl said. She approached Edwina and perched on the ottoman beside her friend's tiny feet. With effort, Edwina dragged her gaze from the near distance and let it drift towards Beryl's anxious face.

"Not with the case, no. But somehow I feel that the universe has become disordered," Edwina said. Beryl reached out and took her friend by the hand. She patted it briskly, noting how cold it was to the touch.

"Truly, you do not look well. What have you been up to while I've been gone?" Beryl said.

"Simpkins has received a visitor," Edwina said.

"Constable Gibbs again? Has he been arrested?" Beryl said. "I thought the case against Frank was still very strong."

Edwina shook her head. "No, it was a legal matter, but not one for the police," Edwina said. "It appears that Simpkins has just inherited a vast fortune."

If anything Edwina's posture became even more relaxed. If something was not done, she would simply ooze into the fabric of the chair and disappear completely.

"That's wonderful news. From whom did he inherit it?" Beryl asked. Such things never bothered Beryl. She was rarely surprised at reversals of fortune for the good or the evil. In fact, it was part of what she felt made life worth living. The very zest of it all, so to speak. It was clear that Edwina did not share her outlook.

"A condiment company," Edwina said.

"You mean like mustard and relish?" Beryl asked. Such a possibility would never have entered her mind. If it wasn't for Edwina's demeanor, she would have had the sneaking suspicion that her imaginative friend was pulling her leg.

"Mustard, yes. I'm not sure what you mean by relish. Chutney, I suppose. Or mixed pickle. Either way, yes, that's exactly what I mean," Edwina said.

"Did he enter a contest? Something on the back of a packet?" Beryl asked. Her mind was agog. Of all the ways she could have considered someone eligible to inherit a great deal of money, the idea of doing so through the auspices of a pickle factory would never have entered her mind.

"The solicitor who came to inform him of his good fortune assures me that Simpkins is a legitimate heir to Colonel Kimberly's Condiment Company and all that entails," Edwina said. "It had nothing whatsoever to do with any contest. It seems to have had something to do with his family."

"How extraordinary," Beryl said.

"Just when you think life cannot get more topsy-turvy, a thing like this happens," Edwina said. "I have no idea what I will do for a gardener now."

So that was it. Edwina was concerned about more changes to her household. It was understandable, really, after the loss of her family members one by one over the course of a woefully short period of time. It wasn't an unfamiliar story, but that did not make it any less painful.

While Beryl was quite sure that Edwina would not consider Simpkins a member of the family in the same way her mother had been, or at least would not admit to feeling that way, she suspected the grizzled old gardener was more important to Edwina than she had previously realized.

"There's nothing to say that he will leave his position here at the Beeches just because he's come into some money," Beryl said. She gave Edwina's hand an affectionate squeeze.

"I rather think it's more than just some money, Beryl," Edwina said. "Colonel Kimberly's is one of the most recognized brands in all the empire. As you would say, Simpkins will be simply rolling in it. I expect he shall want to have a gardener of his own, and one far more suited to the task than he is. For one thing, he'll be able to afford a quality gardener." Beryl noted patches of bright color dotting Edwina's cheeks.

"In my experience, people do not tend to behave differently when they have money and when they don't have it. They're simply the same person, with just a little more jingle in their pockets," Beryl said.

"Do you really think so?" Edwina said with a lilt of hope in her voice.

"I know it's made absolutely no difference to me. Sometimes I'm flush, and sometimes I'm broke. I am always myself. I always want the same sorts of things out of life, the same sort of experiences, the same connections. I can't see how Simpkins would be any different," Beryl said.

"Are you quite certain?" Edwina said.

"I am. Besides, if he's anything like most people who come into a windfall, he'll mismanage it almost immediately and be back where he started in under six months' time," Beryl said.

"But that's ghastly too," Edwina said.

"That may be so, but I've seen it happen more often than not. So where is he? I'd like to congratulate him before he spends it all," Beryl said.

"Come to think of it, I have no idea where Simpkins might be. After he received the news, we were both rather shocked. Simpkins stumbled off through the woods and hasn't been back since. I suppose I should be quite worried about him," Edwina said.

"I shouldn't think it would be too difficult to track him down. Unless I miss my guess, Simpkins will be celebrating at the Dove and Duck," Beryl said.

"I suppose we should go there and make sure, shouldn't we?" Edwina straightened to a more upright position with apparent effort.

"Don't you have your regular appointment with Alma Poole this afternoon?" Beryl asked, getting to her feet.

"When one's gardener has suddenly become a millionaire, there seems little point in bothering with things like maintaining a presentable appearance."

"If you neglect your appointment, you will only feel worse. Besides, I think a bit of a walk in the fresh air would do you a world of good," Beryl said.

"I rather think that hearing I had inherited the controlling interest in a multinational company would do me a world of good. Still, I suppose it will be preferable to a trip into the pub." Edwina hoisted herself from the chair and straightened her skirt.

Chapter 13

Edwina and Beryl separated at the top of the high street. With a cheery wave, Beryl continued along the street to the pub. Edwina watched her as she sauntered down the road. She wished that she were as capable of taking things in stride as Beryl seemed to be. She supposed it was simply not in her nature and that in times of change, she required more time to adapt and to reflect on what such things might mean for the future.

Perhaps Beryl simply did not consider the future as much as Edwina did. Her mother had always admonished her to think how things might turn out, and for the most part, it had felt like sound advice. But from time to time, Edwina wished she could toss her cares to the wind and see where events simply took her just as readily as did her friend.

Still, she liked to think she was capable of changing with the times. She pushed open the door of Alma's House of Beauty and set the bell jingling. Edwina recognized a pretty local girl named Hattie Brooks, who looked up from a sink, where she was rinsing a customer's hair.

Edwina averted her eyes. There was something not quite nice about seeing her neighbors in such a state of vulnerability. She appreciated the fact that Alma had the good sense to cover the bottom half of the windows of her shop in heavy draperies. She could not imagine putting herself on display for all the passersby if the shop had been open to the street.

With a quick nod to Hattie, she took a seat in the waiting area and drew her knitting from her bag. After the distressing day she had had, there was nothing quite like adding a few rows to a project to steady her nerves.

"Mrs. Poole will be with you in just a moment," Hattie said as she placed a towel over the customer's head.

Edwina nodded and felt her shoulders begin to relax down away from her ears as she clicked her needles through the smooth, soft wool. She was not sure for whom she was knitting the small blue hat she held in her hands. That was the way it often was with her projects. She would spot a skein of wool and know that she just had to use it for something or other. Generally, the wool would tell her exactly what it wished to be. Once the project was completed, she invariably found it a home.

As she looked down at the hat, she realized that she had most likely been making it for one of Jack Prentice's younger siblings. She was just mentally inventorying her remaining supply of yarn, with the thought of making small knitted gifts for all the Prentice children, when Alma appeared from the back room.

"I wasn't sure if I'd see you today, Edwina," Alma said, bustling towards her with an outstretched hand. "After all the excitement, I wasn't sure if you would be out on the case." She urged Edwina to the recently vacated sink and waited while Hattie sorted out the potions and products she always used on Edwina's head.

"What makes you think that Beryl and I would be involved in that?" Edwina said.

Hattie pressed her gently back towards the sink, and Edwina felt ill at ease. It didn't feel professional somehow to be discussing her business while gazing at the ceiling and feeling the warm trickle of water dousing her head. Alma seemed to have no such compunctions.

"Well, lately, whenever a crime is afoot, you and Beryl are in the thick of it. I simply assumed that you would be involved in this case as well. Especially since I had understood that Simpkins was one of the suspects," Alma said.

Hattie lathered Edwina's hair and began massaging her scalp with strong bony fingers.

"Whatever led you to believe that Simpkins was one of the suspects?" Edwina asked. While that might have been true, she wasn't about to cast aspersions on her gardener's character, no matter how little time into the future he might be in her employ.

"Everyone knows that Simpkins was the first person Constable Gibbs went to speak with as soon as Hector's body was found," Alma said. "I simply assumed that meant he was a suspect, and the prime one at that."

Hattie leaned even closer and commenced rinsing. Edwina kept her eyes tightly shut against the flood of water cascading near her face.

"As he was Hector's next of kin, she was understandably eager to notify him of Hector's death. It was no more than that," Edwina said.

"People are saying that Simpkins and Hector had a row in the pub only a short time before Hector was murdered," Alma said. "Are you sure there wasn't more to Constable Gibbs's visit to the Beeches than a death notification?"

"What I have understood is that there was no shortage of people who might wish Hector out of their lives one way or another," Edwina said.

Hattie finished the rinsing and urged Edwina to sit up. She

draped the towel over her head and rubbed it through her hair to extract the water. "That's true, miss," the shampoo girl said, before turning to address Alma. "You must be as happy as anyone that he's no longer going to be giving you any trouble."

This was a bit of unexpected information. Edwina had never heard anyone mention a connection between her hairdresser and Hector. Edwina peeked out from under the towel and took note of Alma's expression. It could not be said that it was a happy one.

"I'm sure I don't know what you are on about," Alma said. Edwina's finely honed lie-detecting skills leapt into action. If Alma had been a parlourmaid, Edwina would have made her turn out her pockets in order to check for bits of the family silver.

There was no doubt in her mind that Alma had no wish to speak of her own connection to Hector Lomax. It might have been far smarter not to bring up his death in the first place. But, thought Edwina, perhaps it would have caused more raised eyebrows if Alma had failed to mention the biggest news of the day.

After all, local gossip flowed almost as steadily at the hairdressing salon as it did at Prudence Rathbone's post office–cum–sweetshop–cum–stationer. No, Edwina had always regarded Alma as an intelligent woman, and here was even more proof.

"All I'm saying is he won't be in here causing any more trouble," the girl said.

The girl was not as bright as her employer. Edwina suspected the poor young thing would be in for a stern talking-to by Alma as soon as the opportunity for a moment of privacy presented itself.

"That's quite enough, Hattie," Alma said, waving a comb at her employee. "Why don't you take a seat right here, Edwina, and we'll have you looking lovely in a trice. You'll be wanting your usual wave, I expect." Alma reached for a small cart holding a bowl of strong-smelling liquid.

Edwina's thoughts sprang from musing over what Alma was so eager not to discuss to the question posed. She looked in the mirror opposite her and suddenly realized she had no interest whatsoever in having Alma apply her considerable talents to making Edwina's hair wave.

Curling her hair had been her mother's idea. Edwina had never enjoyed having her head covered in strong chemicals before having strands of her hair clamped between heated metal devices. The entire process took hours, and Edwina had never been able to see the point in all the fuss. She looked over at Hattie and felt an overwhelming surge of recklessness.

"Actually, I have decided it is time for a change," Edwina said. "I should like for you to bob it."

Alma gasped. "Bob it?" she said. "Are you sure?"

"Completely," Edwina said, perching in the chair and folding her hands into her lap. "I should like the same sort of style as Hattie is wearing." Edwina nodded at the younger woman, who gave her a bright smile.

"I must tell you many women regret the decision to bob their hair before I even complete the job. Are you absolutely certain?" Alma said, lifting a long lock of Edwina's hair, as if to emphasize how much there was to lose.

"I appreciate your concern and your warning. But I suddenly feel a great desire for change. Besides, I am sure it will prove practical. Don't you agree, Hattie?"

"My mum nearly threw me out of the house when I first had it done, but now that she has seen how much less fuss my hair is than hers, she is thinking of having hers bobbed too," Hattie said. "Besides, my hair fits so much better under my hats now than it did when it was long, especially when I wear a cloche."

That settled it. Edwina loved her hats more than any other part of her wardrobe. If bobbing her hair would make it easier for her to look well in them, she would be foolish not to do so. There was a certain peacock-blue cloche at the milliner's over in the neighboring market town of Much Dilling that she had had her eye on for some time.

"That is all I need to know. Alma, there is no one I would trust more with the job than you," Edwina said.

It was the truth. While the women in most larger towns and even in many cities were forced to ask barbers to sheer off their long locks, Alma had seen the moneymaking possibility of learning to do so herself. The idea had first occurred to her during the war, when several Land Army girls had asked her if she knew how to maintain their bobbed hairstyles.

She had promptly set off for London, where she'd learned by observing a friendly barber in his shop over the course of several days. When she'd returned home and announced that she was capable of providing bobbed hairstyles, as well as the more traditional ones, she'd begun drawing a steady stream of clients from Walmsley Parva, as well as from many neighboring villages.

"If you are sure, I will fetch my shears," Alma said.

Alma fastened a protective cape around Edwina's neck and gently pulled a comb through her damp hair. Edwina closed her eyes as she felt the cool metal of the shears press against the back of her neck. Her spirits rose with each snip. Her head felt lighter as strand after strand of brown hair fell to the floor. As Alma completed the cutting and loosened the cape, Edwina realized she was holding her breath. She forced herself to exhale slowly, then opened her eyes.

"Well, what do you think?" Alma asked, pointing to the mirror.

Edwina barely recognized the face staring back at her. Her eyes seemed larger; her cheeks fuller. She turned her head slowly from side to side, surprised at the way short tendrils softly framed her face. Released from its own weight, her hair seemed to have discovered a natural wave. She reached up and touched the nape of her neck and was reminded of a most improper but enjoyable incident involving a young man during her youth.

She smiled at her reflection from the utter astonishment of her appearance.

She slid from the chair, thanked Alma for her service, and settled her bill. Hattie crossed the room and handed Edwina her hat, which she promptly placed upon her head. The girl had been right. It was a remarkably comfortable fit. Feeling like an entirely new woman, she set off for the Beeches, wondering what Beryl would have to say when she saw her.

Chapter 14

Just as she had suspected, Simpkins had found his way to the Dove and Duck. However, it had not been a straight path from the Beeches to the pub, if the bits of twig embedded in his beard and the mud spattering his trouser cuffs were anything to go on. Beryl had not thought it possible for Simpkins to look any more disreputable than he usually did. But somehow, he had accomplished just that. She thought a good use of his new-found wealth might be a visit to a bespoke tailor. Or at least for him to make an investment in a new bar of soap.

She stopped off at the bar and ordered a pint of lager for Simpkins and a glass of soda water for herself. Despite the fact that she had no qualms about imbibing at any hour of the day she saw fit, she wished to keep a clear head while speaking with Simpkins. He did not look as though he could be entirely responsible for himself, and Beryl had a sneaking suspicion he might need to rely on her for moral and possibly physical support. She carried the drinks to the table he generally occupied at the far end of the room, and placed the pint before him.

"I hear congratulations are in order," Beryl said, settling into the seat beside him.

"Miss Edwina's been talking, then, has she?" Simpkins said.

"She looked almost as shocked as you do," Beryl said. "I'm not sure she would have said anything if I hadn't pried it out of her. It was easy to see something very shocking had happened in my absence."

"You can say that again. I'm not sure my ticker can take much more," Simpkins said. "I slept on the hard floor of the shed last night, awoke to find a police constable accusing me of murder, discovered my brother-in-law had been murdered, and now find out I'm a man of means."

"I see your point," Beryl said. "You must be completely overwhelmed by the surprise of the news." She took a sip of her soda water and grimaced. She really would have preferred a double whisky. Still, needs must.

"I've been racking my brain and racking my brain, trying to figure out how it is that I came to inherit this money, but I honestly have no idea. Besides, what am I supposed to do with it?" Simpkins asked.

Beryl could tell from the quantity of glasses littering the surface of his table that Simpkins had had a prodigious amount to drink, even for a veteran imbiber like him. She had a sneaking suspicion that he might burst into tears at any moment. He was the sort to become maudlin. She wasn't uncomfortable on her own account. Tears rarely bothered Beryl. They were just another part of life, like laughter or the hiccups.

But men seemed to have a more difficult time with such things, especially British men. She generally preferred men from countries where lips were supple rather than stiff. She let her mind wander for a brief moment to a pleasant fortnight spent in South America. Simpkins let out a rumbling belch, jolting her back to the present.

"I don't think you need to make any decisions straightaway. As a matter of fact, considering the fact you are probably well and truly lubricated, I doubt it would be advisable. There will be plenty of time for you to worry about that once you've gotten more accustomed to the idea," Beryl said.

Simpkins hoisted his glass and drained it, then slammed it down on the surface of the table. Or perhaps it was more that it slipped from his grasp and clattered downwards with a thud. Either way, from the sharp looks the publican was sending his way, Beryl decided it was time to take him home. The only problem was, she couldn't see him being left on his own at the empty cottage he had shared with Hector.

While it seemed clear he and his brother-in-law had not gotten along of late, it was also true that the cottage had once been a place full of warmth and family and supposedly many fond memories. Even someone like Beryl, who had never had such a home to return to or even to lose, could understand that that was not the right place for an elderly man who had suffered several shocks in short duration.

With only the briefest thought to the likelihood of protestations from Edwina, Beryl took Simpkins by the arm and steered him out the door of the Dove and Duck. She led the way down a narrow alley between the pub and a neighboring shop in order to keep out of sight of the beauty salon.

Beryl was glad she had not given in to the temptation and indulged in a few drinks of her own. By the time she had piloted Simpkins back to the Beeches, she had worked up quite a sweat. Steering him up the wide staircase and along the passageway to a back bedroom required more effort than she had expected to expend. Beryl was grateful for her strong stomach and survival skills as she unlaced Simpkins's hobnailed boots and eased them from his feet. She thought once again of the wide variety of soaps he would now be able to afford.

Without a word, he toppled backwards onto the bed, which was covered in a snowy-white counterpane. Beryl did not wish to consider what Edwina would have to say about either Simpkins snoring heartily in one of her guest rooms or the condition of her linens after his dirt-encrusted wardrobe had come into contact with them. At least, she thought, he would be in a position to offer to purchase new bedding should the stains prove impossible to eliminate.

Now that she had conducted her good deed for the day, Beryl felt she deserved that drink she had denied herself at the pub. Besides, Edwina would be back from the hairdressing salon soon, and unless Simpkins managed to quiet down before she returned, she would certainly be aware that someone was snoring on the second floor. The best way to handle Edwina in such cases was directly appealing to her better nature after plying her with a gin fizz. She strode to the parlour and set to work.

By the time she heard Edwina opening the front door to the Beeches, she had chipped the ice for the ice bucket, buffed two glasses until the crystal shone, and had added a fresh cartridge to the soda siphon. She also had run through her prepared remarks in her mind several times.

"Isn't it a bit early, even for you?" she heard Edwina ask from behind her.

"After the day we've had, I didn't think it would do us any harm to bend the rules just a little. Besides, I had nothing whatsoever to drink at the pub."

Beryl dropped three ice chunks into a glass, splashed in a generous quantity of gin, then topped the whole thing off with several squirts from the soda siphon. She fixed a second in exactly the same manner, then carried both to the seating area, where Edwina had stationed herself and taken up her knitting, curiously with her second-best hat still placed firmly upon her head.

"Please tell me you found Simpkins," Edwina said as she reached for the glass in Beryl's outstretched hand.

"He was just exactly where I expected him to be. I found him at his usual table at the Dove and Duck," Beryl said. "He was rather worse for the wear, I would have to say, though." Beryl settled into the wingback chair opposite Edwina and stretched her feet out on the footstool in front of her. She rattled the ice in her glass before taking a sip.

"I'm very glad that you found him. That's one thing off my mind at least," Edwina said.

From the set of her friend's shoulders and the way they had crept up close to her ears, Beryl knew that hearing Simpkins was a houseguest would not be welcomed information. Perhaps she should delay the revelation for a few minutes and ask Edwina about her trip to the hairdresser.

"I cannot help but notice you have not removed your hat," Beryl said. "I must surmise that your head is cold or that your visit to Mrs. Poole was unprecedentedly disastrous."

Edwina lifted her glass to her lips and took a deep drink. Beryl was surprised. Her friend usually made a single cocktail last through an entire evening. Something terrible must have occurred. Surely such an unfortunate turn of events could not have taken place at a worse time.

"Do you promise not to laugh?" Edwina said.

Beryl looked at her with even greater concern. "I should never consider mocking you," she said with feeling.

Edwina nodded and raised her free hand to the brim of her hat. She took another gulp of her gin fizz, then yanked off her headwear. Beryl's mind reeled. For a split second, she wondered if she had somehow forgotten that she had spent the afternoon matching Simpkins drink for drink at the pub. Surely the vision in front of her was the product of spirit-fueled imaginings.

She glanced at the clock on the mantelpiece. Even if she had forgotten throwing back a drink or two, she had not been at the pub anywhere near long enough to have become inebriated. While she prided herself on her ability to entertain a wide range of possibilities in any given situation, she had never given a moment's thought to the chance that Edwina would bob her hair. The pleading look in Edwina's eyes assured her she was not imagining things.

"How smart you look," Beryl said, leaning forward to give Edwina's new look careful consideration. "The very picture of a modern businesswoman."

"Do you really think so?" Edwina asked. Beryl heard the ice rattling in Edwina's glass. Her hand shook, and she nibbled on her lip once more.

"I think you ought to have done it years ago. I would have suggested it if I had had any notion you would be interested in lopping off your locks. I know I have never regretted bobbing mine." Beryl ran her broad hand over her sleek cap of platinum-blond hair. "But whatever made you do it?"

"Something just came over me when Alma asked if I wanted the usual. I suddenly felt all topsy-turvy and utterly rebellious. So I asked her to bob it."

"I understand the nature of rebellions. I spent some time in Russia, you know." Beryl leaned back and considered Edwina's appearance. "But do you like the way it looks?"

"You know, I do rather. My head feels so light, I keep expecting it to float off my neck. It even fits better with my hats."

"To think if Simpkins's inheritance hadn't caused you to question the entire social order, you likely wouldn't have made your discovery," Beryl said.

Edwina scowled at the contents of her glass, and Beryl thought perhaps it was unwise to remind Edwina of Simpkins's good fortune, considering he was asleep on the second floor. She decided to steer the conversation to firmer ground.

"Did you pick up any gossip concerning the case from the other ladies at the hairdresser?"

"As a matter of fact, I did hear something interesting," Edwina said.

Beryl leaned forward. "Do tell," she said.

"Hattie, the shampoo girl, was gossiping about Hector's murder. She mentioned something about Alma being relieved about his death," Edwina said.

"That's interesting," Beryl said. "Did she say why?"

"She did not. As a matter of fact, Alma made it quite plain that she wanted to change the subject," Edwina said. "Fortunately, I had the presence of mind not to pry. If I had forgotten myself and pursued a line of questioning, my hair might look decidedly less flattering."

"Do you have any guesses what the shampoo girl may have been talking about?" Beryl asked.

"I have no idea. It seems like a viable line of enquiry, though," Edwina said. She took another sip of her gin fizz. A bit more small talk and she might be ready to hear the news about Simpkins.

"I would say it's the first surprising lead we've had. All the other animosity towards Hector has been sitting right on the surface," Beryl said. "Speaking of things not on the surface, Simpkins is not one to say a great deal about his personal life, is he?"

"I should think not," Edwina said. She dropped her knitting into her lap, and Beryl realized she might as well just plunge ahead. By the time Edwina had become relaxed enough to hear about Simpkins, she might be too squiffy to comprehend.

"Despite his reticence, the man has had several extreme shocks in the course of just one day. That's quite a lot for a man of his age to endure," Beryl said. "Don't you think?"

"Yes, I suppose it is. I know we are a nation of reserved and stoic people. But I admit, even for me, his news was quite shocking. I can only imagine the extent of Simpkins's own turmoil," Edwina said.

"That's just what I thought you would say," Beryl said.

Edwina squinted at her, and fine lines appeared around her friend's tightly pursed lips. "You've done something, haven't you?" Edwina said. "You might as well tell me. It will only make things more difficult if you wait." She picked up her knitting once more and jabbed the needles through the still forming fabric.

"Like I said, Simpkins was well in his cups when I found him at the Dove and Duck. I didn't think it was the most sensible thing to escort him back to his cottage," Beryl said.

"You haven't put him back in the potting shed, have you? Another night sleeping on the floor will hardly do him much good," Edwina said. Beryl noticed her friend dipping her head to the side, as if training her ears on an unfamiliar noise emanating from the second floor of the house.

"Certainly not. He needed to be tucked up in a proper bed," Beryl said. "Somewhere where someone could keep an eye on him, should the need arise."

"He hasn't any family here in the village. Did you take him over to see his aunt in Pershing Magna?" Edwina asked.

"It was rather too late for that by the time I found him at the pub. He was in no fit state to deposit with an even more elderly aunt," Beryl said. "No, I decided on a far more sensible solution."

Edwina did not look convinced. Beryl had noticed that she and her friend had very different opinions of what constituted a sensible solution. For Beryl, it most often meant taking swift action and employing tall tales and fast automobiles.

Edwina, on the other hand, preferred to mull over possibilities and weigh the pros and cons of each before proceeding down a carefully planned route. In her opinion, they balanced each other out perfectly. But sometimes, it could be a bit frustrating to reach that balance. Beryl was afraid it was likely her friend would take some convincing in order for them to reach an accord.

"And I suppose you're going to tell me you've installed him in one of the small bedrooms at the back end of the upstairs hall," Edwina said before taking another sip of her gin fizz.

Beryl was astonished. Was it possible she was having a

marked influence on Edwina? Then a more upsetting thought occurred to her. Was she herself becoming predictable?

"That's exactly what I've done," Beryl said. "I was sure you wouldn't mind, considering how worried you were about his whereabouts when we parted company this afternoon."

"I am certain the village will have a great deal to say about it, but I am too tired tonight to care. I'm sure you've done the right thing, considering," Edwina said. She held out her empty glass. Beryl hopped out of her chair and hurried to replenish it. "It gives me quite a chuckle to think what my mother would say if she knew Simpkins lay snoring away under one of her prized counterpanes."

"Actually, I left him passed out on top of one."

"Please tell me you at least remembered to remove his boots," Edwina said.

Chapter 15

Both Beryl and Simpkins were still in bed when Edwina heard a knock at the scullery door. She looked up from her toast soldiers and cup of tea and noticed Charles standing there. With a wave of her hand she beckoned him to enter.

"I'm sorry to disturb you again so early in the day, but I wanted to be sure to share some information with you concerning Simpkins before much more time had passed," he said. "I say, whatever have you done to your hair?"

"Not that I need answer to you or anyone else, Charles, but as you can clearly see, I have had it bobbed." Edwina knew her tone sounded strident, but she did not care. There were not all that many compensations for spinsterhood, but not being required to account for oneself to a man was chief amongst them.

"I beg your pardon. I was just taken by surprise. You know, I think you look quite fetching. Like something from the cinema come to our little village," Charles said.

Crumpet pranced around Charles's polished shoes. He was an excellent judge of character, and Edwina found herself forgiving Charles for his impertinence and his interruption of her morning quietude when he bent down to scratch Crumpet beneath his chin.

"Have you breakfasted?" Edwina said, noticing a certain gauntness to Charles's face.

He had lost his domestic help in the autumn unexpectedly and had not found a replacement. It was a common story and one of the reasons Edwina had been so distressed to hear that Simpkins would likely soon be leaving her employ. Servants were almost impossible to find since the war, even if one had the means to pay them. Charles had not been raised to cook for himself, and having no wife or even an unmarried sister who made her home with him, he had grown thinner and thinner in the intervening months.

Charles cast a glance at the cooker and then at Edwina's half-empty plate on the table. "I shouldn't wish for you to go to any trouble," he said.

"Nonsense. I expect you would not say no to an egg and some toast soldiers," she said as she crossed the room and plucked her pinny from a hook on the wall. She tied it around her waist, then motioned for Charles to take a seat at the table. She fetched him a cup and urged him to pour some tea for himself. "Now, what is it that you wanted to tell me about Simpkins?"

"This information is off the record, you understand," Charles said.

Edwina nodded. "You know you can trust me to be discreet, Charles," she said.

"I only meant that you should convey this message as such when you speak with Simpkins," Charles said.

"Of course. It must be rather important," Edwina said.

"I'm afraid it is. You remember my acquaintance Mr. Petti-grew?" Charles said.

"I am unlikely to forget a stranger from London bearing news of a vast fortune for my jobbing gardener," Edwina said, banging the iron skillet for the eggs on the cooker with a bit more ferocity than she had intended. Charles, with his usual unflappable good manners, ignored her unseemly outburst.

"He has advised me that Simpkins would be well served to engage a solicitor of his own. He indicated that the interests of the Kimberly family are unlikely to align with Simpkins's own and that he would be foolish not to retain individual counsel," Charles said.

Edwina turned away from the cooker and gave Charles her full attention, a smooth brown egg clutched in her hand.

"Does Mr. Pettigrew represent either the Kimberly family or the corporation?" Edwina asked.

"Neither. He represented Colonel Kimberly himself in his private affairs. He has represented Mrs. Kimberly and even Colonel Kimberly's nephew in the past but feels it is unlikely that they will retain him in future, as he was the bearer of such unexpected financial news when the will was read," Charles said.

"Were you surprised that he confided such a thing to you?" Edwina asked.

"I was, rather. Pettigrew is a close-to-the-vest sort of man. His reputation is that of an exclusively by-the-books sort of solicitor. I think the whole situation had him more than a little rattled," Charles said.

Edwina turned back to the cooker and cracked the egg into the hot pan. She watched as it sizzled and began to firm up. As it did so, thoughts similarly coalesced in her mind.

"You don't suppose that Simpkins's windfall is likely to lead to rather a lot of difficulty, do you?" Edwina said.

"From what Pettigrew had to say, the Kimberly family did not take the news well at all. Pettigrew indicated Simpkins should be prepared for them to try to keep ahold of the money one way or another," Charles said.

Edwina cut two slices from a fresh cottage loaf and placed

them under the grill. She watched them carefully as they turned a golden brown, then sliced them into soldiers and placed them, along with the fried egg, on Charles's plate. She took her own seat and topped up her cup of tea, which had grown cold.

"It would seem that Simpkins would be well served to have a solicitor of his own," Edwina said. Edwina had spent enough time as a girl at her father's chambers to know that disputes about a family's money could turn nasty very quickly. It had hardly mattered about the amounts involved. Edwina could see, however, that the stakes were much higher, considering the size of the fortune. Simpkins was going to need all the help he could get. "Would you be willing to act on his behalf?"

Charles looked up from his breakfast. A bit of egg yolk clung to his chin. It was rather endearing.

"While I am not an expert on the ins and outs of corporate law, it would be my great pleasure to assist Simpkins in protecting his interests, should he prevail upon me to do so," Charles said.

"I'm sure that if there's anything you do not know, you will make every effort to find out. Simpkins will be most fortunate to have you on his side," Edwina said, reaching out with a serviette and dabbing the yolk from his face.

Chapter 16

When she had first arrived in Walmsley Parva some months earlier, Beryl had been surprised at how much village life revolved around the small rituals of the day. She was even more astonished at how easily she, too, had fallen into a course of predictable behavior. But surprising or not, the fact remained that she had fallen into the habit of walking into the village most days either to purchase a copy of the newspaper, to pick up produce for a meal, or even just to window-shop amongst her fellow villagers.

While she had felt no need to bustle off much before noon, she had found herself awake slightly earlier that morning than was her habit. Perhaps it was the sound of Simpkins's snores reverberating through several horsehair plaster walls that had roused her ahead of schedule.

No matter the cause, she found herself once more smiling and nodding to passersby as she strode along the high street, Edwina's sturdy wicker shopping basket draped over her arm. With Simpkins in the house, Edwina had insisted that they would require additional comestibles.

Her first thought was to head straight for the butcher shop. She crossed the street and peered at the window display. The offerings were no more inspiring than usual, although to be fair, no less so. Two paltry chickens and a sad excuse for a leg of lamb hung from iron hooks in the window.

She found herself longing for a thick porterhouse steak served rare, like the ones at her favourite steak house in Chicago. She pushed open the door and set the bell jangling. Sidney Poole, purveyor of fine meats, or so his shop's sign would have one believe, looked up from a brown paper packet he was wrapping up for the vicar's wife, Muriel Lowethorpe. He neatly tied a double knot around two pork chops, then slid them across the counter.

"Good morning, Miss Helliwell," Muriel Lowethorpe said. "How is Simpkins this morning?"

"I haven't the foggiest notion," Beryl said.

She knew that Edwina would not be pleased to discover news of Simpkins's installation at the Beeches had already made its way around the village. She was not entirely sure if there was some sort of prohibition on such a cohabitation by the Church of England. Edwina was an upstanding member of Vicar Lowethorpe's flock and would be loath to sully her reputation as a parishioner of sterling character. Although, even the nastiest of minds could not have entertained the notion that something untoward was afoot between Edwina and Simpkins no matter how closely they may have passed the previous night.

"But surely you've heard about his windfall, have you not?" Muriel said. "It's all around the village."

Beryl had often wondered in the past how such news had spread around Walmsley Parva. But this time, she felt quite certain the news had come from the source itself. Simpkins was not a man to hold back about the things on his mind when he was well into his cups. Judging by his behavior at the pub the previous afternoon, he probably had told each and every patron about his newfound wealth.

"You have heard about that, then, have you?" Beryl said.

"I'd reckon everyone in the village has heard," Sidney Poole said, crossing his beefy arms across his rotund chest. Beryl had often thought that the creature with the most meat on its bones in all the shop was Sidney Poole. "With the way he was crowing about it at the Dove and Duck yesterday, it would be a wonder if they hadn't. Not that anyone begrudges him his good fortune."

Sidney shot a look at the vicar's wife. Beryl seemed to recall he was also a regular attendee at the local place of worship, and she remembered once having heard some sort of proclamation that envy was considered a sin.

"I don't know as it's entirely accurate to state that no one begrudges him his inheritance," Muriel said.

Beryl wondered if there was a similar admonition about gossip in the good book. If there was, Muriel had conveniently put it out of her mind. Fortunately, Beryl had no such qualms. As an investigator, it was her duty to use whatever means necessary to get to the truth. Even if it meant indulging in a bit of sin with a vicar's wife.

"I find that hard to believe. Simpkins seems to be so well liked in Walmsley Parva," Beryl said unashamedly. She propped her shopping basket on the counter and leaned against it, as if prepared to stay for a while.

Muriel and Sidney exchanged a significant look.

"The source of animosity does not come from anyone well acquainted with Simpkins. As you say, he is well liked in the village. I'm sure all of us are delighted for him," Muriel said.

"It's them folks from up in London," Sidney said.

"Folks from London?" Beryl said. "Speaking ill of Simpkins?" She wondered if Mr. Pettigrew, the solicitor, was the person to whom Sidney referred. From what Edwina had said, Mr. Pettigrew seemed to have Simpkins's best interest at heart.

"That's right. People who seem to think he had done them out of their fair share," Sidney said. "Mrs. Kimberly, for one."

"Would that be the widow of Colonel Kimberly of condiment company fame?" Beryl said.

"Exactly the one. Although, I do confess I was a bit shocked that a man of as much position as Colonel Kimberly would be married to someone who seemed more suited for the dance halls than ballrooms," Muriel said.

Beryl had long suspected there was a sharp side to Muriel, which Edwina never seemed to notice. Beryl was always leery of persons so doggedly devoted to good works. She felt they were most certainly covering up for some sort of wickedness simmering just below the surface.

Beryl found that her ideas of wickedness very often did not align with those of more traditionally minded people. She rather prided herself on her capacity to enjoy several of the seven deadly sins. What she could not tolerate were close-mindedness, grudge holding, miserliness, an unwarranted sense of superiority, or false modesty.

"You said folks from London. Is there anyone else here besides Colonel Kimberley's widow?" Beryl said.

"There was a solicitor and also a man who mentioned being on the board of directors for the company," Muriel said. She turned to Sidney, who nodded in agreement.

"That's right. A man stopped in here yesterday, asking if I knew of any place that offered lodgings in the village," Sidney said. "And where I might find Albert Simpkins."

"And what did you tell him?" Beryl said.

"I mentioned the Beeches for Simpkins. As for the lodging, I recommended the Dove and Duck since it is the only place in town that lets rooms," Sidney said.

"Unless one knows a resident and can prevail upon him or her, Sidney is quite right. Walmsley Parva is not exactly a sightseeing destination," Muriel said. "And I thank the Lord for that."

"And you say they were speaking disparagingly of Simpkins?" Beryl said.

"Not so much disparagingly as slyly. As if they wanted to plant the seed in the minds of his fellow villagers that Simpkins had somehow acquired his inheritance in an underhanded manner. No one came right out and said anything you could quite put your finger on. It was more what they implied," Muriel said. "Rather wicked, I thought it was."

Beryl understood exactly what Muriel meant to convey. Perhaps there was more depth to this woman of good works than she had previously considered.

"Do you mean there was nothing he could actually refute because there had not been anything said outright?" Beryl asked.

"That's it exactly. It was clever but quite nasty of them," Muriel said.

She made a tut-tutting noise that was particular to the English population. It was as close as many of them got to complaining overtly. Beryl thought she might add tut-tutting to her list of seven deadly sins. In her mind, if one had a complaint, why would one not just get it off the chest? To her way of thinking, it was ever so much better to air things out. With that in mind, she determined to complete her shopping quickly and to track down the people from out of town who were doing their best to discredit Simpkins.

"Well, as we have much to celebrate at the Beeches on Simpkins's behalf, I'm here to purchase some celebratory items for the table. No matter what people from London have to say about any of it. What would you suggest?" Beryl said, turning to Sidney.

Muriel lifted her parcel and placed it in her own shopping basket before taking her leave. A few moments later Beryl followed suit, a stringy-looking duck, a beef tongue, and a half pound of sausages weighing down her own basket.

She made her way farther up the street and paused in front of the Dove and Duck. Peering through the window, she noticed the owner, Bill Nevins, behind the bar, wiping it down with a cloth. She rapped on the window. He looked up and beckoned her inside. Her enquiries after his overnight guests yielded no positive results.

According to the publican, he had had two guests overnight, but neither of them was still within. Bill had remained in business for many years partly by knowing which questions not to ask of his customers. He had no idea whatsoever where Beryl might find either of them. Nor did he know when they were likely to return.

She stopped in at the greengrocer for a pint of strawberries, a bunch of radishes, and a quantity of peas. With her basket heavily laden, she determined to return to the Beeches. Perhaps Edwina would be more likely to know where out-of-town visitors might choose to spend the day. At the very least, she should be informed that they had arrived. Beryl had a suspicion it would not be long before Simpkins would need to deal with them.

Chapter 17

Beryl had been right to head back to the Beeches. She entered the house through the scullery door and placed Edwina's shopping basket on the table. Her friend stood pouring hot water from the kettle into a china teapot. Not the best one, mind you, but certainly a serviceable and attractive piece, nevertheless. Something in the set of Edwina's shoulders told Beryl there was something afoot.

"You'll never guess what I heard down in the village," Beryl said.

"Is it that visitors from London are here and wish to speak with Simpkins?" Edwina said.

So that was where they had gone, Beryl thought to herself.

"That's it exactly. Those city people waste no time in getting straight to the point, do they?" Beryl said.

"I would rather that they had wasted even less time," Edwina said. "As it is, I find that I am fixing tea for a woman I would not have hired as a parlourmaid. I would prefer that they would just get on with whatever it is they wish to say and stop beating around the bush about it."

Edwina placed the lid on the teapot with a clatter. Beryl could not help but notice a lack of home-baked goods placed on the tray. Edwina opened a cupboard and pulled down a packet of store-bought biscuits. Beryl could only surmise that Edwina was well and truly affronted at the behavior of their uninvited guests. She had never before seen packaged biscuits on offer when visitors were present. It was rarely done when just she and Edwina were on their own.

As a matter of fact, there had been no such thing in the house until Beryl had arrived on scene several months earlier. She felt peckish now and again and did not wish to bother Edwina with preparing something from scratch. Given her own culinary skills, packaged goods were the only way to keep up her strength.

"Shall I take the tray in for you? You look as though you would rather not," Beryl said.

"I would be very grateful if you would do so," Edwina said. "It had been my intention to simply leave them to it, but I didn't have the heart to leave Simpkins on his own with them. He is rather an innocent about people of that sort, and it felt wrong of me to leave him to fend for himself. But there's just something about their superior behavior that puts my teeth on edge. I'm not sure I can trust myself not to point out that Mrs. Kimberly has difficulty not dropping her aitches."

That settled it. Beryl could not wait to meet them. She patted Edwina on the shoulder and then hoisted the tea tray.

"I'll take it from here. You go on out to the garden and keep out of sight."

"But what will you give as an excuse?" Edwina said. "It should be horribly rude for me to abandon guests mid-visit."

"They're not your guests, are they?" Beryl said.

"I suppose not. They are here to see Simpkins, after all," Edwina said with a hopeful lilt to her voice.

"I don't intend to tell them anything. I make it a policy never to explain things I do not wish to explain. As far as I can see, you owe them nothing, not even this tea," Beryl said. "Now scoot, before they come in and find you." With that, Edwina bustled out the back door, Crumpet capering close at her heels.

A half hour in her beloved garden ought to set things right, Beryl thought.

She pushed open the kitchen door with her hip and set off down the long hallway to the parlour. The door was open, and voices floated towards her as she approached. Beryl was a sizable woman both in height and, after a winter of a sedentary lifestyle, she had become a bit larger in breadth as well. That did not mean, however, that she was not light on her feet. After all, Beryl had spent so many years in the bush, making her way quietly through in order not to disturb the permanent inhabitants or expose herself to dangers unseen, that she found it quite natural to move silently as she approached the room.

The tone of the widow Kimberly's voice grated on Beryl's nerves. While she was not one to consider any of the social classes more worthy than the others, she was able to recognize the differences in their manner of speaking and their comportment. It was obvious even to her that Edwina had been correct in her assessment of Mrs. Kimberly. Beryl thought it likely she was hearing a cunning chorus girl who had captured a wealthy older man's heart.

First and foremost on her mind was the idea that the widow not be allowed to do so a second time. Simpkins was not for sale. She strode through the door, the tea tray held out in front of her, a bright but firm smile plastered on her face. Simpkins looked up in relief as she crossed the room and placed the tray on the low table in front of him.

"I see you are entertaining without me," Beryl said. "Won't you introduce me to your friends?" Beryl sank down proprietarily onto the sofa next to Simpkins and gave him a reassuring smile. She slipped her arm through his for good measure.

"This here is Mrs. Kimberly, the widow of Colonel Kimberly. And with her is Mr. Armitage, who says he's the chairman of the board of directors for Colonel Kimberly's Condiment Company," Simpkins said.

Beryl thought he had done rather well to keep their names straight, considering that a decidedly green hue tinged his skin. Simpkins was in no condition to be out of bed, let alone wrangling with the sort of circling sharks Beryl was quite certain these two would turn out to be.

"A pleasure to meet you both, I'm sure," Beryl said. "I'm Beryl Helliwell, and do allow me to extend my own welcome to Walmsley Parva. I understand you're staying in rooms above the pub."

She released her claim on Simpkins's limb, hoisted the teapot, and inclined her head towards Mrs. Kimberly, who nodded. She poured out a cup for the other lady, then turned to Mr. Armitage, who nodded that he would appreciate a cup as well.

"That is correct," Mr. Armitage said. "There were no other accommodations to be had."

"Who would have thought the best we could do was to take poky little rooms above a pub?" Mrs. Kimberly said. "It's not what we are used to, not in the least."

"Village life is quite different from that of the city, Mrs. Kimberly," Mr. Armitage said. "I have found it quite charming. I understand you are *the* Beryl Helliwell, celebrated adventuress and thrill seeker. It's a pleasure to make your acquaintance." Mr. Armitage inclined his head in a semblance of a slight bow. Beryl noted that Mrs. Kimberly looked decidedly unimpressed.

"You have me at a decided disadvantage there. You seem to know exactly who I am, but I know nothing about you besides your connection to Colonel Kimberly's company. What brings you to Walmsley Parva? As I'm sure it's not the view from the rooms above the pub."

She passed a cup of tea to Simpkins, having added two lumps of sugar but no milk. She doubted his stomach could take it.

"We are here on business," Mr. Armitage said. "There are any number of matters to discuss with Mr. Simpkins."

"I expect you wanted to see for yourself the new head of the company, did you not?" Beryl said. She heard Mr. Armitage stifling a guffaw.

"That's just it exactly. At least it is as far as I'm concerned," Mrs. Kimberly said.

Beryl noticed for the first time the rather wide gap and stiff manner Mr. Armitage maintained between himself and Mrs. Kimberly. Perhaps he thought no better of the young widow than Edwina did. Beryl held out no illusions that either of them was there with Simpkins's best interest in mind. But she did wonder if their own perceptions of their own best interest differed from one another.

"Mr. Simpkins may be just what we need to bring a breath of fresh air into what I don't mind saying is a rather stodgy atmosphere at Colonel Kimberly's," Mrs. Kimberly said.

Beryl noticed the young woman batting her eyelashes flirtatiously in Simpkins's direction. Unless she missed her guess, Mrs. Kimberly had no intention of relinquishing her claim to part of the Kimberly wealth to an outsider.

She seemed inclined to employ her strengths unabashedly. If Simpkins thought the stress of the day before had taken its toll, Beryl greatly feared he had no idea what he was in for. Beryl's first thought was to whisk Simpkins off somewhere far from their clutches. Her second thought was that keeping him under her and Edwina's watchful eyes at the Beeches was perhaps the best course to take.

"Let's not go getting ahead of ourselves," Mr. Armitage said. "What I wished to impress upon Mr. Simpkins is that the company is well in hand and that he can have full confidence in our ability to see to his interests without him needing to go to the trouble of learning the ins and outs of the world of commerce."

"What do you think, Simpkins?" Beryl said. "These two seem

to have very different takes on how you should handle your situation. I think the only one who really matters here is you."

Simpkins turned towards Beryl and looked directly into her eyes. She could see that he felt dreadful. No wonder Mr. Armitage had every reason to wish Simpkins as far from the boardroom and corporate headquarters as humanly possible. His appearance made her grudgingly admire Mrs. Kimberly's overtures of a romantic nature. It took a certain sort of gumption to look on the hungover Simpkins and determine it worth the effort. She hoped there was enough grey matter still firing away inside his head for him to have something to say that would protect his own interests.

"For now, I am going to rely upon the advice of my trusted solicitor. You'll have to excuse me. I'm going to go and have a lie-down," Simpkins said.

He rose to his feet, and as he did so, Beryl could hear the joints of his knees creaking and popping. What he needed was a hot bath and at least eight hours of sleep. Even so, he had done an admirable job of deflecting decision making.

She had to wonder at his reliance on a solicitor to get him out of difficulties. Had he actually hired one? It would be a question for Edwina, she thought as she watched his shambling progress out the parlour door. She turned back to their guests.

"As I'm sure you have plenty of matters to attend to, as do I, please allow me to see you out," Beryl said. She rose and pointed towards the door.

Chapter 18

Edwina felt quite restored after removing herself to the garden. The birds were twittering in the trees and the bushes. The roses were at the height of their bloom. Decorating the banks of her beloved koi pond were tall stands of Japanese irises unfurling deep purple blossoms atop rich green stalks. From her seat on a bench next to the clear water, she watched the flash and sparkle of sunlight playing upon its surface and upon the scales of the school of koi sliding just below the serene pond surface.

Once, the pond had been nothing more than a boggy depression where frogs and toads and mosquitoes gathered in their search for moisture. While her mother had been ill, Edwina had stolen moments here and there, digging and mucking about, using the damp low area to its advantage. Despite the fact that most physical activity had been discouraged by her mother, they had shared a love of gardening, and Edwina had always made her excuses for leaving her mother's side in order to go and work on the pond.

She was quite pleased with the fact that it appeared to have been there for decades rather than only a couple of years. So much had changed in so little time, and not all of it had been for the worse. While there had been so many losses and so much grief during the war years, there had also been the opportunity to grow, to rise to the occasion, to find out what one was made of. She thought about the change of Simpkins's fortune and what it might mean to her own life, and she decided she would concentrate on what good might come of it rather than the fact that she was likely to lose her garden help and one of the only constants left in her life.

Simpkins had joined her in creating the boggy pond more often than not. While he had been content to leave much of the heavy lifting to her younger and more willing back and arms, he had been filled with notions, suggestions, and queries that, as she gave it thought, had helped her to clarify her own wants and beliefs about the project. As much it had felt like a goad in her side at the time, in some ways Simpkins had done her a service by his needling. In fact, if it had not been for many of his argumentative suggestions, Edwina might have given up on the project long before she had completed it. Truly, it had been a great deal of work.

She wasn't used to thinking of him in this way. More often than not, he simply struck her as someone who did not remember his place and who made it his business to provoke her at every opportunity. What was it about the possibility of such a large life change for her gardener that made her consider him with fresh eyes? Was she really so shallow as to value someone based only on their financial standing? No, that couldn't be it. She had met many vulgar millionaires, and she had not come to consider them as more worthy of her acquaintance because of their financial position.

Edwina realized with a jolt that it was his new capacity to abandon his job at the Beeches that had forced her reconsideration of his worth. Like it or not, she would miss him, should he choose to go. That most likely explained why she had not put up more of a fuss when she discovered that Beryl had installed him in one of the back bedrooms, hobnailed boots and all. As she reflected on this, she heard the sound of someone clearing his throat just behind her. She turned, expecting to see Simpkins or Charles Jarvis.

"I do hope I'm not disturbing you, but I was irresistibly drawn to the beauty of your garden," Mr. Armitage said.

Edwina felt instantly wary. While she was inclined to pridefulness as concerned her garden, there was something about Mr. Armitage that instantly put her back up. He did not wait for an invitation but drew near and took a seat on the bench beside her.

"Have you concluded your business with Simpkins, then?" Edwina asked.

"Mr. Simpkins concluded his business with us, and rather abruptly. But I'm sure you are most familiar with his rather unorthodox manner," Mr. Armitage said.

Edwina suspected that had he been a member of a lower class, he might have rolled his eyes. It would not matter to Edwina how many compliments he bestowed upon her garden. She was disinclined to warm to him.

"I expect he's not at all the sort of person you are used to dealing with at Colonel Kimberly's," Edwina said. "Still, one must learn to change with the times and to learn different ways of doing things, wouldn't you agree?"

A sleek koi slid closer to the edge of the pond where they sat. Edwina leaned forward and admired its pleasingly smooth form and the way it gracefully swished its tail.

"Not to argue with a lady, but I am inclined to feel differently. I'm not quite sure Colonel Kimberly's should have to become accustomed to an unfamiliar manner of operations. The company is in fine, fine shape and needs no adjustment to our way of doing things," Mr. Armitage said.

"Surely every good businessman is interested in growth," Edwina said.

"Growth indubitably, but not always change. When your hand is on the rudder and you are on course in the right direction, change is entirely undesirable."

"Are you implying that Simpkins is somehow undesirable?" Edwina asked. She pulled her attention from the pond and looked Mr. Armitage in the face. His full head of silver hair was cut into a sophisticated and expensive style. His bright blue eyes bored into her own, and the way he cocked an eyebrow in surprise said he felt the two of them ought to be in accord.

"I'm sure Mr. Simpkins is perfectly well suited for many things. Mucking out stalls, dividing dahlias, swilling lager at the local pub. But heading a large corporation, or even owning one, seems unlikely to be the destiny of a man like him," Mr. Armitage said. "On that, I am certain we can agree."

"You are aware, sir, that you are discussing a company that makes it their business to sell items made of vegetables and fruits. Who better than a gardener to know about such things?" Edwina said.

"My dear lady, I can only assume that you are making sport of all this for reasons of your own," Mr. Armitage said. "Certainly a gentlewoman such as yourself can easily understand that Mr. Simpkins must be dissuaded from participating in any of the activities at Colonel Kimberly's. I implore you to use what must be considerable influence upon your employee to remove himself utterly from any expectation of interfering with daily operations. In fact, I beseech you to convince him to sell his interest in the company as soon as he is able to do so."

Edwina felt roiling indignation fill her stomach. Simpkins was often someone who she felt unfit for a wide variety of activities. She also felt he was *her someone* to consider unworthy of those activities, and not anyone else's.

"Mr. Armitage, I fear you have overstepped in your assumptions. It is not my place to tell Simpkins how to conduct his own considerable business. Should he ask me for my advice, I would be glad to give it. But you mustn't make the mistake of believing I would thrust myself upon him with opinions that were not solicited," Edwina said. She tried to keep her voice even and devoid of the shrill tone she knew it often held when she spoke of Simpkins.

"Surely you must feel as though a gardener from this piddly little village is doing the entire society an affront by getting so far above himself," Mr. Armitage said. "What will it take to convince him to sell up his shares and leave those qualified to get on with the job at hand?" He drummed his manicured fingers against the arm of the bench.

Edwina found him entirely repellent. Who was he to say that anyone from Walmsley Parva was not good enough to take an interest in or to hold on to anything he or she chose?

"I have always found Simpkins to be a man with a mind of his own. But should I have the opportunity to influence him in any way, you may rest assured that I will tell him to take every opportunity to educate himself on every aspect of Colonel Kimberly's Condiment Company in order to best involve himself in it. Now, I am afraid you will have to excuse me, as I have a meeting to attend at our piddly little village hall." Edwina stood, forcing a man with manners to get to his own feet. "I bid you good day."

Chapter 19

As soon as Edwina left for her meeting of the Women's Institute, Beryl turned her attention to making good on her boast of writing an adventure guide. She realized with a jolt that she had not done so merely to distract Simpkins from the distressing news about Hector. She had felt a bit disconnected from her old life of late and had a hankering to revisit her gadabout lifestyle, if only on paper.

A small voice in the back of her head told her she had been foolhardy to put forth such an outlandish idea without giving it due consideration. Although she knew it was a weakness in her character, she had difficulty backing down once she had announced an intention to tackle something new. As soon as Edwina had suggested she might find writing a book more difficult than she assumed, she had telephoned the local stationer's and ordered a Remington portable typewriter, to be delivered at the shop's earliest convenience.

The stationer's had proven lamentably efficient in its delivery service. Beryl glanced down with gnawing regret at the typewriting machine in front of her. Beryl's hopes for a career as a celebrated author had been somewhat dimmed by the wretched machine. When she had lifted it from its wooden crate and given it pride of place on the small desk in the morning room, she had expected to master it just as easily as she had the controls of an airplane or those of her beloved motorcar.

But such was not the case with the typewriter. Every time she tried to press on one key, at least two clicked forward and entangled themselves, marring the surface of her sheet of paper. It put her in mind immediately of her ineptitude with a sewing machine at Miss DuPont's Finishing School for Young Ladies. If it had not been for Edwina's surreptitious assistance during the lessons devoted to household management, Beryl might have found herself a captive of Miss DuPont to that very day.

It wasn't just the machine that was troubling her, though. Determined to get her ideas out of her head and into written form, Beryl had dug a notebook from a drawer in a cabinet in the library. But every time she set out to put pen to paper, she found her thoughts would not run out of her brain and down through her hand. Still, she could not credit Edwina's admonition that in order to be an author, one ought to first be a reader. Beryl decided that the muse was simply not with her and that she ought to be taking action on something else while awaiting its arrival.

She rolled the sheet of spoiled typewriter paper out of the machine, folded it in half, and tucked it under the blotter, where it would be unlikely that Edwina would see it. Beryl was in no mood to discuss her lack of progress on her new project. She decided to kill two birds with one stone and head to the village to speak with Alma Poole.

While Edwina lived in constant fear of offending Alma and alienating herself from the village's only hairdresser, Beryl felt no such compunctions. As much as she was well aware that her appearance was one of the secrets of her celebrity, Beryl was perfectly capable of attending to her own grooming needs.

Many was the time she had made do with a hunting knife in the bush when it came time to trim her own hair. In fact, a new style of asymmetrical bob named the Seesaw had taken the world by storm after she appeared in a newspaper photograph after having done so.

Beryl set out at a rapid pace and arrived in the village in good time. She strode into the hairdressing salon and looked around. Alma, a shampoo girl, and a woman from the village whose name Beryl could never remember were all assembled inside. The shampoo girl looked up expectantly as Beryl advanced towards her.

"Do you have an appointment?" she asked.

"I don't happen to have an appointment, but I did hope that you might be able to squeeze me in. Are you available for a wash and set?" Beryl said.

The girl motioned Beryl forward after glancing at Alma, who nodded with approval. Beryl settled herself in the reclining chair and gave over to the relaxing twin ministrations of warm, sudsy water and firm fingers. By the time she sat upright once more, a fluffy towel draped over her damp head, she had formulated an idea.

"I wanted to ask if any of you knew of someone here in Walmsley Parva who would be willing to give me typing lessons?" Beryl said. She looked expectantly from face to face.

Alma scrunched her eyebrows together thoughtfully. The nameless village woman simply shook her head. Fortunately, the shampoo girl seemed to be in the know.

"You'll be wanting to talk with Geraldine," the shampoo girl said, wiping her hands on a second towel.

"Where might I find this Geraldine?" Beryl asked.

"Geraldine is a telephone operator, so I suppose you could simply lift up your handset at home, that is, if you've got one," the girl said. "You could simply ask her."

"Yes, I suppose I could do that. But I do tend to prefer to do business face-to-face. Do you happen to know when I might find her at the telephone office?" Beryl said.

"She's there most days since she is one of the two full-time operators."

"If she's a telephone operator, why would you recommend her to give typing lessons?" Beryl said.

"Because she knows how to type," the girl said, her voice tinged with exasperation.

"Is that a common thing with most telephone operators?" the village woman asked.

"I have no idea. I just know Geraldine knows how to do it. She has something of a side business writing up letters for businesses and even transcribing handwritten notes from time to time," the girl said. "She does put on airs about that just a bit."

"You've been very helpful. Thank you," Beryl said.

"Why are you interested in learning to type?" Alma said. "Does it have to do with your private enquiry agency?"

Beryl saw no reason to share all that she knew. Besides, she was not quite sure she was ready to speak with the public about her creative endeavor. The work was advancing more slowly than she had anticipated, and she felt surprisingly reserved about mentioning it. The agency made a remarkably believable excuse for wishing to acquire typing skills of her own.

"As ours is quite a modern business, Edwina and I felt it best to embrace up-to-date standards in both technologies and methods. While a handwritten invoice or report to a client is certainly an acceptable method of running one's business, we both felt that typewritten correspondence would help to elevate our professional standing. As Edwina already does so much for our partnership, I thought I would offer to learn to type," Beryl said.

"Any little advantage a woman can have in business seems sensible to me," Alma said.

This was just the opening Beryl had been looking for.

"Of course, you would know all about that, wouldn't you, Mrs. Poole?" Beryl said. "Even though yours is a business that specializes in female clientele, I'm sure you have had your share of trials and tribulations on the road to success."

Alma held a pair of shears aloft as she thought on the question. She lowered the shears and tapped the nameless woman on the shoulder with the flat side of them.

"You certainly can say that again. My Sidney was not as supportive as he might've been when I announced my intention several years ago to open the shop. He seemed to think it offended his pride if his wife needed to go out to work. Besides, I think he enjoyed having me at his beck and call if he didn't think I could claim more important obligations outside of the butcher shop," Alma said.

"I always think it best for a wife to know her own mind and go about conducting herself as she sees fit," Beryl said. "I suppose that's why my own marriages have not lasted as long as some other people's."

The nameless woman looked slightly scandalized. Beryl was almost glad to see Alma begin to snip away at the woman's hair. She left a decidedly uneven course across her forehead in an attempt to create a fringe.

"I understand your meaning. My Sidney is a good man, but there've been times when we haven't seen eye to eye," Alma said.

"Like the other day," the shampoo girl said. "It's not as though you haven't had other offers, now is it?"

"Now, that's just what I like to hear," Beryl said. "Just because one is paired off doesn't mean they don't appreciate an admiring glance from another now and again, now does it?"

Two faint spots of color appeared on Alma's pale cheeks. If Alma Poole had an admirer, Beryl was not likely to criticize her for it either out loud or in her own mind. She was all for taking life's pleasures wherever they could be found so long as they did not hurt others.

"I wouldn't call them *offers*, although it does do the heart good to know one is appreciated from time to time," Alma said. She snipped off an especially long section of hair from the woman's forehead. Beryl noticed a flicker of fear pass over the woman's face as she spotted the hair cascading down the front of the cape draped over her shoulders to protect her clothing.

"I know just what you mean. I should think you'd have to be beating them off with a stick. A woman like yourself, in the prime of life, with a vocation that gives her access to all the secrets of beauty. Tell me I'm not right," Beryl said.

Mrs. Poole blushed a little more deeply. "I shouldn't like to say anything as boastful as that. But I have been the recipient of one or two admiring glances," she said.

"She's being far too modest, isn't she?" Beryl said, turning to the shampoo girl with an encouraging smile. "I bet you could learn a lot from Mrs. Poole about letting gentlemen down gently after inflicting disappointment."

"I don't know about gently. Mrs. Poole was anything but gentle in her refusal of Hector Lomax," the shampoo girl said.

"My understanding was that Hector wasn't easily dissuaded from anything he set his mind to," Beryl said. "I shouldn't think a gentle word from a lady like Mrs. Poole would be enough to discourage him."

"It certainly was not. Even a harsh word didn't seem to get rid of him," the girl said. "Although, I thought she ought to let him keep on with his attentions, considering the present he brought her."

"That sounds intriguing," Beryl said.

"It was really nothing," Alma said.

Another jagged chunk of hair dropped to the floor. Beryl was quite certain she heard a squeak escape from the client's lips. If Alma kept on the way she was going, her client would find herself sporting an uneven and very modern-looking bob. Beryl had been right to ask simply for a wash and set while questioning Alma. Clearly, she was the sort of person who was best suited to focusing on one thing at a time.

"If a ring like the one he brought you was nothing, I would like to see the sort of present you think is worth noticing. I would have accepted it if I were you," Hattie said.

"Don't be daft, girl. I have my reputation to think about," Alma said. Beryl noticed her hands trembled. "I'm not likely to go ruining my life over a flashy bit of costume jewelry."

"You don't know that it wasn't real," Hattie said, rolling her eyes.

"Of course I do. How could a man like Hector have afforded a ring covered in real diamonds, rubies, and emeralds?" Alma asked.

"I'm sure no one thinks ill of you for Hector's interest," Beryl said. "Although I can see how it would be bothersome. To both yourself and to Mr. Poole."

"Sidney was not best pleased," Alma said. "I tried to tell him that in my line of work, one must be polite to the public, but he told me that I was the only game in town and that it was not necessary. Especially since Hector frequented the local barbershop instead of my establishment."

"Do you mean to say he bothered you here in the shop?" Beryl asked.

"In here practically every day, he was," the girl said. "In fact, it quite disturbed the ladies to have a gentleman hanging about. Isn't that right, Mrs. Poole?"

Alma nodded. "The hairdresser's is meant as a refuge for women. No one wants to be seen by the gentlemen of the village with their hair in disarray. I told him he was costing me business with all his foolishness."

"He wasn't in bothering you right before he went and got himself murdered, was he?" Beryl asked. "I expect the shop would have been closed by then."

"Well, of course it was. I need a bit of time to tend to my life outside the shop. The cooking and cleaning, not to mention the bookkeeping I do for Sidney's business as well as my own."

"The working woman's duties are never done, are they?" Beryl said with what she hoped was a sympathetic tone.

She had been trying to pick up on a few of the finer points of friendly interaction between women from Edwina, who seemed to manage such things with no effort whatsoever. Beryl had no practical experience in running a household. She had always prided herself on having the good sense to marry only such men as could support a large number of trained staff. She felt rather sidelined in the world of women and experienced a familiar sense of being an outsider. Still, she must be learning the ropes, as Alma was nodding at her conspiratorially.

"Isn't that the truth? I expect you and Edwina have no end of fun without any gentleman getting under your feet and leaving newspapers and cigar ash strewn about the Beeches like they were born to the royal family," Alma said.

Beryl guiltily considered the coffee cups cluttering the surface of her dressing table and the pile of newspapers she had seen Edwina gather up from beside Beryl's favourite chair that very morning. Perhaps she had been the reason for much of the staff turnover at the homes she had shared with former husbands. She made a note to ask Edwina if she ought to do more to help with the household chores or at least to do less to create them.

"You must value spending a little time on your own away from here. I thought that very thing the other evening, when I saw Mr. Poole was at the pub," Beryl said. "He left earlier than I expect you would have preferred, about the same time as Hector."

Alma's hand froze in midair, her scissors poised above the client's head, as if she needed to concentrate on her response. She cast her gaze up towards the ceiling, as if the right answer could be found written on the cracked plaster and water stains.

"It was a sore trial to me, of that you can be sure, when he arrived back home, but there was nothing to be done but to set the bookkeeping ledgers to one side and to make the man his tea," Alma said.

"There is much to be said for a cozy domestic scene," Beryl said. "Still, I hope you managed to get a bit of time to yourself before the day's end."

Alma looked her directly in the eye and used a tone that brooked no argument. "Not a moment to myself did I have the entire rest of the evening. Sidney talked my ear off about who won the Derby and what the chances were for his favourite in the next race. I kept right on working on the books, but he nattered away in my ear until bedtime. I could hardly hear myself think. It will serve him right if his accounts are all off at the close of the week."

With that, Alma turned her attention back to the head in front of her. Beryl looked at Hattie's reflection in the mirrored wall across from the shampoo station. The girl was eyeing her employer with an uneasy look.

Was she worried for the client, or had Alma said something that had given the girl pause? If so, what had she said that was not to be believed? Hattie managed to hold her tongue, but Beryl was quite certain there was something she could add to the conversation if she was less concerned with the status of her employment.

Chapter 20

With her hair freshly dried and set in place, Beryl settled her bill and swept out the door. As much as she did not think it necessary to rely on a hair salon, one could not deny the spring it put in one's step to feel freshly coiffed. Although, she expected by the time she motored home, her hairstyle would have blown away. She considered wrapping a brightly colored scarf around her head to preserve her hairdo but thought better of it.

As she approached the automobile, she noticed a well-formed young man in a bespoke suit overtly inspecting her prized possession. In fact, he made so bold as to run his finger over the driver's side door handle, as if he were about to let himself in and slide behind the steering wheel. She quickened her pace. Beryl could not abide the thief. Especially of any form of conveyance.

Although, truth be told, she had been the one doing the taking on rare occasions. Her thoughts turned fleetingly to an occasion in the Arabian Desert, where she had helped herself to a sure-footed camel in a desperate effort to escape the clutches of an enthusiastic suitor who refused to be rebuffed almost as strenuously as had Hector Lomax.

"I see you have exemplary taste in automobiles," Beryl called out as she approached. She patted her pocket to assure herself that her pistol was safely ensconced in its depths. Despite his appearance, he might be quite desperate.

The young man looked up. "Is this yours?" he asked.

"It most assuredly is," Beryl said, stepping up beside him and placing her hand on the windscreen.

"I hope you won't be offended by my perusal. I have one of these black beauties of my own, and I couldn't help but admire how favorably yours compares. Allow me to introduce myself," the young man said, pulling a silver engraved card case from an inside jacket pocket. Beryl took the card he offered and read his name from it.

"Rupert Fanhurst," she read. "It's a pleasure to make your acquaintance. My name is Beryl Helliwell."

"*The* Beryl Helliwell?" the young man asked, a look of astonishment crossing his face.

"The very one."

"Whatever are you doing in a quiet little backwater like Walmsley Parva?" he asked. "Shouldn't you be off gallivanting across the globe somewhere?"

It was a question Beryl often found herself being asked. It was not one she always answered. She could not understand why anyone thought that just because a person often did something, they were required to always do that very same thing. Wasn't life meant to be an adventure, and weren't adventures made up of changing one's way of doing things?

Gallivanting across the globe could become just as routine as staying put if one didn't exercise caution. Still, he was quite young and could not be faulted for having both strong opinions and little wisdom. As he was a rather handsome specimen, she decided to take pity on him.

"I have started out on a new sort of adventure," Beryl said.

"You have something extraordinary planned here in this quiet place?" he asked.

"As a matter of fact, the adventure is not just planned but rather is already well under way. My dear friend Edwina Davenport and I have started a private enquiry agency," she said, pleased to see Mr. Fanhurst's eyes strain forward in his long, slim face.

"How absolutely extraordinary," he said. "Have you actually had any clients?"

Beryl felt her hackles start to rise. She was not easily provoked to anger, but Mr. Fanhurst's obvious dismissal of the new venture was difficult to endure without comment. She reminded herself that not everyone was as capable of expansive thought as either she or Edwina, and decided to stick to the high road.

"I am pleased to say we've been involved in several cases thus far. In fact, we are currently working on a murder enquiry," she said, enjoying the look of absolute astonishment the poor young man could not disguise as it crossed his face.

"Murder?" he asked. "Isn't that a job for the police?"

"I am afraid I cannot discuss the details that brought the case to our attention. I am sure a man of breeding like yourself comprehends that some situations call for discretion."

"Of course. How rude of me," he said. "Please accept my apologies."

"Consider it forgotten," Beryl said. "Tell me, what brings you to Walmsley Parva, Mr. Fanhurst?"

"I am here on business," he said.

"I confess you have my detecting skills in high gear. Very few people venture to this little hamlet on business," Beryl said. "What is it that you do?"

Mr. Fanhurst raised his hands in a gesture of futility. "I'm sorry to disappoint a lady, especially as lovely and accomplished a one as you. However, my business is also of a discreet nature, and my lips are, for the moment at least, sealed."

"Very well, Mr. Fanhurst. As we seem to have little about which we may freely converse, I will bid you a good day," Beryl said, stepping down from the curb.

"Will you allow me to ask for your advice before you go?" he asked.

"Certainly."

"Is there anywhere at all in this village besides the pub to find a place to stay?"

"Are the accommodations not to your liking?" Beryl asked.

"Assuredly, they are not. The bed is lumpy, the windows chatter in the frames at the slightest suggestion of a breeze, and there is a most peculiar smell emanating from the cupboard. I daren't unpack my trunk," he said.

Beryl suddenly found Mr. Fanhurst a far less attractive man than she had previously. If there was one thing she could not abide besides a gossip, it was a man who was incapable of roughing it with good humor, should the need present itself. She squinted at him and tried to imagine how he would fare on a monthlong trek through the interior of Brazil. All she could conjure up was a sort of constant whining from him, which drowned out the buzz of the mosquitos. Any interest she might have had in getting to know him better was utterly forgotten.

"I can't say I have anything encouraging to say on the hostelry front. The pub is the only place for short-term accommodation in the village," Beryl said. "Unless you know someone who invites you to stay in his or her private home, you are entirely out of luck."

"Do you live in the village?" Mr. Fanhurst said, leaning closer than Beryl found she liked.

"I am happy to say that I do," Beryl said. "At the home of my friend Edwina Davenport."

"A large and rambling country house, I would guess," Mr. Fanhurst said. "Perhaps one with a large number of spare rooms?"

"I am afraid I could not possibly expect a man of your discriminating taste to find satisfaction anywhere in the village, even at a house with as much to recommend it as the Beeches," Beryl said before giving him a stunning smile and continuing along the pavement.

Chapter 21

There was no doubt about it, Edwina thought. Muriel Lowe-thorpe, the vicar's wife and dedicated leader of all charitable projects in the village of Walmsley Parva, was not up to her usual standard of cajoling and rallying volunteers for all those unpleasant tasks that needed doing in any volunteer organiza-tion. At the conclusion of the Women's Institute meeting, Edwina made a point of lingering. She wished to speak to Muriel alone. Not only in her capacity as a friend but as per-tained to the case against Frank.

Muriel's usually tidy hair had been scraped back haphaz-ardly. Stray tendrils crept out from beneath the brim of her re-spectable but uninspiring hat. It was the sort of headwear of which Edwina could not entirely approve. While she under-stood that a vicar's wife, especially one in a small village like Walmsley Parva, must comport herself with dignity and clothe herself in a manner that was beyond reproach, Edwina har-bored the belief that even the most upright of women might show a little flair in the millinery department. Muriel did not seem to share her convictions.

Her oatmeal-colored day dress was neither flattering nor reproachable. It served the sole purpose of ensuring that it could be said that the vicar's wife was clothed. She had pinned a brooch made of carved ivory and silver to her bosom upside down. It was not like Muriel to look anything but serviceable and efficient. In fact, Edwina could not think of a time in which she had ever seen the unflappable paragon of village virtue looking anything but uncompromisingly tidy.

In addition to her appearance, Muriel had forgotten to bring along a typewritten copy of the meeting's agenda and had allowed the previous week's meeting minutes to be approved without squabbling incessantly over the minutest of details, as was her usual habit. Without a doubt, something was on Muriel's mind. As a friend, Edwina was concerned. As a newly minted private enquiry agent, she was intrigued.

She felt her hand itch for the tiny notebook and pencil that she had come to keep in the pocket of her summer frock. She found that making detailed notes of her conversations with clients and those people she interviewed on their behalf helped her to keep her thoughts in good order. While she had not reached the point that she felt her memory had entirely abandoned her and gone off on holiday to some fleshpot resort along the Riviera, she had noticed it tended to wander off of its own accord now and again.

However, many of the people with whom she spoke did not feel comfortable having their every word jotted down for posterity. After the first case she and Beryl had undertaken as professionals, Edwina had learned to commit conversations to paper just after they had concluded rather than taking notes during the event. While she doubted from the looks of Muriel that she would much notice anything that was happening, Edwina decided not to risk putting her off. For now, her trusty notebook would remain secreted away in her pocket.

"I don't suppose you have time to come back to the Beeches for a cup of tea and a wander through my garden?" Edwina asked.

She knew that Muriel was also a gardening enthusiast, and it was one of the many points of interest she and Muriel shared. As a vicar's wife, Muriel could not be expected to engage a gardener, and for the most part, Edwina did not consider Simpkins to be a great deal of help. She found she and Muriel had much to convey to each other on the subject of staking delphiniums and turning compost piles. It should be an easy enough thing to tempt her to the Beeches for a stroll around to see what was in bloom.

"As much as I wish I had time, I daren't leave Wilfred alone for long," Muriel said. "Although I do confess I have been hankering to see how those phlox cuttings I gave you last autumn have settled in."

Edwina's thoughts bounced between a desire to enquire after the vicar's surprising level of neediness and her desire to boast about the success of the transplanted phlox cuttings. The parent plants from which they had been cut had suffered greatly from powdery mildew, a condition Edwina felt showed a lack of vigilance on the part of the gardener. She prided herself on the fact that such a loathsome and telling disease dared not rear its ugly head in any of the garden beds at the Beeches.

In the end, she reminded herself that her duties to her client superseded any petty feelings on her part. Although Muriel was inclined to think her husband incapable of functioning without her direction in every facet of his life, she felt it behooved her to at least make a polite enquiry after his troubles.

"I do hope the vicar has not fallen ill," Edwina said.

"No, not ill exactly," Muriel said slowly. She stopped straightening the chairs around the table in the middle of the village hall and gave Edwina her undivided attention. "It's just that he's terribly upset by what has happened to poor Frank Prentice."

"Surely Frank's arrest has very little to do with the vicar," Edwina said. She could not imagine why he would be more upset about Frank than he was about Hector Lomax's murder.

"That's exactly what I said when he wouldn't stop nattering on about it this morning," Muriel said, nodding vigorously. Two more stray tendrils of grey hair slipped out of their pins and fell across her high forehead. "But he said he cannot help but blame himself in the matter."

"Did he say why?" Edwina asked.

"Wilfred believes that if he had not dismissed Frank from his position as sexton, none of this would've happened," Muriel said.

"But surely the vicar can't believe that Frank Prentice would kill someone over a perceived slight," Edwina said. "And even if he did, why would the vicar hold himself accountable for the deeds of another?"

"Wilfred feels that he's been rather an old fool," Muriel said. "He dismissed Frank because he was unreliable. Of course you know the man drinks like a fish."

A look passed between the two women that said more than words ever could. Many men had spent too much time with the bottle prior to the outbreak of the war. Edwina was sorry to say that upon returning home, even more men had joined the ranks of those determinedly dissolute.

She did not blame them for seeking solace where they could find it after all that they had suffered. But she did think it a shame that their loved ones were forced to endure suffering of their own on account of the men's preferred form of oblivion.

"I had understood from what was said round the village that the vicar dismissed Frank after a pattern of dereliction of duty had developed. I had thought that Hector's complaint was simply the final straw." Edwina felt her hand creeping towards her pocket. She forced herself to smooth the skirt of her summer white frock instead.

"That is accurate, at least up to a point," Muriel said. "Perhaps I should not speak ill of the dead."

"I should think, as practically a member of the clergy, you would feel it your duty to prioritize the needs of the living and possibly the wrongly accused," Edwina said. Sometimes Muriel could use a little coaxing.

"I see just what you mean. Frank is the one who requires advocacy at this point. I'm sure that Constable Gibbs is doing all that she can on Hector's behalf," Muriel said.

"That's exactly what I mean," Edwina said. "Now you are saying?"

Muriel cleared her throat and looked about the village hall conspiratorially. "Wilfred had reason to believe that Hector's complaints about Frank were not entirely based on his disappointment with the services Frank rendered."

"What else could it have been about?" Edwina asked. She was surprised to consider there had been any other motivation for Hector's desire to see Frank relieved of his duties. Did he bear the man a personal grudge?

"Only hours before Hector's body was found, he had approached Wilfred about taking over the job of church sexton himself," Muriel said.

"What did the vicar say?" Edwina said.

"He agreed to hire him. After all, a church cannot go without a sexton for long, and he had not yet found someone to replace Frank," Muriel said.

"Did Frank find out about Hector being given his previous post?" Edwina asked.

Muriel nodded slowly, setting her soft second chin awobble. "Hector approached Wilfred in the church early in the afternoon of the day that he died. He asked Wilfred if he had filled the empty position, and when my husband said that he had not, Hector suggested himself for the role."

"But how did Frank find out about that?" Edwina asked.

"As soon as Wilfred agreed to give Hector a trial run at the job, Frank sat bolt upright in one of the pews only a few feet from where they stood chatting. Apparently, he had been taking a nap stretched out on one of them, and neither of the other two men was aware of his presence," Muriel said.

Edwina wasn't sure exactly what the world had come to when people could be emboldened to use the church as a place to sleep off too much drink. But the sad truth remained that over the past few years churches had lost much of their utility for their supposed purpose.

Despite the fact that churches had played a central part in village life for centuries, the Great War had changed all that. With so many young men having joined up and having died for their country, there had been far fewer weddings for the church to perform. Without weddings, there had been a sharp decline in the number of births and thus the need for christenings. As a final blow to the value the church establishment provided to the community, the decision by those in charge to refrain from recovering bodies and returning them to British soil for burial had eliminated the need for funeral services.

It was no wonder that appeals for funds to support the church roof repair had fallen on such deaf ears. From Sunday to Sunday, Edwina found herself saddened by the small number of fellow villagers who felt the need to attend services on a regular basis. It was a small step from a lack of regard for services to a repurposing of the pews as a space not for spiritual solace but for sleep.

"Did Frank confront them about it?" Edwina asked. She shuddered to think of a confrontation taking place within the sanctity of the church itself, but she supposed that anything was possible.

"Wilfred reported that Frank did not say a word. He simply sat up, scowled at Hector, then turned a look of reproof on Wilfred himself. Wilfred mentioned that Frank did raise a fist and shake it in Hector's general direction."

"I do hope the vicar will not continue to blame himself for what has happened. The duties of a village vicar are onerous enough without adding to them by self-recriminations," Edwina said. "Please send him my best, won't you?"

"I'm sure he will be glad of your support, but he would not approve of me gossiping about his worries with his parishioners. I hope that you will refrain from mentioning it to him," Muriel said, a deep groove appearing between her eyebrows.

"My lips are sealed. In my capacity as a private enquiry agent, I have learned to be entirely discreet," Edwina said. "When you find the time, I do hope you will come by to see the gardens. Perhaps I can persuade you with the offer of some softwood cuttings Simpkins has taken from a rather fine quince specimen."

Muriel nodded absentmindedly, her eyes darting towards the door. If the offer of a prized flowering quince did not ignite her interest, Edwina was certain the vicar was truly in a bad way. Muriel had been hounding her for a piece of her magnificent flowering shrub for years. Edwina wished to distress her neighbor no further. She hurriedly made her good-byes and headed out the door and on into the sunshine of a warm summer's morning.

As she headed back towards the Beeches, striding along at a rapid pace, she felt she could hardly wait to share her findings with Beryl. It was more information about the case but not good news for their client. The more she discovered, the guiltier Frank Prentice looked.

Most people would not be inclined to kill someone over a

job digging graves in the local churchyard. But by all accounts, the Prentice family was in dire straits, and perhaps Frank had been pushed to the snapping point by Hector's actions. As she made her way home, she couldn't help but feel there was little likelihood their newest case would end in success.

Chapter 22

Beryl decided to take advantage of the fact she was still in town and to go discreetly in search of Geraldine, the telephone operator. As the telephone office was situated not far along a nearby street, Beryl found herself peering in through the plate-glass door of the small brick building in short order.

Beryl strode into the small office, and a young woman seated on a low stool spun around to face her. Some sort of a headset with a mouthpiece and earphones sat upon her head. She held a plug attached to a length of cord in her hand, as if Beryl had interrupted her in the midst of her duties. Beryl could not help but notice that despite the girl's impeccable posture and stylish attempts at a modern cropped hairstyle, her face looked as though it had been hastily constructed by a sculptor about to clock out for the day and eager to hurry along with his mates to the local pub.

Her small eyes were set far too close together, and her irises were a blue so pale as to be almost unsettling. Her nose, overly large and bulbous, dominated her face. Thin lips perched above a receding chin. Despite the fact she was old enough to hold down a responsible position in the village, she was still unfortunately sporting a bumper crop of spots and blemishes on her skin.

A less prepossessing young woman, Beryl thought, she had never encountered in all her life. Still, she was not interested in hiring Geraldine Howarth for her beauty but rather for her practical skill set. She crossed the room and stuck out her hand.

"I do hope that I'm not bothering you, but your friend Hattie from Alma's House of Beauty suggested that I make your acquaintance," Beryl said. "Are you Geraldine?"

The girl's eyes widened, which merely brought them to the size of those of a normal individual. Her appearance did not improve upon closer inspection. Beryl thought she looked unsettlingly like a sleepy lizard.

"Yes, I am."

"Allow me to introduce myself. I'm Beryl Helliwell."

"Everyone knows who you are. I've been just dying to meet you," Geraldine said. "But why did Hattie send you to find me?"

"Your friend suggested you as just the right person to help me with a predicament I've gotten myself into," Beryl said, lowering her voice conspiratorially.

Geraldine let the switchboard plug fall from her fingers and clatter to the surface of the makeshift desk in front of her.

"I'd be happy to help any way that I can," Geraldine said. "Do you need to place an overseas call? Perhaps a coded message for the king?" Geraldine lowered her voice with each word that passed her lips.

When Beryl had first arrived in Walmsley Parva, she had deliberately shared the information with the village's biggest gossip, Prudence Rathbone, that she had on occasion done some work for His Majesty. Prudence had promptly spread the news to the rest of the population. Every now and again, Beryl found herself in the position of explaining to yet another resident of

Walmsley Parva that she and the king were not working on any joint projects at the moment. Geraldine was just the latest such person.

Beryl hated to disappoint any of her adoring public, especially when it took so little to entertain them. Still, any communications she had with George were not to be conducted in the open, over a telephone line, where any member of the public might listen in.

"As ably as I'm sure you could assist me with contacting the king, I'm here for another sort of skill you possess," Beryl said. "Hattie led me to believe that you were an expert typist."

Geraldine nodded, with her mouth hanging open widely. "I can type, take dictation, and even do a bit of light bookkeeping," she said. "Are you hiring someone for your enquiry agency?"

Beryl felt quite heartbroken at the look of eager anticipation on Geraldine's face. She understood the yearning for adventure that many young people felt. Why should Geraldine be any different simply because she was a plain-looking girl from an isolated village? Beryl hated to disappoint her and did her best to play up the opportunity she had on offer.

"I do need something in connection with the enquiry agency, but we are not yet looking to add staff to our partnership," Beryl said. "I'm sure you can be relied upon for your discretion, having been placed in a position of trust as a telephone switchboard operator, can you not?"

"I know enough not to go carrying tales, if that's what you are asking," Geraldine said. "Are you looking to have some letters typed?"

"I'm afraid that our business is of such a delicate nature that our clients would prefer us not to allow anyone other than Edwina or myself to know the specific details of their difficulties. Which is what brought me to you," Beryl said. "I had hoped you would be able to teach me to type."

Geraldine looked Beryl up and down, as if trying to decide

how best to answer. When her gaze fell upon Beryl's large, broad hands, she tipped her head to the side and squinted.

"I certainly could try, but you understand I cannot guarantee the results," Geraldine said. "I shouldn't want you to get your hopes up. Not everyone finds it easy to learn."

"I am delighted to hear you say that. My first attempts with the machine have not proven successful. Is there some sort of a trick to bashing only one key at a time?" Beryl asked.

"Having slim fingers is probably the best thing," Geraldine said, eyeing Beryl's hands for a second time. "A great deal of practice may be what you require."

"Would you be willing to take on the job of trying to help me?" Beryl asked. "I can pay you for your time. Shall we say at the same rate as you earn here at the telephone office?"

Beryl was gratified to see the young woman's eyes light up with pleasure.

"How soon were you hoping to start?" Geraldine asked.

"How about in two days' time?" Beryl said. "I'm in the thick of a case at present and may not be able to devote myself to the lessons immediately."

"Did you want to bring your machine here, or would you like me to meet you somewhere else?" Geraldine asked, looking around the small telephone office.

Beryl looked around, too, and decided that there was nowhere in sight that seemed an auspicious place to set up shop. Besides, anyone might wander in at any time, and Beryl was not quite sure she wanted the world to know what difficulty she had been experiencing operating such a simple machine. It was the sort of thing that might make the newspapers.

"Would it be possible for you to call on me at the Beeches? I have the typewriter already set up in a quiet room there, and we would not be in anyone's way at that location."

A light blinked on above a jack on the switchboard, and Geraldine reached for a cord. "Number please?" Geraldine said clearly and with authority into the mouthpiece of her headset. She slipped the end of the plug into the switchboard, then turned her attention back to Beryl.

"Mostly, I work the evening shift into the night. Shall I call on you at around ten in the morning?" Geraldine said.

While Beryl did not prefer to leave the comfort of her bed before ten o'clock in the morning, she was eager to begin her lessons and understood that other people had schedules that were far more fixed than her own. Another call lit up the board and urged Beryl to conclude her arrangements quickly.

"I look forward to seeing you then," Beryl said before taking her leave.

Chapter 23

Beryl returned from her trip into the village with a triumphant look stamped on her face. Edwina was never quite sure whether Beryl's high spirits were to be celebrated or discouraged. Beryl was enough of a force of nature even when not flushed with triumph.

"You look pleased with yourself," Edwina said.

"I have had a fruitful outing into town."

Edwina felt a cold, nagging finger of dread as she wondered what Beryl might be up to. She desperately hoped it did not involve the motorcar. Or their still strained finances. "You haven't gone placing more wagers with Chester White, have you?" she asked.

"No. Nothing like that. What would you say if I told you that Hector offered Alma Poole a ring matching the description of the one he stole from Simpkins?" Beryl asked.

"I would say that such a thing was shocking and that Alma would have been well within her rights to do away with such a vulgar man," Edwina said. "Her husband, Sidney, could hardly be blamed if he had done away with him given the slightest opportunity."

"I thought the same thing. To my way of thinking, the Pooles are the strongest suspects," Beryl said.

"Except for Frank Prentice," Edwina reminded her.

As if on cue, Crumpet announced with full voice that a visitor had appeared at the door. Beryl returned to the kitchen a moment later, followed by an anxious-looking Jack Prentice. Edwina knew Beryl far too well to be fooled by her forced cheerfulness.

"What brings you to see us again so soon, Jack?" Beryl said.

"I hoped you might have some good news to tell me about my father and the case," Jack said, peering up at the two women.

Edwina noticed the frayed cuffs on his shirt and the threadbare condition of the flat cap he turned round and round in his small, ink-covered hands. She thought once more of the knitted items she was planning for his siblings and him, knowing full well a warm jumper or a pair of thick socks was little comfort as a replacement for a father.

"It's early days yet, Jack," Beryl said. "There's no sense getting yourself worked up so soon." Beryl looked over at Edwina with a look of pleading in her eyes.

"You're far too sensible a lad for us to tell you anything but the truth," Edwina said. "As of yet we have no new information to help your father's case. We have not given up investigating, but everything we have found so far has not turned up an alternate suspect."

"That's what my mama said you'd say," Jack said. "She thinks he did it." Jack's thin shoulders sagged beneath his cotton shirt.

"We don't necessarily think your father is guilty," Beryl said. "We just don't have anything to prove the contrary. You can see how that's different, can't you?"

"So you just need more time?" Jack asked.

Edwina did not believe in lying, least of all to children. It was far better to tell the truth, sooner rather than later. Still, there were ways of saying things that were not cruel.

"As far as anyone is able to tell at present, your father has the strongest motive for Hector's murder. He cannot account for his whereabouts at the time the crime was committed, because of his drinking bout. For your sake, we are working diligently on discovering whether or not someone else had equal opportunity and motive to commit the crime," Edwina said. "We cannot truthfully say anything more encouraging than that."

Jack looked her straight in the face, and Edwina thought how old he looked despite his lack of years. He slapped his cap against his leg, then settled it back on his crop of unruly curls.

"You can't say more fairly than that," Jack said. "I'd best get back to work." With Crumpet close on his heels, he turned and headed out the back door and into the garden. Edwina watched his retreating form as he slipped off through the woods and out of sight.

"I'm not entirely sure I like this job of ours," Edwina said as she turned back towards her friend.

"Nor do I," Beryl said. "Frank's chances don't seem very good, but there is one thing we can say."

"Which is?" Edwina asked.

"They are better than they would be if we hadn't taken on this job," Beryl said. Edwina noticed her friend had entirely lost her look of triumph that she had been sporting only moments earlier.

"I feel as though we've hit a dead end," Edwina said. "I have no idea which line of enquiry to pursue at this point." She reached for a linen tea towel and began absentmindedly buffing a water glass she plucked from the drying rack. She always thought best with something to busy her hands.

"I've been racking my brain and racking my brain about the whole sordid affair. I am in great need of a distraction," Beryl said.

"I hardly know what to suggest," Edwina said.

"You needn't worry about that. I've already thought of something," Beryl said.

"Which is?"

"I'm rather afraid I've been going soft over the past few months by living entirely indoors, sleeping in a comfortable bed, and eating your well-prepared meals. If I am to write this adventure guide, I need to recall the details of a life spent living rough," Beryl said.

"What does that mean?" Edwina said.

"I think I shall camp out tonight," Beryl said.

"Camp out?" Edwina said, her heart filling with dread. She dearly hoped Beryl was not intent on setting up camp herself in the potting shed.

"Yes. I've decided to take a bedroll and a rucksack full of provisions and to spend the night camped out at Hector's place," Beryl said.

"Surely that's not necessary, is it?" Edwina said. "Especially with a murderer about."

"If Doris Gibbs is right, there isn't a murderer on the loose. He's locked up tightly in the Walmsley Parva jail cell," Beryl said. "I wish to bring a real spirit of adventure to my manuscript, so I feel that it behooves me to give myself a bit of a refresher course."

Edwina placed the water glass on a shelf in the cupboard and threaded the linen towel through a drawer handle to dry. She untied her pinny from around her waist and hung it on its hook. As much as the idea of spending the night outside, sleeping on the ground under the cold stars, did not appeal to her, she knew she must make the offer.

"What do you suggest that I pack to take with us?" Edwina asked.

"My dear friend, I in no way expect you to accompany me," Beryl said.

"I couldn't possibly allow you to go alone. Even if there isn't a murderer on the loose, it's hardly the done thing for a woman alone to sleep outdoors, especially on a dead man's property," Edwina said.

"I'm afraid I must insist on going it alone," Beryl said. "It will only have the ring of authenticity if I camp out on my own. Walmsley Parva is hardly the most dangerous place I will have found myself in such circumstances."

"Are you quite certain?" Edwina said, trying desperately to hide her relief. "I should never forgive myself if anything were to happen to you."

"My dear Ed, you're far too good to me. If you would be willing to wrap me up a packet of sandwiches and perhaps a piece of fruit or two, I shall be completely content to head out on my own. After all, when one has spent so much time navigating the sands of the desert, the densely forested jungle, and even the high seas, a fallow field on a fruit farm holds no terrors."

Edwina heard the determination in Beryl's voice, but she also noticed her friend patting her pocket, as if she was reassuring herself that her tiny pistol lay inside it.

Chapter 24

Edwina had not slept well. Between her worries about Beryl spending the night all alone in such close proximity to Clifford Hammond's property and being forced to endure the sound of Simpkins's reverberating snores, she had spent the night tossing and turning. Even Crumpet looked the worse for the wear when he lifted his small head from the cushion in his basket and blinked sleepily at her the next morning.

She quickly dressed and hurried to the kitchen, where she boiled water and prepared a flask of tea. She had saved two scones from tea the afternoon before and placed them, along with a pat of butter and a small jar of fruit preserves, into a small basket. Despite Beryl's preference for sleeping late, Edwina could not imagine her friend managing to lounge about long after the sun had risen. It was one thing to remain asleep tucked up in bed with the drapes drawn. It was quite another to be sprawled out on the ground in the open.

Another thought had worried her as she had lain in bed the night before. She imagined Beryl attempting to make breakfast for herself over an open fire. Between Beryl's lack of cooking skills and the severity of the drought, Edwina was concerned that Beryl might light the district on fire.

Edwina's imagination was a powerful one, and she had dreamt over and over that her dear friend had set the entire region ablaze. In one dream Jack had stood just in front of a billowing cloud of soot, hocking a newspaper with the headline FORMER ADVENTURESS FOUND GUILTY OF ARSON.

She decided to take pity on Crumpet and left him sleeping in his basket as she slipped out the back door and headed for Hector's cottage. The sun was high in the sky, and the day grew warmer and warmer with each step she took. Wild roses bloomed in the hedgerows, and up ahead of her, she noticed a small brown rabbit scurrying beneath a hazelnut thicket.

After about fifteen minutes of walking, she spotted Hector's cottage up ahead. Once again, she felt a wave of sadness wash over her as she thought of the condition of the Lomax farm. The fruit trees had not been properly pruned at the end of the winter, and no one had seen fit to mulch beneath the strawberry plants. It was so dry, she caught herself imagining that something had burst into flame.

She sniffed the air delicately, wondering if her imagination had run away with her completely. She stopped stock-still and drew in a deeper breath. No, she had imagined nothing. The smell of smoke was very near and very real. She lifted her hand to shield her eyes and scanned the scene in the distance. She was unable to see anything to indicate what might be burning.

She rushed towards Hector's cottage, spilling her basket in her haste, quite certain Beryl would prove the cause of the difficulty. Beryl was nowhere to be found as she approached the small cottage and mounted the front step to the door. She pressed on the latch and found it gave way easily in her hand. Despite her loathing to enter without permission, she was alarmed by the smell of smoke that seemed to be coming from within. She flung open the door and stepped inside.

Her nose had not deceived her. As she moved from the entryway deeper into the home, the smell grew stronger. The kitchen did not reveal the source of the smoke, nor did the small sitting room, where she had sat with Simpkins and Beryl the day they had heard of Hector's murder. She moved farther into the small cottage. Her eyes began to water, and she felt an overwhelming desire to cough.

The small room in front of her was rapidly filling with smoke. In its center sat a large brass bed piled high with clothing. The clothing was smoldering, and right before her eyes, a tower of flame grew and began to lick at the low-beamed ceiling. She turned around and raced back towards the kitchen.

The sink was fitted with a hand pump rather than a modern set of taps. Edwina grabbed a filthy kettle from the cooker and filled it with water as quickly as she could operate the pump. She raced back to the bedroom and threw the water at the smoldering pile of clothing. She returned to the kitchen several more times, filled the kettle, and doused the fire repeatedly with its contents.

When she was satisfied that the fire was well and truly extinguished, she leaned back against the wall and caught her breath. Her knees felt weak as the shock of what had happened sank in. Suddenly she realized she had no idea what could have caused the fire and whether or not Beryl was in any danger.

Edwina raced outside and swept her eyes over the open fields, in search of her friend. She wondered if she should head over to Clifford Hammond's property to ask if he had seen her, but thought better of it. For all she knew, he was the person who had set the fire and possibly even murdered Hector. Alerting him that Beryl might be alone and vulnerable was perhaps the worst thing she could do.

She worked her way around the side of the house and allowed her gaze to move slowly along, as if she were forming a search grid. Up ahead, something caught her attention by fluttering in the slight breeze. She strode off purposely in the direction of a hedgerow comprised of currant bushes. About halfway up the row stood a magnificent European beech tree. There, on the ground beneath it, Beryl lay stretched out on her back, her arm slung over her head in a preposterously unladylike position. Even though the sun fell fully on Beryl's face, she gave no sign of consciousness. Edwina hurried towards her more quickly, hoping that nothing nefarious explained her complete oblivion to the coming of the day.

As she approached, the sound of Beryl's rumbling snores floated across on the morning breeze. Edwina slowed her pace and gave herself a moment to catch her breath. She went so far as to retrieve a delicately trimmed handkerchief from inside her sleeve and used it to dab an unladylike sheen of perspiration from her forehead.

She looked back out across the field for the presence of any intruders, ones that could be responsible for setting the fire. As far as she could see, she and Beryl were the only people in the vicinity. Other than the birds in the trees and a pair of butterflies flitting from bush to bush in search of nectar-filled flowers, nothing stirred except for the breeze.

She bent over Beryl, reached down, and shook her friend gently by the shoulder. She knew from previous experience it would do no good to simply call her name. Edwina wondered what explained her friend's capacity to sleep anywhere at any time.

Edwina was not so fortunate in her quest for a good night's sleep. More often than not, she lay awake on her bed, sleep eluding her for an hour or more as she ran through what had happened that day and what she anticipated of the next. Even if she managed to fall asleep promptly, she often awoke in the night, plagued by the same sorts of anxious thoughts.

Since Beryl's arrival, she had slept better, it was true. But interrupted sleep was a habit of long standing and one she found was not easily broken. With Beryl in the house, she felt less lonely, but her anxiety had not decreased. Rather it had shifted from worries about expiring with no one but Crumpet to know she had gone to worries about expiring by being jettisoned through a motorcar windscreen or as the result of a confrontation with a criminal. Life was far more exciting with Beryl in residence but at least as woefully bereft of restorative rest.

Edwina thought that Beryl had learned to sleep wherever she could whenever she could as a result of her global ramblings. If her friend had not learned to blot out the rest of the world in order to rest, she could not have maintained her hectic pace. Although Edwina did not wish to behave as wildly as her friend, she did understand some of the necessities for making that happen. Chief on the list was a good night's sleep.

Edwina thought it most likely that Beryl would have no valuable information to contribute about whom the intruder in Hector's cottage could have been. Edwina suspected she would have been far too deeply asleep to have noticed a thing. She shook Beryl's shoulder more vigorously, and the other woman's eyes fluttered open, then blinked slowly.

"Good morning, Ed. What brings you out at such an early hour?" Beryl said, stretching languidly before raising up on one elbow.

"I thought to bring you breakfast after your adventure, but it seems I've had an adventure of my own instead," Edwina said.

"I ought to go away more often if it opens the opportunity for adventures of your own," Beryl said. "What happened?"

"I think you'd best see for yourself," Edwina said as she pointed towards Hector's cottage.

"Has something happened in the night?" Beryl asked.

"I think it must have happened just before I arrived," Edwina said. "Let's gather up your things. I'll tell you on the way back down to the cottage."

Beryl expertly rolled her bedroll into a neat bundle and tucked it under her arm. Edwina gathered up the few items that remained outside the rucksack and stuffed them down inside it. In a flash they were on their way across the field, and Edwina explained what she had found when she had arrived.

"No, I didn't see a thing. Or hear anything either," Beryl said in response to Edwina's question about a possible arsonist.

"I thought it was hoping for too much to think you might have been conscious."

"You certainly couldn't have imagined that I would have noticed someone skulking about the cottage and not confronted him or her, could you?" Beryl asked. "Surely you think better of my courage than that."

"Of course I do. I was just hopeful that you might have important information to share," Edwina said.

"Now that we're here, show me what you found," Beryl said.

The two women entered the cottage and followed the same route that Edwina had used when she discovered the fire. But this time, with no concern that something was on fire, Edwina had time to notice the condition of the small home.

She had been too worried and too busy on her earlier visit to notice the disarray. While it was true that the cottage had been untidy the day before, this morning it appeared absolutely ransacked. Edwina could not believe she had not noticed it before.

"You didn't do this, did you?" Beryl said, pointing to a refuse bin in the kitchen that had been overturned and its contents spilled across the floor.

"Certainly not," Edwina said. "As a matter fact, this is the first I noticed it."

As Edwina looked around, she noticed that cupboard doors sagged open and items were strewn about haphazardly. She proceeded from the kitchen into the parlour, where the mess was also noticeable. Once again a wastepaper basket was tipped out. Ashes in the fireplace had been raked forward and spilled across the hearth, as though someone had been examining them for the remains of something burnt.

"How bizarre," Beryl said. "You say the fire was in the bedroom?"

"Follow me," Edwina said. She led the way into the small bedchamber and pointed at the brass bed, with its sodden heap of clothing piled in its center. She took a moment to glance over at the dressing table, where a photograph of a young woman and a young man wearing their Sunday best stood. She crossed the room and lifted the photograph in its frame for a closer look.

To her surprise, she was staring at the face of a far younger Simpkins. He had been handsome in a way, she had to admit, with his clear, steady eyes and strong jaw. The woman in the photograph looked up at him adoringly. This must be a youthful version of his beloved wife, Bess.

"This must be Simpkins's room," Edwina said, holding the photograph out to Beryl.

"Why would anyone want to deliberately set fire to this cottage?" Beryl asked. "And were they trying to send a message to Simpkins?"

Chapter 25

"I haven't the faintest idea," Edwina said.

"I should have thought Hector would be the one more likely to have created enemies intent on ravaging his property," Beryl said.

"Are you thinking of Clifford Hammond?" Edwina asked.

"He would be in the best position to start the fire without being detected, since all he had to do was cross the property line and sneak inside," Beryl said. "And he would have been in a good place to observe whether or not there was anyone at home at the time of the break-in."

"Do you really think he would have risked damage to his own property by lighting a fire on the neighboring one?" Edwina asked. "After all, if anyone would know how dangerously dry the conditions are, it would be Mr. Hammond."

"He seemed concerned about a crop failure for this year as well as into the future. Do you suppose he subscribed to some sort of insurance scheme?" Beryl said.

"Surely you don't think he would be likely to risk his own livelihood for the future by burning his property for an insurance payout?" Edwina asked. "Or that he would do something so unfeeling to all his plants."

Edwina thought of her own gardens and the plants housed within them, and her heart gave a wrench. She could not bear to think of the hardship Mr. Hammond's trees and bushes were forced to endure. Edwina had an intimate knowledge of each of her own plants and looked on them almost as members of her family. She could not imagine another gardener being so brutish as to consign his charges to wholesale slaughter. The very notion was barbaric.

"I am sure I cannot say, but from the looks of his plants, this year's crop is unlikely to yield a profit. Men do any manner of unexpected things, should they become desperate enough." Beryl turned her attention to the clothing on the bed. "If it wasn't him, then who would have done it, and why?"

"We know it wasn't Simpkins, because he was tucked up in the spare room at the Beeches all night. And there is no reason he should wish to destroy his own home that I can see," Edwina said.

"Frank could not have done it, since he spent the night under the watchful eye of Constable Gibbs," Beryl said.

"You don't think it could've been one of Frank's family members, do you?" Edwina asked. There was something quite mischievous about the whole situation. Could it have been the work of a child, like Jack?

"I suppose we cannot dismiss the notion that someone from the Prentice family was involved, but I can't see what they would have to gain by setting a fire, can you?" Beryl asked.

"Who is to say anyone has to gain by what occurred here? Isn't it possible that somebody was just venting their spleen?" Edwina said.

"Anything is possible, I suppose, but I prefer to work from the theory that unusual happenings connected to a murder are unlikely to be a coincidence," Beryl said.

"I suppose we shall have to report this to Simpkins, at the very least," Edwina said. "I suppose we ought to consider reporting to Constable Gibbs too."

Beryl shook her head vigorously. "She would only arrest us for breaking and entering. She would probably accuse us of setting the fire as well. No, it would be far better simply to keep this to ourselves for now."

"You don't think we should tell even Simpkins?" Edwina asked.

"I can't see how it will do him any good to know that someone has broken in while he was away from home. I thought we had agreed it would be best to keep an eye on him. If he hears about damage to his property while it's empty, he might feel obligated to return to his cottage to protect it."

"I suppose you're right. After all, there is nothing that he needs to do in response to what has happened. At least not if we clear out these clothes and tidy up the wastepaper baskets," Edwina said.

"I think that would be the best course of action. After all, Simpkins might be in danger out here on his own. We were assuming that whoever set the fire knew that he was gone overnight, but that may not have been the case. Someone may have been making an attempt on his life," Beryl said.

That did it. Edwina was not about to send any employee of hers into harm's way. What Simpkins did not know wouldn't hurt him. She stepped up to the bed and gathered the sodden clothing into her arms. With Beryl's help, she carried the lot of it outdoors and spread it out on the grass in order to inspect the damage. Those pieces that were simply wet, they pinned to a clothesline strung at the back of the house.

The items that were singed beyond salvaging, Edwina bundled up and wrapped in a tablecloth she found in the kitchen. While Beryl took the load of clothing to the motorcar in order to dispose of it discreetly later, Edwina moved about the cottage, tidying those things she knew had been disarranged by the intruder.

In the kitchen she closed the cupboard doors and returned the rubbish to its bin. That task completed, she moved into the parlour and used the fireplace brush to return the ashes to the grate. She repeated the task of scooping up wastepaper and righting the basket next to a small table. Stacked on the table were several books she recognized as property of the Walmsley Parva reading room.

In fact, the one on top was a book she had been looking forward to reading. Edwina had a hidden passion for the romance of the American West, and the popular novels written by Zane Grey were amongst her favourite reads. She felt it her civic duty to return the volumes to the reading room without delay. She knew for a fact that Simpkins was not much of a reader, if one discounted accounts in the racing world news. She had no doubt that Hector was the one who had borrowed the towering stack of novels. He clearly had no use for them now.

She lifted the Zane Grey book from the stack and could not resist thumbing through it for a peek. As she did so, she noticed the edge of a piece of paper extending slightly beyond the volume's pages. She turned to where the book had been marked, and realized that Hector had shared a habit with her. He had marked his place in the book by inserting a used envelope in it.

On the back of the envelope was written a list of groceries. Edwina did the same thing herself more often than not. She could not see wasting valuable paper on something that was destined only to be thrown away or burnt up in the stove. The list included produce items and meat from Sidney Poole's butcher shop. She turned it over and was surprised to see the name Albert Simpkins written on the front.

Hector had used Simpkins's mail for his list making. Edwina noticed the handwriting on the front was quite distinctive and unfamiliar. The name of the cottage and its location—Daisy

Brook Farm, Walmsley Parva, Kent—were clearly written on it in deep blue ink. Edwina clucked her tongue as she noticed the letter *y* in *Daisy* and in *Walmsley* were ill formed. Rather than the loop being formed on the left side of the stem, the writer had formed it on the right. Edwina imagined what Miss DuPont from her finishing school would have had to say about such a poorly formed hand.

Not only was the handwriting odd, but Edwina was also surprised to see that the envelope had been postmarked in the popular tourist town of Tunbridge Wells. While she did not claim to have a comprehensive knowledge of all Simpkins's friends and relations, she had never known him to mention having any acquaintance from that town. She certainly thought it unlikely he would have failed to mention it if someone in his circle of acquaintance had traveled there for pleasure and had thought to send him a letter. It was one of the things that most annoyed Edwina when Simpkins was at the Beeches.

She supposed, upon reflection, that he was as lonely as she had been before Beryl had arrived and taken up residence in her home. She'd often noted that lonely people blathered on and on about the smallest of details concerning their lives whenever they had the opportunity. A letter from Tunbridge Wells would certainly count as an item of note that he would have been eager to share.

The postmark clearly displayed the name of the town, but the date had smeared, and Edwina could make out only that the letter had been sent in the month of May. The envelope did not look to be an old one, and as it was still only early June, Edwina wondered if it had been sent the month before.

She supposed it possible that this was the last grocery shopping list that Hector ever wrote. On a whim she carried the stack of books and the envelope to the kitchen. Beryl mounted the stone step in front of the cottage and arrived just in time to witness Edwina wrenching open the door of the icebox.

Edwina peered inside and spotted a partially eaten roasted leg of mutton, a carton of eggs, and the better part of a pound of butter. She consulted the list. All those items were written upon it. She made her way along the cupboards and opened them one by one, searching for the other items on the list. She found most still intact.

"What are you doing?" Beryl asked. "I hope you're not planning to cook anything in here."

"Certainly not. I was just wondering if the groceries on this list had been purchased recently. Considering most of them still seem to be here in the house, I would say that they had," Edwina said.

"Why should that matter?" Beryl said.

"Because I think that we may be able to get a better sense of Hector's movements during the last hours of his life from this list," Edwina said. "I have a postmark date on the envelope and could consult Sidney Poole and the greengrocer about the approximate time these items were purchased. It may give us a better sense of what he was up to during his last days."

"Are you sure it's a wise idea to go to the greengrocer's?" Beryl asked with an arched eyebrow.

Some weeks before, Edwina and Beryl had run afoul of local greengrocer Gareth Scott. Edwina had made a practice of avoiding his shop whenever possible.

"Perhaps we can rely on Simpkins to tell us all we need to know. After all, he might know when the groceries were purchased. It could save us a trip."

"Excellent suggestion, Ed," Beryl said. "Let's jump in the old bus and head back to the Beeches. So long as he is out of bed, we can ask him right away."

Chapter 26

By the time they returned to the Beeches, Simpkins had made his way downstairs from the guest room, where he had made himself thoroughly at home. Beryl was pleased to see he seemed more like himself than he had in the past twenty-four hours. The color had returned to his pale cheeks, and there was a spring in his step that spoke of soberness.

They found him in the kitchen, clad in a pair of carpet slippers and one of Edwina's aprons. Beryl had not gotten quite used to Edwina referring to an apron as a pinny. Nevertheless, he was wearing one with tucks and frills and a bit of embroidery.

After the goings-on at Hector's cottage, they had not attempted to salvage the breakfast Edwina had brought. Beryl found that she was starving, and was more than pleased to see Simpkins was showing off one of his best skill sets at the stove.

The smell of crisp bacon and grilled tomatoes filled the air. While Beryl was not enthusiastic about tea or many of the other culinary choices she had encountered while in the British Isles, she felt quite pleased with their notion of a traditional breakfast. If she had to start her day earlier than she preferred, she liked to do it with a full English fry-up.

Edwina had made several pointed comments about the injurious effects of the daily consumption of such things, but Beryl had wisely ignored her. She and Simpkins shared an enthusiasm for eggs and sausages and little cooked mushrooms. Edwina waited until they had all settled at the kitchen table, with steaming plates of food before them, before she broached the subject of the groceries at Hector's cottage to Simpkins.

"I wondered if you happen to remember when you got this letter?" Edwina asked, removing the envelope from the book she had taken from Hector's cottage and sliding it across the table to him.

Simpkins lifted it and inspected both the front and the back. "I've never seen this before in my life. Where did you find it?"

Beryl and Edwina exchanged a significant glance. Fortunately, Simpkins would not be surprised to hear that his brother-in-law had been up to more incidents of unsavory behavior. After all, if he was willing to steal and sell his dead sister's wedding ring, what would it matter to him to pilfer the post?

"Edwina found it at your cottage. It was tucked inside a book she assumed Hector borrowed from the reading room," Beryl said, reaching for her steaming cup of coffee.

It could be said that her morning routine would be vastly improved if Simpkins remained in charge of the coffeepot. As much as she appreciated Edwina's culinary skills, her friend could not seem to get the hang of brewing a decent cup of coffee, no matter how hard she tried.

Her efforts always ended up like a watered-down version of tea or something so strong and gritty, it stripped the enamel off one's teeth. Beryl should not have been surprised that Simpkins would be the one to produce a quality cup of strong drink. After all, it was his specialty.

"Any books in the cottage were sure to have been Hector's," Simpkins said. "You say that he used my post as a bookmark?"

"Yes. At least I think he did. It was tucked inside, with the grocery list written on the back," Edwina said.

"Are you quite sure that you did not read the letter that was inside it and simply leave the envelope lying around for Hector to use?" Beryl asked.

"I am sure I've never seen this before," Simpkins said.

"Do you know anyone who lives in Tunbridge Wells?" Edwina asked. "Or someone who would have been likely to be visiting there?"

Simpkins shook his head slowly. "I had some cousins who visited there once when I was a young man, but no one more recently that comes to mind."

"What about businesses or seed merchants or memberships in some sort of a club whose headquarters might be located in Tunbridge Wells?" Beryl suggested.

Simpkins reached for a pot of gooseberry preserves and fished around in the bottom of it with his knife. "What the devil do you think Hector was doing reading my post?"

"I have no idea. The reason we brought it to your attention was not to upset you about his invasion of your privacy but to try to ascertain when that letter arrived at the cottage. We inspected the larder and noticed that most of the foodstuffs listed on the back of the envelope are still present in the house," Edwina said.

"What's that got to do with the price of eggs?" Simpkins asked.

"We thought perhaps it would make it easier to trace Hector's movements over the last day or so of his life if you were aware of the letter and when he might've had the opportunity to get ahold of the envelope," Beryl said.

Simpkins looked at the postmark and tapped it with a gnarled, grubby finger. Beryl hoped that Edwina was not taking note of the condition of his fingernails, but then she feared that Edwina had as she watched her friend push her plate away from her slightly. Edwina was far too fastidious to enjoy meals cooked by someone who could plant potatoes under their nails.

"I haven't seen it, so I would assume that he took it as soon as it came in. I was here at the Beeches most of the time over the last couple of days of his life, so if it came in recently, he would've had plenty of opportunity to help himself to my post without me noticing. I really can't be more help than that," Simpkins said.

"Then I shall just have to go down to the village and make enquiries. I'll return the books to the reading room and then stop in at the butcher shop to ask Mr. Poole when the last time was that he saw Hector," Edwina said.

"I think I'll accompany you into the village. I have an errand I'd like to do myself," Beryl said.

Edwina arched an eyebrow at her, but she kept her thoughts to herself. Beryl wanted to stop in and inspect some of the other models of typewriting machines on display at the local stationer's. She wondered if some of them might have more widely spaced apart keys than the model she had purchased. Even with her upcoming lessons with Geraldine Howarth, she wasn't sure there was much cure for her troubles if she didn't find something that better accommodated her hands.

But there was no need for Edwina to know that. She had not been as supportive of Beryl's enthusiasm for writing her adventure guide as she would have liked. There was no reason to give Edwina the satisfaction of knowing she had been right to caution Beryl about the venture.

They finished up the breakfast in record time and left Simpkins at the Beeches. He offered to do the washing-up and mentioned that there were a few hardwood cuttings he wished to pot that afternoon. He and Edwina conferred briefly about the value of forsythia and flowering quince before Edwina could be convinced to fetch her hat and be bundled into the car.

Chapter 27

The reading room was empty when Edwina pushed open the heavy door and stepped inside. As always when she entered the light-filled space, with its shelves and shelves of books, she felt perfectly at home. If there was one place in the world she loved almost as much as the Beeches, it was the Walmsley Parva reading room.

Her mother had not approved of many of the sorts of books that Edwina enjoyed and had not allowed them to be stocked in the library at her home. Edwina's father had been far more encouraging of her thirst for adventure novels but had found it difficult to stand up to his overbearing wife. As a compromise, when she was still quite a young girl, he had taken Edwina to the reading room and introduced her to the delights of popular fiction.

While Mrs. Davenport had been convinced of the value of improving literature and nonfiction, Edwina's mild-mannered, bespectacled solicitor father had shown a surprising side to his character when he suggested to Edwina that he had always delighted in the works of Sir Arthur Conan Doyle and Wilkie

Collins. He had admonished her not to tell her mother unless she asked directly about their trips to the reading room.

Edwina had made a point to select some things that her mother would believe were suitable on every visit in order to have a truthful but not entirely revelatory conversation with her mother about her current reading list. Over the years she had managed to work her way through much of the reading room's collection. It was not until several months after her mother's death that she had finally allowed herself not to add a cookery book or a history of the Visigoths or some such thing to her reading stack in order to fend off her mother's admonishments.

It should have felt like a liberation to no longer need to continue the deception, but in fact, the first time she had not selected an improving book from the stacks had been a low point in Edwina's life. It was as if in that one small act, she had accepted that her mother was well and truly gone from the face of the earth. Fortunately for Edwina, Beryl had appeared on the scene not long after and had raised her spirits considerably.

Edwina carried Hector's books back to their spots and replaced them neatly on the shelves, sliding each carefully in next to its neighbor, except for the book she wished to keep for herself. That she had left back at the Beeches. But she reminded herself to update the reading room logbook so that others would know where the volume had gone and when it was expected to return.

As she ran her finger along the column and looked for Hector's name in order to mark that his latest loans had been returned, she was not surprised to see that the book she wished to take out had been borrowed several weeks prior. She knew that she had been waiting for what seemed like forever, but Edwina had considered it possible that she was simply being impatient and unreasonable.

It was gratifying to realize that she had not. In the past, reading had taken up much more of her free time, and she had found it far more difficult to wait for her turn with popular volumes. Now that she and Beryl were involved with their private enquiry business, she had far too many distractions to spend much energy chomping at the bit for others to hurriedly return books.

Hector had borrowed the book more than six weeks earlier. *How like such a man of poor character to be so selfish*, she thought, tapping forcefully on the line in the ledger where he had written his name. She lifted the pen and marked the date when she had returned it.

The lengthy time during which the book had been in Hector's possession certainly did not help to narrow down the time frame for the letter she had found tucked inside it. Still, she felt slightly proud of herself that she had thought to double-check such a thing. She made her own entries in the logbook, cast a fond glance around the reading room, and headed off to the butcher shop.

Sidney Poole stood behind the counter of his shop, looking as though he had nothing whatsoever to do. There were no other customers in this shop, and Edwina felt her timing was impeccable. She pulled the grocery list envelope from her handbag and stepped up to the counter.

"Good day to you, Miss Davenport," Sidney said. "I've got a nice bit of lamb set aside if you're interested."

He inclined his head towards the back room, and Edwina understood that he was trying to offer her something special. She wondered at his motives. Did he have a guilty conscience about Hector's murder? Sidney was not in the habit of treating her with special consideration. At least he hadn't been over the course of time when her finances had fallen into arrears.

Beryl's arrival and additional sources of income—gambling winnings and generous, albeit sporadic, alimony payments— had put her housekeeping accounts back on solid footing. But she didn't think they had improved to the point where Sidney

Poole would be holding back choice bits of lamb on her account. This was worthy of investigation.

"While that sounds simply lovely, it's not, in fact, why I am here," Edwina said, tapping on the envelope and sliding it across the counter. "Do you remember when you sold these items to Hector Lomax?"

Sidney picked up the envelope and squinted at it. Hector wrote in a clear hand, and Edwina was surprised to see Sidney taking his time over the handwriting. Was he having the sort of vision trouble so many people did in the middle years of life? Or was he using it as a ruse to buy some time to concoct a response to her question?

"Let me pull out my ledger," Sidney said. "Hector usually put things on account, to be billed later. But I don't have to tell you how that goes, do I?" Sidney gave Edwina a look that at one time would have brought a flush of shame to the back of her neck. Fortunately, Edwina found that she had been feeling much bolder since Beryl's arrival. Was it the constant influence of her courageous friend or the newfound self-confidence she felt from her work as a private enquiry agent? Perhaps the source of the confidence did not matter as much as the fact that it had become a habit and a way of life.

Unfortunately, so had the tendency of tradesmen to become far more outspoken with the upper classes than ever they had been before the war. Edwina was all for changes of her own but was not always so inclined to be in favor of those embarked upon by others. This would never do. She would need to find a way to put him in his place if she wished to trade with him without trepidation.

"Yes, why don't you do that," Edwina said. "I haven't much time to wait, so if you would attend to it immediately, I would appreciate it."

"Busy with another investigation, are you?" Sidney said, lifting the ledger from beneath the counter and spreading it out between them.

"As a matter of fact, I am," Edwina said.

"Isn't this the sort of thing that Constable Gibbs should be asking?" Sidney said, running his finger along the ledger and then turning the page.

"I'm working on behalf of the client, who is not being served well by Constable Gibbs's line of enquiry," Edwina said.

"Young Jack Prentice, I believe, isn't it?" Sidney said.

"Where did you hear that?" Edwina said.

"Everyone in the village is talking about it. No one thinks it likely that you and Miss Helliwell will come to any sort of success with this case. Here it is, a leg of mutton. Purchased six days ago. Was that all?" Sidney asked.

"It's everything from the butcher on Hector's list, but not everything I wanted to ask you about," Edwina said. She stepped a little closer to the counter and looked Sidney directly in the face. "It's my understanding that you had an argument yourself with Hector not long before he died. I was curious what it was about."

"I am not in the curiosity business," Sidney said. He closed the ledger with a bit more vigor than Edwina felt it required.

Good, she thought. She was getting under his skin.

"I understood it was likely that it had something to do with your wife," Edwina said.

"Who said that?" Sidney said.

"I wasn't sticking my nose in. I just happened to be at Alma's beauty parlour when the subject of Hector came up. Your wife did not seem very happy about his behavior, and I assumed that you are the sort of husband who would be interested in defending her honor," Edwina said.

Sidney was the kind of man who would not be able to resist flattery, especially where it concerned chivalrous behavior. She had often noticed him helping elderly women cross the street or brushing grit from the knees of small children who had taken a tumble outside his shop. Despite the fact that his business was one that dealt with the grizzlier side of food production, she knew him to be a man with a very tender heart.

"As much as I hate to say it, you're right about the argument with Hector," Sidney said.

"What exactly was he doing?" Edwina asked.

"He kept coming into the shop and bringing her gifts and cards," Sidney said.

Despite having heard from Beryl that Hector had offered Alma a ring, she felt a slight shock of indignation. To bring gifts to another man's wife, at her place of work, in front of the rest of the village, was outrageous. No wonder Sidney had been angry about the incident.

"What sorts of gifts?" Edwina asked.

"Flowers, baskets of fruit, even bits of jewelry," Sidney said. "Alma was beside herself about the whole thing."

"Well, of course she was. No decent woman wouldn't have been," Edwina said. "What did he hope to gain by that kind of behavior?"

"He seemed to think he could convince her to leave me," Sidney said.

Edwina thought she had never heard of something so ridiculous in all her life. Alma and Sidney Poole had been married for over twenty years. The notion of her running off with another man seemed entirely preposterous. But from the look on Sidney's face, he did not share her complete faith in his wife's ability to resist the clumsy wooing of another man.

"I shouldn't have thought you would have anything to worry about on that front," Edwina said soothingly.

"You'd think so, wouldn't you?" Sidney said, running a fleshy hand across his brow. He exhaled deeply, and Edwina found she felt quite sorry for him. "But you never know, do you? You know, I've been worried about something like this happening my entire marriage."

Edwina was even more shocked. The Pooles had always seemed

like a solid example of a successful and prosperous marriage. The idea that Sidney felt some trepidation as to its constancy provided Edwina with a remarkable insight into the lives of one of her fellow villagers.

"I certainly would not be one to tell you how to run a marriage. After all, it's not as though I'm an expert on such matters," Edwina said. "But I do know that Alma never has anything but supportive and fond things to say about you whenever I'm in the beauty shop."

"Things like this just make me crazy," Sidney said.

"What is it that you think could happen? Why are you so worried?" Edwina said.

"My Alma is so glamorous, I'm constantly afraid that she'll feel too good for me. After all, I'm no Douglas Fairbanks, am I?" Sidney gestured to his watermelon-sized stomach and gave Edwina a sad grin.

Edwina had never given much thought to whether or not Alma was glamorous. Although, by the standards of Walmsley Parva perhaps, it could be said that she was a well-turned-out woman. Until Beryl had arrived in the village, Edwina supposed an argument could be made that Alma was the most fashion-conscious, sophisticated, and glamorous-looking woman in the village. Her position as proprietress of the only beauty salon in town required she project a certain sort of image.

"I can see why you would be upset. Did something bring it all to a head that night at the pub?" Edwina asked.

"Alma told me that Hector asked her to run away with him. He said they could make a new life together somewhere far from here," Sidney said.

Edwina noticed a slight wobble in his lower lip. His tender-hearted nature extended to his marriage, from the looks of it. She felt an overwhelming urge to pat his hand but of course refrained from doing so. It was hardly the behavior of a savvy investigator to comfort those being interrogated.

"Hector had plans to up and leave Walmsley Parva?" Edwina asked.

"For all I know, it was just so much banter on his part. Alma told me that he made the same sorts of propositions to all sorts of women and that I shouldn't be so concerned that he had singled her out for any special attention," Sidney said.

"But this happened just before your argument at the pub?"

"It happened earlier that day. He stopped into her shop and made the suggestion in front of the shampoo girl, Hattie. Alma told him to get out and then came right over to let me know. I couldn't believe it when Hector had the gall to come in here and try to buy some sausages from me."

"You refused to sell him anything?" Edwina said.

"In fact, I did. I told him that from now on he needed to get his meat somewhere else, since this butcher shop was off limits to the likes of him," Sidney said, crossing his arms across his chest. "He didn't take my words too kindly."

"So you took up the argument again at the pub later that day?" Edwina said.

"Just the sight of him pushed me nearly over the edge, but when he started making comments about Alma's legs and comparing them to the leg of mutton he had purchased at the store a couple days earlier, I lost my temper," Sidney said.

"I should think you would have. Did anyone else in the pub hear his comments?" Edwina said.

Even if Sidney were not the one to have killed him, he would make a very fine suspect if anyone else knew the extent of Hector's effrontery towards Mrs. Poole.

"I was in a blind rage, so I haven't any idea who heard what. I know he leaned forward when he said it to me, so it's possible he was speaking in a low tone. Hector was someone who enjoyed being sly," Sidney said.

"I don't suppose you have an alibi for the time of his death, do you?" Edwina asked.

"I shouldn't think so. I took my time getting home after I left the pub. I wanted to cool down before I saw Alma. It always upsets her to see me so angry," Sidney said. "Not that I needed to worry about that."

"Why? Wasn't Alma home when you returned?" Edwina said.

"She didn't arrive for quite some time afterwards," Sidney said. "Does it matter?"

Edwina wasn't sure how much to tell him. Alma being away from home could be very significant to the investigation indeed. She seemed to remember quite distinctly that Alma had said she was at home with her husband at the approximate time of the murder. She was going to have to discuss the matter with Beryl. If neither of the Pooles could give an alibi for the other, either one of them made a very fine suspect.

Chapter 28

The Palais Cinema, owned and operated by one Clarence Mumford, sat in a position of prominence on the high street of Walmsley Parva. The afternoon matinee was scheduled to start momentarily, and Beryl spotted the ticket girl, Eva Scott, making change for a final patron. Her timing could not have been more perfect to stop by and ask the young woman a few questions.

Beryl pushed open the heavy glass door with its polished brass handle and allowed it to swish shut behind her. As she crossed the plush carpeting and delivered a beaming smile to Eva, she wondered what her life would have been like if she had accepted the repeated invitations by a well-known film director to star in one of his many productions.

She had toyed with the idea from time to time and had even gone so far as to visit one of his sets in order to be better informed about the ins and outs of the industry. While she did not feel proud of those things that were not of her doing, but rather were gifts of nature, she realized that she had a highly photogenic face. Whenever she appeared on newsreels or in newspaper articles or magazines, she was well aware that she looked every bit a starlet.

But the film director, handsome though he was, had set her internal alarm ringing. She had made one or two foolish decisions with men in her earlier years and through hard-won experience had learned not to repeat them. After all, what fun were mistakes if you kept making the same ones? She vastly preferred all new mistakes. She was all the more certain she had made the right decision when, after turning him down for a fifth time, a scandal broke involving him and a cruel assault on a very young girl.

Beryl was all for people having the sort of fun they chose behind closed doors. But she only approved if all parties involved were consenting wholeheartedly. Still, she couldn't help wonder about the path not taken whenever she looked up at the large posters with their leading ladies splashed across them, doe eyes and red lips staring down at her, as if to say she could have been amongst their ranks.

All in all, she thought, she was far better off living the sort of footloose life she had embarked upon. Even if that life had surprisingly taken her wandering feet to a tied-down place like Walmsley Parva. Beryl was a great believer in the unimaginable occurring. Just because the average starlet was barely out of her teens did not mean that she and Edwina would never make a splash on the screen.

For all she knew, someone would wish to commit their exploits to film one day, and perhaps the pair of them would play themselves on the silver screen. With that happy notion in mind, she threw back her shoulders and crossed the now empty lobby to where Eva Scott leaned against her fist across the glass-topped counter.

"Quite a crowd today, Eva," Beryl said.

Eva straightened up and smiled back at her. The two of them

had gotten to know each other when Beryl had first come to Walmsley Parva. Eva had an acquaintance with some of the people involved in the very first case she and Edwina had solved. They had been fast friends ever since. Beryl saw a bit of herself in the younger woman, who seemed to chafe at the strictures small village life constantly sought to impose upon her. Beryl thought it her civic duty as a woman of the world to give encouragement to those whose wings looked likely to be clipped.

"Are you here to see the show, Miss Helliwell?" Eva asked, stepping closer to the till. "If so, you'd best hurry. That music says the show is about to start." Eva cocked her head and tipped her ear towards the hallway leading to the theater.

"Actually, I'm here to see you. I don't suppose you were working on Saturday, were you?"

"I was. You know I work most Saturdays. It's one of the most popular days of the week at the cinema, and Mr. Mumford hates for me to have that day off," Eva said, looking over her shoulder towards a wooden door at the far side of the room.

Mr. Mumford's office was situated directly behind it, and Beryl was willing to bet that the owner of the cinema was unlikely to be in there alone if he could help it. Beryl thought no more of Mr. Mumford than she had of the propositioning film director.

"You didn't happen to see Sidney Poole going past that evening while you were here at the counter, did you?" Beryl asked, turning slightly to face the plate-glass windows overlooking the street.

Eva had an advantageous position for watching all the goings-on once the tickets had been sold and the films were under way. Occasionally, a straggler would enter the cinema or a patron would come out to purchase cigarettes or some sort of refreshment, but in general, Eve's responsibilities were confined to ticket sales just before the show commenced. In fact, it was common to see Eva sitting on a little stool behind the counter, trying to hide a book from view.

"I did see Mr. Poole. He came along right after Hector Lomax," Eva said.

"Did you see the two of them interacting?" Beryl asked.

"As a matter fact, I did. Even from a bit of a distance, it was clear that they were having an argument," Eva said.

"Did it get physical?" Beryl said.

"Mr. Poole might have jabbed Hector in the chest a few times," Eva said. "Both men looked very angry."

"Did Hector shove Mr. Poole back?" Beryl asked.

"I don't think so. But he looked as though he was laughing. It looked as though Mr. Poole was the only one who was actually angry," Eva said. "Why do you ask?"

"It's connected to a case Miss Davenport and I have been hired to investigate," Beryl said.

"Aren't you working for Jack Prentice, trying to get his father off the hook?"

"We are looking at a number of other suspects in Hector's murder besides just Frank Prentice," Beryl said.

"I wouldn't want to get Mr. Poole into any trouble," Eva said.

"Surely you must have already told the police what you saw that evening," Beryl said.

"No, Constable Gibbs never asked me about it," Eva said. "Do you think Mr. Poole is involved?"

"I wouldn't like to say that, but I think that the argument he had might give us a better idea of what happened to Hector that night," Beryl said.

"Mr. Poole is one of my father's good friends," Eva said. "I wouldn't like to get him into any trouble."

"If Mr. Poole has done nothing wrong, he has nothing to fear," Beryl said. "It's your duty to tell the truth."

"I guess you're right. Besides, it's not as though the police don't already have the murderer in custody," Eva said.

"They definitely do have someone in custody. So I'm sure you won't mind telling me if anything else happened between Hector and Mr. Poole that you could see," Beryl said.

"There really wasn't very much more to it than that. Hector laughed, Mr. Poole shoved him, and then they both went out of sight before anything else happened," Eva said.

Beryl looked out the window once more. From her vantage point near the ticket counter, she saw there were a few places the two men could have gone where Eva would no longer be able to see them.

"Did you see which direction they went? Did they go off in the same one?" Beryl asked.

"They did. Hector seemed to walk away from the situation, and Mr. Poole followed him, still waving his arms and shouting," Eva said.

"Could you hear what he was shouting?" Beryl asked.

"I couldn't. The glass is quite thick, and the music from the film was very loud, even all the way out here. I suppose I assumed he was shouting because of the way he was waving his arms about."

"Did you see where they went exactly?" Beryl asked.

Eva stepped out from behind the counter and walked towards the glass. Beryl followed her and watched where the girl pointed her finger.

"Hector turned right down Little Hempfield Lane. Mr. Poole went right along after him, and then the two of them were out of sight," Eva said.

"Little Hempfield Lane leads to the church, does it not?" Beryl asked.

"On the south side, yes," Eva said. "There is a gate leading from the lane directly into the churchyard. You cross it and enter the church from there."

Just then a young man emerged from the theater and made his way to the ticket counter. Eva smiled her apologies at Beryl and went back to her job. Beryl gave her a slight wave and then pushed open the heavy door once more.

She stood on the pavement outside the cinema and looked off in the direction of Little Hempfield Lane. Unless she missed her guess, that was exactly the side of the churchyard on which the vicar had noticed the headstone with the pipe ash littering its surface. Her thoughts were brought back to her surroundings when she heard her name being called. Edwina was determinedly making her way along the street, doing her best to capture Beryl's attention without making too much of a scene.

"You look like the cat that swallowed the canary," Beryl said.

Edwina's face was flushed, and she was struggling to breathe normally. She must have hurried from the butcher's at an unseemly pace. It was as much of a public display of excitement as Edwina was ever likely to make. Beryl felt the pleasurable tingle of an investigation making progress as she looked at her friend's sparkling eyes. She tucked her hand in through Edwina's arm and pulled her sedately along the sidewalk.

"Sidney just admitted that his wife was not at home when he returned from the pub the night of the murder," Edwina said in a voice barely above a whisper.

Her eyes darted back and forth, up and down the street, as though she was absolutely intent on not being overheard. Beryl could hardly fault her for that. Gossip moved through Walmsley Parva at much the same speed the influenza epidemic had and sometimes with similarly devastating consequences.

"She wasn't at home when he arrived?" Beryl said. "So that means he doesn't have an alibi for the approximate time of the murder."

Edwina nodded her head in a most unladylike way. "But it

also means that Alma does not have an alibi either. And she's the one who lied about it. What do you think it means?"

"It could be nothing except that she confused one day with another," Beryl said.

"You don't believe that, do you?" Edwina said as a flicker of disappointment moved over her delicate features.

"A good investigator must examine all possibilities, including those that are disappointing or unpleasant. People do forget things and misremember dates."

"I doubt very much that anyone would forget where they were when a fellow village resident was murdered," Edwina said. "While I understand that your life may have been filled with people dropping like flies here, there, and everywhere, it's not the sort of thing we are used to here in Walmsley Parva."

"Don't get yourself all dithered up. I was merely pointing out that it was a possibility. It's far more likely that she meant to be deceptive. The question is, Why?" Beryl said.

"She as much as admitted that Hector was costing her business and creating trouble in her marriage," Edwina said.

"Those certainly would be compelling reasons for me to do away with unwanted attention from a suitor," Beryl said.

"But were they enough to cause her to murder him?" Edwina asked.

"I think that depends entirely on Alma's temperament," Beryl said. "You know her far better than I do. Do you think she would be likely to take such matters into her own hands? Or would she have implored her husband to act on her behalf?"

"I would say that Alma was capable of doing either one. She's a woman who knows her own mind and is willing to take action to get what she wants. Not everyone would have the ambition to start up a business like she has. I can't imagine her wanting it to go to pieces for someone like Hector Lomax."

"Do you think that her business was really in danger from Hector?" Beryl said.

"Yes, I think it really was. For two reasons," Edwina said. She held up her fingers one at a time. "Firstly, the ladies of Walmsley Parva would not have appreciated the presence of a man during their appointments. Since he had become quite dependably likely to be present, it would give them pause when it came time to book another appointment."

"What was the second thing?" Beryl asked.

"People would be inclined to say that there was no smoke without fire. They would have started to mention that Hector would not have continued to pursue Alma if she had not given him some sort of encouragement. Even though it was widely recognized that Hector was a cad and a pest, Alma, as a woman, would be expected to take the higher road," Edwina said. "She would be the one to bear the responsibility for making it absolutely clear that she had no interest in him. People would say that if he continued to pursue her, it was because she had not done an adequate job in rebuffing him."

"That doesn't seem fair," Beryl said. "It isn't as though she asked him to start harassing her at her place of business."

"It's not a question of whether or not it was fair. It's a question of whether or not it would be a reason for her to kill him. It wasn't just that he was costing her money. He was costing her, her reputation," Edwina said. "When there isn't a lot of news, people feast upon mere morsels and are able to make quite a meal of them."

"There's another possibility, though, isn't there?" Beryl said.

"You think that she had made up the idea of being at home with Sidney in order to give him an alibi?" Edwina said.

"It's just as good a theory as her killing Hector, isn't it?" Beryl asked.

"Of course it is. Alma's reputation is no better off if her husband turns out to be a murderer," Edwina said. "She would be ruined."

"She also may love him and wished to protect him," Beryl said.

"Yes, of course that could be part of it too," Edwina said.

From the look on Edwina's face, Beryl thought her friend found it unlikely she could consider Sidney Poole a desirable mate. Beryl had to agree with her. None of her ex-husbands had resembled Sidney in even the most cursory of ways. Still, she could see how he might be of value to Alma.

"I was just speaking with Eva Scott, and she said that she saw Sidney and Hector arguing just outside the Palais after they left the pub the night of the murder," Beryl said.

Edwina pulled her notebook from her pocket and began to scribble down a few notes. Beryl took it as a good sign that the case was making enough headway that Edwina was worried she might forget small details.

"Was she able to hear what they were arguing about?" Edwina said.

"No, she was not. But she did say that they turned off along Little Hempfield Lane," Beryl said, raising an eyebrow significantly.

"So Sidney may well have followed Hector to the churchyard. That makes a decent case for Alma to be the one giving Sidney an alibi, doesn't it?" Edwina said.

"One of us is going to have to go back and question Alma again about her alibi," Beryl said. "I think you should be the one to do it."

"Why me?" Edwina said.

"You have a longer acquaintance with Alma, and you aren't an outsider like me. I think she will feel that you are more likely to understand her reasons for stretching the truth," Beryl said. "Besides, you have such a tactful way of dealing with such things, and there's no one whose ability to separate the truth from fiction I would trust more than yours."

Edwina's eyes widened. "I think you're just saying that to convince me to be the one to do an unpleasant task." Edwina slipped her notebook back into her pocket and scowled.

While it was true that Beryl was not above a well-placed bit of flattery in order to convince others to do her bidding, Edwina's ability to ascertain the truth was one of the things Beryl most admired about her. She had an uncanny knack for putting her finger on untruths, and even why those untruths were offered in the first place. If anyone could get Alma to open up about her misstatement, it was Edwina.

Chapter 29

Edwina reluctantly agreed to speak with Alma again about her alibi statement. She would likely have protested and would have tried to think of some excuse to fob off the task, but as fate would have it, Alma exited the nearby fish-and-chip shop just as Edwina was about to volley her first excuse. Beryl patted her on the arm and delivered one of her knowing winks.

"Strike while the iron is hot, my dear Ed," Beryl said. "I shall head back to the Beeches and eagerly await your news." She spun Edwina around and gave her the slightest of pushes in the direction of the chippy. Edwina squared her shoulders, adjusted her hat, and reminded herself that she was on the job.

She slowed her pace but kept Alma in sight. She wished to speak with the other woman out of the way of prying ears. Alma might be able to forgive her for asking impertinent questions in private. She would be unlikely to do so should Edwina embarrass her in front of others. Alma crossed the street and struck off in the direction of the village green. Edwina followed at a leisurely pace, keeping her quarry well within sight. She was pleased to see Alma head for a bench near the duck pond.

When it became clear that Alma intended to sit in the sunshine to enjoy her lunch, Edwina quickened her pace and joined her on the bench.

"Care for a chip?" Alma said, extending a cone of newspaper tantalizingly filled with perfectly browned bits of potato.

She had breakfasted several hours earlier, and Edwina felt her stomach rumbling at the sight of one of the world's best culinary inventions. Her conscience suggested she decline, as it might be a conflict of interest to accept gifts from a suspect. Her taste buds and her stomach clamored for her to be reasonable. Edwina reminded herself that she was the moral rudder in her partnership with Beryl, and politely declined.

"Suit yourself," Alma said. "Perhaps I shouldn't admit it, but I sneak off and buy a nice bit of fish from time to time. The butcher's wife is expected to happily consume all manner of sausages and chops, but the truth is, I don't think you can beat fish and chips when they are properly done."

"I'm sure that Mr. Poole wouldn't begrudge you a bit of culinary diversity from time to time," Edwina said, regretting her refusal as she watched Alma break off a piece of golden-brown batter-encrusted fish.

A flock of ducks waddled towards them, and Edwina wondered how soon it would be before they would encircle the bench in search of a portion of Alma's lunch. Edwina was quite fond of ducks, birds of all sort, for that matter, and she wished she had brought the bag of stale bread that she kept on hand to feed them.

It was little things like that that made her remember the war years with sharp pangs. While she had never felt hungry throughout those terrible times, she had felt a chafing at the restrictions rationing had brought towards the end of the war. It was a small thing, really, but Edwina had long since discovered that the small things were often the most important ones.

The pressure of the group to conform to expected behavior

was always intense in a small village like Walmsley Parva. But during the war, the village had thrown itself fully behind the war effort and all that entailed. The residents of Walmsley Parva, at least publicly, had fully embraced the idea of food conservation and rationing. The notion of wasting good bread on wild ducks was not to be entertained. Edwina felt that the friendly flock that inhabited the village green in her own corner of the empire had suffered along with the rest of them. She was inordinately relieved when Alma broke off a piece of potato and tossed it towards the gobbling flock.

"Sidney doesn't know about it," Alma said, tossing another piece of chip into the fray. "My husband doesn't hold with fish." She gave Edwina a look that said such a thing was not to be comprehended.

"It must be very difficult in a marriage to know what to keep to oneself and what to put out for discussion," Edwina said.

"It can be a bit of a trick, that's for sure," Alma said. "Although the truth of the matter is, the vast majority of husbands spend so very little time listening that it doesn't much matter. Although, I daresay, if I came home with this to serve for tea, he would notice right sharp like."

"It seems to me that some men are far more attentive than others," Edwina said. "Hector Lomax, for instance, was far more attentive than one would perhaps appreciate." Edwina held her breath and kept her eyes fixed firmly on the ducks as she waited for Alma to reply. In her experience, people often opened up of their own accord if one did not insist on glaring at them.

"You and Miss Helliwell seem to have a whole hive of bees in your bonnets about my connection with Hector Lomax. Is there something you want to come right out and ask me?" Alma said, turning on the bench to face Edwina full on.

"As you likely already know, Jack Prentice has hired us to see if it's possible that anyone other than his father could have murdered Hector. I would not be doing my job if I did not make enquiries of all those who have had reason to dislike him of late," Edwina said.

Alma looked at her for a moment, studying her face the same way she did when she was considering how best to implement a new hairstyle. Finally, she let out a deep exhalation and seemed to have come to a conclusion.

"At least you're not just trying to dig into my personal life for your own gossiping pleasure," Alma said. "Every morning I see Jack out on the corner, selling newspapers on account of his no-good father. What is it that you want to know?"

"I want to know where you really were at the time of Hector's murder. Your husband told Beryl that you were not at home when he arrived after leaving the pub. Which means neither of you has an alibi," Edwina said.

"I was still at the salon. In my business one has to take care of ones looks, and I needed to color my hair," Alma said.

"Why wouldn't you just have said that in the first place?" Edwina said.

"Because I'm vain about it, that's why," Alma said. "I shouldn't like anyone to know exactly how old I've gotten to be, and coloring one's hair is practically as good as admitting that one is getting long in the tooth."

Edwina wondered about the truth of that statement. And she wondered about Alma's ability to see herself with any degree of clarity. It was obvious to Edwina, a woman who admittedly did not spend much time fussing about with cosmetics and beautifications beyond the use of wide-brimmed hats and toilet water, that Alma colored her hair. In all Edwina's days, she had never seen someone with the naturally occurring hue that covered Alma's head. She did not expect anyone else in the village had been more easily fooled than had she.

She also entertained the idea that Beryl had not been made aware that coloring one's hair was as good as admitting to aging.

Beryl's own shade of platinum blond, Edwina was sure, had far more to do with the marvels of modern chemistry than it did with any benevolence on the part of Mother Nature. Beryl's hair color hadn't changed much since the two of them had become friends at Miss DuPont's finishing school so many years before.

She felt disinclined to believe Alma's latest version of her whereabouts at the time of Hector's murder. In fact, she felt rather insulted that Alma would wish her to believe her excuse. While she might be convinced that Alma was at her place of business, she remained skeptical as to her reason for keeping it a secret.

"I don't suppose anyone can confirm that you were there at the time? If you wanted to keep it a secret, I'm sure you were not eager to let anyone know your whereabouts," Edwina said.

"As a matter of fact, Geraldine Howarth spotted me just as I was heading in. I'm sure she could confirm my story, if you aren't willing to take my word for it," Alma said, tossing a final piece of chip at the ducks before folding the newspaper into neat squares.

"I'm not trying to offend you, but I would point out that you have already changed your story. And, after all, a man has been murdered," Edwina said.

Alma got to her feet and collected her handbag. She shrugged her shoulders. "Everyone has their little secrets, Edwina. Even you. As far as this matter goes, ask Geraldine if she saw me that night at the salon. I didn't kill Hector, but I can tell you one thing that won't change," she said.

"What's that?" Edwina said.

"Whoever did it did the whole village a favor," Alma said.

Chapter 30

Beryl had sent Simpkins out to the garden shed for a bit of pottering about before Edwina was expected to return. In her estimation, Simpkins was far more likely to be watering himself from a flask than he was the perennial seedlings he had started that spring with an eye to planting them out in the open garden later in the season.

In front of her, on the morning room desk, sat the infernal typewriting machine. She had wanted to practice her typing skills without being overheard by Simpkins or anyone else. She had gone so far as to close all the windows in order to block the noise of her laborious plunking on the instrument.

After a valiant half hour's struggle, she had leaned back in the chair and wondered if her writing career would be over before it had begun. She pulled a notebook from a drawer and uncapped her fountain pen. Edwina made it look so easy to take notes about the case, and Beryl thought perhaps she ought to try her hand by that means rather than slowing herself with the typewriter.

But try as she might, no thoughts would come out. When

Beryl looked down at the notebook, she realized she had simply created a series of swirls and doodles. Obviously, the sooner she conquered the typewriting machine, the better.

Beryl had realized early on that one of the secrets of her success was to play to her strengths and utterly avoid her weaknesses. Some people felt it was virtuous to try to improve on their areas of weakness, but Beryl was not amongst them. She had never felt that she could improve upon a shortcoming enough to pull it up to scratch.

By playing to her strengths, she found life to be easier and more fun. And, she felt the strategy had proven to be successful. She had never even felt inclined to turn her hand to those things for which she was not well suited. That was until she got the notion to create an adventure guide.

It was an extraordinary feeling to realize she wished to do something, and to do it well, which did not come easily to her. Beryl had never thought anything of hopping into a fast-moving vehicle, jumping on an already moving train, or cutting the sandbags from a barely tethered hot-air balloon and drifting off to God knows where with barely enough provisions and the minimum of gear.

She had entered romantic relationships, confronted criminals, and consorted with royalty with ease and panache. She had long ago realized that keeping house, staying put, or heading volunteer organizations would never be her purview. So she avoided such things entirely and admired those who did not seem to mind them.

It was a curious sensation to realize she might have met her match in a Remington portable typewriter. Or that she might have found a way in which she was not the most entertaining storyteller in the room. Could it be that Edwina had been wise to suggest that she spend a little more time reading books before she thought she could write one?

It was with some relief that she heard Edwina coming along

the hallway and calling her name. Beryl replaced the notebook in the drawer and capped her fountain pen. She quickly pulled the disastrously error-ridden sheet of typewriting paper from the machine and crumpled it into the wastepaper basket. Just as Edwina was entering the room, she cranked a new sheet along the roller bar and attempted to look busy.

"I hope I'm not interrupting the artist at work," Edwina said.

Beryl thought she caught a touch of irony in Edwina's voice. She had the uncomfortable feeling that Edwina did not have full confidence in her proposed venture. The sooner she could meet with Geraldine Howarth for her typewriting lessons, the better.

"I was just finishing up a bit of work and would be happy for the break," Beryl said. "How was your chat with Mrs. Poole?" Beryl pushed away from the desk and crossed the room to join Edwina in the seating area positioned before a long stretch of windows. It overlooked the garden and a charming view of Edwina's cherished koi pond.

"Alma says that she was at her salon instead of at home," Edwina said.

"Why wouldn't she just say that in the first place?" Beryl asked.

"She says she didn't want anyone to know that she was coloring her hair," Edwina said.

"That sounds rather a flimsy excuse. Can anyone confirm her story?"

"She says that as she was entering the shop, she was stopped by Geraldine," Edwina said. "I didn't take the time to track down Geraldine to ask for her side of the story."

"I shall make a point to do it myself," Beryl said.

She took that as a sign that everything would be moving along nicely on her project. Beryl believed in signs. Many was the time she owed her life to following her instincts and to reading and interpreting what was happening around her. The fact that Edwina pointed her in the direction of Geraldine just as she had been thinking of her was all the confirmation Beryl needed that her project would be a success.

"Where is Simpkins?" Edwina asked.

"He's out in the garden, doing some work. I thought a spot of fresh air would be good for him," Beryl said, thinking of Simpkins huddled up in the shed, slipping nips from his flask, and reclining in a rickety basket chair tucked into a corner, with his feet propped up on an overturned milk crate.

"I'm glad to hear it. I think having as much of the normal routine as possible might be good for him at this point," Edwina said.

"I'm not sure how much of a normal life Simpkins can expect going forward with his inheritance," Beryl said.

"That's exactly why I think he needs the structure of his regular routine," Edwina said. "I'm not sure how much change he can take all at once, given his age."

"He's going to need some help no matter what, isn't he?" Beryl said.

"Exactly. That's why I was so relieved when he agreed to engage Charles as his solicitor," Edwina said.

"I was thinking about navigating the shark-infested waters of the Kimberly Company principals," Beryl said. "He's in a great deal over his head with that lot."

A dark shadow crossed Edwina's face. Beryl thought once again how complicated her friend's relationship with Simpkins must be. She herself had no great attachment to her own home or even her elderly parents. Although, if she were faced with the loss of her parents, as Edwina had been with her own, she might feel differently.

"I've been giving some thought as to how to deal with them. I think it would be best to keep them as far from Simpkins as is possible," Edwina said.

"That might be a way of protecting him," Beryl said.

"But you don't seem to think it's the best way, do you?" Edwina said.

"I think this might be a matter of keeping one's enemies closer than one's friends," Beryl said. "How would you feel about inviting them around for an evening of bridge?"

"I sent Mr. Armitage, the chair of the board of directors, away with rather a large flea in his ear the day we met," Edwina said. "I'm not quite sure how to turn around and invite him to my home for a few friendly rubbers."

"I'm sure you'll think of something. You always are good for pouring oil on the troubled waters," Beryl said.

"I suppose I could apologize and blame it on some sort of female hysteria because of the murder in the village," Edwina said.

"Well, I do hate to play into stereotypes about women, especially those that would weaken our position in business, but that would likely be an expeditious way to sweep the whole thing under the carpet," Beryl said.

"I'm sure Mr. Armitage is no more broad-minded than the average man of his class and age," Edwina said. "When do you propose that I should invite them?"

"I would say in this matter there is absolutely no time to waste. Why not send them an invitation for this evening?" Beryl asked.

"I'm rather afraid I will have missed the post," Edwina said.

Beryl knew that this was Edwina's excuse for not wanting to spend the rest of the afternoon tidying the house and preparing the lavish array of snacks she would undoubtedly feel required to concoct even for a simple evening of bridge. As sorry as she felt for her friend's level of self-imposed hospitality, she could not allow her to wriggle out of her responsibilities on the investigatory front.

"I'll tell you what I'll do," Beryl said. "You pen a note, and I will hand deliver it as soon as it's dry. I would like to go into the village to confirm Geraldine's account of Alma's alibi as it is. I can stop in at the pub and deliver the card. I'll even await their reply, so you'll know whether or not to expect them as soon as possible."

"I was afraid you'd say something like that," Edwina said as her attention was drawn to the door of the potting shed creaking open.

Simpkins staggered out, clutching at the doorjamb as he carefully attempted to place one foot in front of the other in an effort to exit the small building.

"As you can see for yourself, Simpkins needs all the help that we can give him," Beryl said, leaning her head towards the unsteady journey the elderly man was taking towards the koi pond. "I'll see to Simpkins while you see to the note."

Chapter 31

With a creamy envelope addressed in Edwina's firm, neat hand, Beryl hopped once more into her automobile and set off in the direction of the village. With the cost of petrol, she really ought to undertake such jobs on foot, she told herself. But her mission required haste, and she could not see breaking into a trot.

Even when at the peek of physical prowess, running had never been one of her passions, at least not if she was not being chased by a large predator or an unwelcome suitor. As neither was the case, she delighted in putting her cherry-red machine through its paces.

In record time, she pulled up next to the curb in front of the pub and then walked back in the direction of the telephone office. She peered through the side window. Edwina would have been too short to look in. The window sat at a height that would have disallowed many of Walmsley Parva's citizenry from peering through it.

Geraldine sat with her back to the window. Beryl didn't know much about the running of a telephone office, but she was familiar with the idea of listening in, having had her fair share of briefings on surveillance during the war years. She was absolutely certain from the tilt of Geraldine's head that she was overhearing a juicy bit of gossip. Beryl wondered if Geraldine was in the habit of doing such things often. She could not see why the girl would be inclined to listen in on one conversation but not another.

Beryl made a mental note not to say anything over the telephone line that she would not wish to have repeated. She was all the more pleased to think that she had encouraged Edwina to write out an invitation rather than to choose to telephone down to the pub and request to speak with one of the Kimberly company party.

Beryl gave a fleeting thought to hiring someone else to tutor her on the typewriter. If there was one thing she could not abide, it was a gossip. She certainly had no interest in lining the pockets of one. Still, she knew of no one else in Walmsley Parva whom she could ask for lessons, and it would hardly advance their cause of solving Hector's murder if she alienated someone she needed to question.

Geraldine pulled the headphones from her head with a guilty look on her plain face as Beryl stepped through the door.

"Miss Helliwell, I thought our appointment was for tomorrow," Geraldine said. "Have I misremembered the time?"

"No, nothing like that. I just had a question I wanted to ask you," Beryl said. "Do you have a moment right now?"

Geraldine looked back at the switchboard, and Beryl thought she noted a glance of regret.

"So long as it doesn't interfere with my duties, I'm free to speak with you," Geraldine said. "What is it that you wanted to ask me?"

"I wondered if you happened to speak with anyone after your shift on Saturday, in the early evening?"

Geraldine's posture stiffened, and her expression became guarded. "On the telephone, you mean?" She spun her wooden stool away from the switchboard and crossed her arms over her chest. Once again, Beryl wondered what sort of conversation the young woman had been listening in upon just as she arrived.

"No. I meant after you left the telephone office that evening. Someone you would have met in person," Beryl said. She did not want to influence Geraldine's response in any way. If Alma had invented an encounter with Geraldine, it would not further the investigation to put ideas in her alibi's head.

"I headed straight home after I left work," Geraldine said.

Beryl felt the buzz of excitement that accompanied progress or at least a new avenue of exploration in a case.

"But now that I come to think of it, I stopped in at Alma's to ask if she had any appointments available this week. My mother telephoned just before the end of my shift to ask me to put in a call to Alma at home, since it was after hours at the shop. There was no answer at her number, but I happened to see her entering her shop just as I was leaving, so I popped by to ask about the appointment in person."

Beryl wasn't convinced that Geraldine was telling the truth. She did not have the same ability to sniff out untruths as Edwina did, but she was rather well versed in nonverbal communication. It came in handy in parts of the world where one did not speak the language. And when playing cards. Her almost legendary ability to know when to go all in and when to play conservatively was based entirely on her knack for reading body language. If she were betting on Geraldine's truthfulness, she would assuredly not bet everything.

Still, she couldn't prove that the telephone operator was lying. She could only suspect that either she was holding something back or she was shading the truth. Either way, the interview left her with more questions than answers. Perhaps Geraldine would slip up and reveal something more useful during their typing lesson in the morning.

"I appreciate your help in my investigation. I trust you are still available tomorrow for the typing lesson?" Beryl said with far more enthusiasm than she actually felt. There was something subtly repellent about the girl, and the more time Beryl spent with her, the more she regretted hiring her.

"I wouldn't miss it for the world," Geraldine said.

The switchboard lit up once more, and with a sense of relief, Beryl excused herself and withdrew to the street. She checked the pocket of her long silk duster for the invitation from Edwina and headed off to the pub with much on her mind.

The Dove and Duck was empty save for a rosy-cheeked barmaid named Annie, who stood behind the bar, polishing glasses with a white cloth. When Beryl asked after the visiting Londoners, Annie rolled her eyes and informed Beryl that both Mrs. Kimberly and her nephew had retired to their rooms after complaining loudly about the items on offer for lunch. Beryl slid a sixpence across the bar, along with Edwina's invitation, and asked if the girl would deliver the message to whichever one of the party she found least offensive.

"If you don't mind, I will pour myself a drink while I await a reply," Beryl said.

Annie gestured towards the taps, pocketed the money, and headed for the stairs to the rooms on the second floor. Beryl scooted around behind the counter and expertly filled a still water-spotted glass to the top with her favourite local cider. While she had no taste at all for beer, she did enjoy hard cider. It was a specialty of the region, and she believed firmly in supporting the local economy. When the barmaid returned a moment later, she shook her head when Beryl asked to have it added to her tab.

"Let's put it on the slate for his nibs," she said under her breath. The girl inclined her head towards the staircase. Beryl could only imagine how rudely the Kimberly party must have behaved to provoke such a response from Annie, who was usually a straight arrow and a bastion of good humor. It must have been something especially egregious, as the young woman picked up her tray of glasses and carried them to the back room as soon as a member of the party appeared at the foot of the staircase.

"Hello again," said the man Beryl had found admiring her car the day before as he approached the bar and perched on the stool beside her. "I am delighted to accept your friend's invitation for bridge on behalf of my companions and myself."

"Are you connected to the Kimberly party?" Beryl said.

"Indeed I am. Colonel Kimberly was my mother's uncle," Rupert Fanhurst said. "Which makes Florrie my step-great-aunt, I suppose. Will my presence disarrange your plans for the table?"

"Think nothing of it. You are all very welcome this evening," Beryl said.

She was an avid bridge player, as was Edwina, and Mr. Fanhurst's attendance would upset the numbers. Beryl's initial reaction was to consider who else could be invited to make up the numbers for a second table. Charles Jarvis could always be counted on for a rubber.

Beryl had no idea whether or not Simpkins knew how to play. She rather thought it unlikely. Even if he had a firm grasp of the rules, he was liable to be too well lubricated to focus on the game by evening.

Beryl discounted the idea of inviting the vicar or his wife on the grounds that they would put an even greater crimp in the gambling than Edwina was inclined to do. She briefly considered her other acquaintances from Walmsley Parva before deciding that it was best not to expand the guest list. Edwina would be rattled enough to discover there would be one extra member of the party. Adding any more would surely distress her.

Besides, she thought upon further consideration, if she or Edwina sat the games out, they would be in an ideal position to observe the play. In Beryl's opinion, nothing revealed character so quickly as a crash landing from an airplane or a heated game of bridge. Perhaps Rupert Fanhurst's unexpected appearance would be the best thing that had happened to the investigation thus far.

"Until this evening, then," Mr. Fanhurst said, sliding off the stool and reaching for Beryl's hand. He bent forward and raised it to his lips.

As she watched his retreating back, Beryl wondered if his courtly manners were intended to get into her good graces on account of her celebrity or because of her connection to Simpkins.

Chapter 32

Crumpet barked from somewhere along the front hallway, and Edwina cast a glance around the parlour for a final time. Simpkins had helped her to place a card table in the center of the room before announcing he had no intention of socializing with the Londoners and leaving the house for the pub.

A pad of paper and a pen to keep score as well as a pack of cards lay on the table's smooth surface. She ran the list of refreshments she had prepared through her mind as she nervously plumped a pillow on the sofa.

She most assuredly had not liked Mrs. Kimberly or Mr. Armitage when she had made their acquaintance earlier. She could not imagine either of them would have improved since last they met. Edwina had been thrown off kilter by the news that an additional member of their party would be joining them.

It made things rather more difficult for someone to need to sit out the game. She had managed to convince herself that the evening would not be intolerable if she had the chance to enjoy the game. But now it seemed that someone would have to offer to sit out. Edwina had insisted that she would observe the others from her favourite spot on the sofa.

Beryl had offered to be the one to sit idly by, but Edwina had reminded her that as the superior cardplayer, she would be better at creating the sort of strain during a game that so often revealed character. No, Edwina had said, it would be far better for her to sit on the sidelines with her knitting and to observe all the goings-on. She would use the opportunity as the hostess to chat with whoever was serving as the dummy in any given game. Beryl had reluctantly agreed, and the whole matter had been settled before the doorbell sent Crumpet into a frenzy.

The Kimberly company party swept into the room with wide smiles. Edwina could not get over the sense that Mrs. Kimberly was nothing more than a dance-hall girl who had made a fortunate match. Edwina could make out the faintest hint of a lower-class accent, despite the younger woman's designer gown and luxurious fur wrap. Her clothing was another giveaway as to her origins. A well-bred lady would not have made the mistake of being so overdressed for an evening of bridge in the country.

Mr. Armitage, Edwina thought, was exactly what he purported to be. As a well-heeled solicitor and man of the city, he wore clothing that was understated, and his manners were solicitous but reserved. She was quite certain from their previous encounter that his purpose in attending that evening was not simply to enjoy a game of bridge. He had the best interests of his board of directors in mind and was likely looking for a way to pressure Simpkins to heed his advice in all matters pertaining to the company.

Mr. Fanhurst was effusive in his appreciation of the invitation. He made it sound as though he had been in actual danger of dying from boredom, should he have found himself left to his own devices for another evening at the village pub. He presented Edwina with a box of chocolates and said that he had enquired of the shopkeeper as to her preferred confections.

Edwina lifted the paper lid from the box and noted without

surprise that Prudence Rathbone had recommended sugared al-
monds and Turkish Delight, her two least favourite sweets to
be found anywhere in Great Britain. Prudence had still not
quite recovered her good humor over the difference of opinion
she and Edwina had had concerning the inclusion of members
of a nearby mining community in Walmsley Parva's May Day
celebration the month before. Edwina thanked the young man
for his gift and placed the opened box on the table, along with
the variety of finger sandwiches and fairy cakes she had prepared for the evening's refreshments.

Beryl brought up the rear as the party entered the room, and
made her way directly to the drinks table, where she set about
filling a cocktail shaker with chips of ice and splashes of spirits.
Over the sound of her vigorous rattling, she enquired after
their plans.

"I'm so glad you were able to join us this evening, as I'm sure
you will all have business back in London soon, won't you?"
Beryl asked. "You must be eager to figure out how best to run
the business with a new man in charge of it all."

"I'm sure that it will be worth it to stay in the village for a
few more days," Mr. Armitage said. "After all, I think it's safe
to say we are all still trying to figure out how best to proceed."

"Do your business interests take you away from London
often?" Edwina said, retrieving her latest knitting project from
the basket beside the sofa.

"I'm happy to say that Colonel Kimberly's company enjoys
widespread renown and is stocked all across the empire. I have
seen a great deal of the countryside during my tenure as chairman of the board of directors."

"We're not going to spend the whole evening talking business, are we?" Mrs. Kimberly asked, glancing over at the card
table.

"Certainly not," Beryl said. "If you all will take your seats
around the table, I'll finish making the drinks and then join you."

"Do you not intend to play, Miss Davenport?" Mr. Armitage said.

"Beryl is the real bridge enthusiast of the two of us. I'm perfectly content to simply observe. Besides, I'd like to get this jumper finished before the child I'm making it for has outgrown it," Edwina said, lifting the tiny sweater for all to see. Mrs. Kimberly's eyes lingered on the small blue object in Edwina's hands.

"What shall we do for partners?" Beryl asked as she expertly poured the cocktails from the shaker into five awaiting glasses.

"I propose that Mr. Fanhurst and Mrs. Kimberly play against the two of us, Miss Helliwell," Mr. Armitage said. "They have played together often and are a formidable pair. I think they might even be able to give you a run for your money."

Beryl squirted some soda water from the siphon into each of the partially filled glasses, then handed the drinks around to their guests. As she passed one to Edwina, she gave her friend a sly wink. Edwina felt quite certain their guests did not know what they were in for.

"I am looking forward to the challenge," Beryl said. "Mrs. Kimberly, would you like to be the first to deal?" Beryl slid the pack of cards across to the younger woman, and before Edwina knew it, the evening was in full swing.

Edwina watched covertly from her place on the sofa, her knitting needles clicking through the fabric of her project more slowly than was her habit. The bidding and the playing were so fast and so furious that her attention was diverted to a greater extent than she would have thought possible.

It was obvious from the very beginning of play that Mr. Fanhurst was an audacious bidder. Mrs. Kimberly and Mr. Armitage both seemed far more hesitant in their play. Several times during the first game, Mrs. Kimberly let it be known in so many words that she was not entirely pleased with her partner's performance. Mr. Armitage was better at hiding his concern when Beryl threw caution to the wind and bet heavily on her hand. Still, Edwina was quite certain from the way he twitched the side of his mustache that he was none too comfortable with her style of play.

After the first hand, Mr. Fanhurst served as dummy, and Edwina took the opportunity to speak with him while he sat it out beside her on the sofa.

"Please accept my condolences on the death of your uncle," Edwina said. "A terrible loss, I'm sure."

Mr. Fanhurst swirled the contents in his glass and took a sip before answering. "I hadn't realized how much I would miss the old reprobate until he was gone," he said.

"The two of you were not close?" Edwina asked.

"I think it's safe to say we merely tolerated each other. He felt I was a dilettante, and I thought he was a stodgy old goat who had no notion whatsoever of what it's like to be young in the world of today," he said. "I suppose you think I'm heartless for not being more bereaved, but I would rather be considered heartless than to go to the effort of pretending something I do not feel."

Edwina felt rather shocked at his forwardness. She had not become entirely accustomed to how jaded the young people seemed these days. Perhaps they always had been, and she was the one who had changed. Perhaps her age was catching up with her, and she no longer understood what it was like to be young and trying to discover one's own way of being in the world. Certainly, the younger generation had been through a great deal, and much of the future looked bleak.

They called the Great War the war to end all wars, but somehow she doubted that that would prove to be the case. It had taken something from all of them, but in many ways, she felt it had stolen the most from those who were youngest. How cruel to be under thirty and to realize that the economy was in dire straits, jobs were few, and for the vast majority, the notion of

God was entirely dead. No, she did not think Mr. Fanhurst was heartless. She thought that he was heartsick, like so many other young men just like him.

"I make it a point not to judge the relationships of others," Edwina said. "Elderly relatives can be demanding and difficult, and oftentimes they forget what it's like to be young."

"You sound like you're speaking from personal experience," Mr. Fanhurst said, leaning in towards Edwina and fixing his light blue eyes on her face.

"Suffice it to say, I've had my fair share of interactions with my elders that were not entirely enjoyable. You appear to get on much better with his wife than you claim to have gotten along with him," Edwina said. She indicated towards Mrs. Kimberly with her free knitting needle.

Mr. Fanhurst followed her gaze and glanced over at his aunt. "Florrie's been like a breath of fresh air in that moldering old pile of a house. Until she arrived, the place was like a mausoleum. I still can't believe my uncle convinced her to marry him."

"Where did they meet?" Edwina asked.

"Theirs was a shipboard romance. She had tragically lost her husband to an outbreak of malaria overseas and was returning home. My uncle had been abroad himself on business and apparently was instantly smitten. They were actually married by the ship's captain before they returned to Southampton," Mr. Fanhurst said. "You could have knocked me over with a feather when he returned with such a pretty young thing on his arm."

"You hear about such things happening, but I don't know that I've ever met anyone in real life to have enjoyed such a storybook romance," Edwina said. "Although, it does seem that Mrs. Kimberly's luck with her husbands is rather poor."

"I expect she'll be okay before long," Mr. Fanhurst said. "A woman like that finds a way to land on her feet without much difficulty."

He got to his own feet and returned to the table as the hand drew to a close and the tricks were counted up. Before long, it was Mrs. Kimberly's turn to play dummy, and she perched in the same place her nephew had sat not long before.

"May I interest you in a plate of sandwiches or a fairy cake?" Edwina said, laying her knitting aside.

"That's very kind of you, but I find I have no appetite this evening," Mrs. Kimberly said.

"Grief has that effect on many people, I have noticed," Edwina said.

"I don't believe it's the grief over my departed husband that is responsible for me feeling so poorly," Mrs. Kimberly said. "I think it more likely that I am feeling the ill effects of discovering my husband thought so little of me as to leave the vast majority of his estate to a stranger rather than to his devoted wife."

Edwina hardly knew what to say. While she was certain that Simpkins would find his life vastly improved by the sudden influx of wealth, she realized that his good fortune came at another's expense. It was obvious that Mrs. Kimberly had had expectations and that they had been thwarted. Her willingness to place Edwina in an awkward conversational position served only to reinforce the idea that she had not been raised as a lady.

"I'm sure it all came as quite a shock to you. It's no wonder you have not felt quite yourself," Edwina said.

"I don't mind telling you, I can't eat, I can't sleep, and I have palpitations and dizziness," Mrs. Kimberly said.

Edwina thought it likely that Mrs. Kimberly didn't mind telling anyone anything at all. She seemed the sort of woman who habitually unburdened herself to strangers on a train. If it had not been for her feeling of responsibility towards Simpkins, she would have been pleased never to have encountered Mrs. Kimberly again. She was exactly the sort of woman Edwina most liked to avoid. Still, one could not be rude to a guest in one's own home.

"Perhaps you should avail yourself of the services of our local doctor. I am not one to often suffer ill health myself, but Dr. Nelson is well respected in the village," Edwina said. In point of fact, Edwina had been less than satisfied with her own dealings with him back in the autumn, but there was no need to besmirch his reputation with an outsider.

"As we will likely be here for a few more days, I will take you up on your suggestion," Mrs. Kimberly said. "I should like to be feeling well for the return journey."

"Do you have something special awaiting you when you return home?" Edwina said, picking up her knitting once more.

"I've made plans to stop in at Tunbridge Wells on my way back to London. I should hate to feel unwell during my visit there."

Edwina tried not to show any emotion at the name Tunbridge Wells as she wrapped the light blue yarn around her needle. She did not wish to spook her quarry.

"Will that be your first trip to that town?" Edwina asked.

"Yes, it will be. I had planned to visit it with my husband before he became ill, and I decided not to deny myself the pleasure of the journey, even though he is now sadly unable to make it with me," Mrs. Kimberly said.

"What made you decide that you wish to visit there?" Edwina said. "Was there anything special that called your attention?"

Mrs. Kimberly shifted in her seat and cleared her throat. "I was quite eager to visit the rock formations at Wellington Rocks. I have been told that they are not to be missed," she said.

Edwina found that hard to believe. If Beryl had said that she wished to spend a day scrambling about sightseeing at a famous rock formation, Edwina would not have batted an eyelid. But a woman such as Mrs. Kimberly, with her stiffly coiffed hair and inappropriate fur stoles, did not give off the impression that geology was one of her passions. Edwina could well see her being interested in visiting rocks if they were diamonds, sapphires, or rubies, but other than that, her interest seemed quite implausible.

"I expect you shall find it to be quite lovely. I visited there as a child with one of my aunts. You will certainly want to make the effort to feel well, though, if you are going to be traveling about sightseeing or taking the waters," Edwina said. "When you call the doctor's surgery, be sure to mention my name, and I expect they will be able to fit you in easily."

Mrs. Kimberly gave Edwina a sly smile, leaned forward, and tapped her playfully on the arm. "Now, why would the doctor be so willing to accommodate you, I wonder?" she said. "Have you been up to some sort of mischief here in this stagnant little backwater?"

Edwina felt the back of her neck flush warmly. She wished fleetingly that her hair still fell to her shoulders. There was simply no response that she could think of to such a suggestion. While she did know that some spinsters were known for forming inappropriate attachments to various members of their communities, Edwina had never considered herself to be in danger of someone believing her to be one of them. She was careful to comport herself in such a way as not to draw criticism from her fellow villagers and was startled that an outsider would be so boldly offensive, especially as she had no reason to be.

Edwina's earlier dislike of Mrs. Kimberly intensified, and she found herself hoping the doctor would not be able to squeeze her in for an appointment. Edwina was not sure if she felt more offended that someone would think her capable of such wanton behavior or that Mrs. Kimberly was eyeing her as though they had something in common.

With a sense of relief, she realized that the hand had come to an end, and Mrs. Kimberly rejoined the others at the table. By the time Beryl joined her on the sofa, she was ready for the evening to be over. Beryl took one look at her and suggested another round of drinks. The others gladly accepted her suggestion, and Edwina noticed that Beryl skipped the soda water in the glass that she offered to Edwina.

Beryl served the drinks to the others, then carried Edwina's to her and leaned over her friend closely as she pressed it into her hand.

"Have you learned anything important?" Beryl asked, her voice pitched low.

"Only that Mr. Fanhurst did not care much for his uncle and that Mrs. Kimberly has been feeling unwell for some time," Edwina said. She could feel that her neck was still hot and hoped Beryl had not noticed it.

"Nothing else?" Beryl asked. "You seem a little on edge."

"Mrs. Kimberly claims that she intends to head to Tunbridge Wells when she leaves here, for a visit to the Wellington Rocks. I find that very hard to believe," Edwina said quietly.

"Why do you not believe her?" Beryl asked.

"Does she seem the sort to hike about in search of geological wonders?" Edwina said.

"Not particularly. But we don't know her well enough to say."

"I thought it was a bit of a coincidence that she is planning a trip to the very same town from which the letter to Simpkins was posted," Edwina said.

"Tunbridge Wells is a popular tourist spot, though, isn't it?" Beryl asked. Edwina had to admit that it was. There had been visitors to the town for ages upon ages, looking to take the waters and visit the local abbey.

"It still caught my attention," Edwina said. "As an investigator, it is important not to allow one to believe too often in coincidences."

"Agreed. I shall keep my ear to the ground about any other nefarious trips Mrs. Kimberly or any other member of her party might be planning while I relieve them of some more of their money," Beryl said, giving Edwina an exaggerated wink before heading back to the table.

Edwina felt miffed at being teased about her attention to detail. Cases were solved by noticing where the pieces all fit and where they did not. No matter what Beryl or Mrs. Kimberly had to say, there was something about the entire party that just wasn't quite right.

Chapter 33

The day started off decidedly on the wrong foot. Both Beryl and Simpkins had arisen at an hour far earlier than Edwina would have preferred that they do. Each had seemed intent on consuming a full English breakfast. Simpkins had offered to assist in its preparation, but Edwina did not wish for him to feel entirely at home. She felt it best to relegate him to the sidelines in her own kitchen. At least for the moment.

She had slept poorly herself after the bridge party the evening before. She had lain awake for much of the night, mulling over what the future was likely to hold. Beryl looked no worse for the wear after her adventures the evening prior.

While she would be loath to admit it, Edwina had been delighted with the amount of winnings her friend had pocketed by evening's end. Beryl truly was an astonishingly adept player. While Edwina had a passion for the game, she would never be able to bring herself to place a wager for anything more valuable than a pile of matchsticks. It was simply not in her nature to gamble.

But Beryl seemed to thrive on such experiences. She bet aggressively and somehow managed to make it pay off, taking trick after trick, rubber after rubber. In fact, Beryl's constant run of luck seemed to have increased the tension in the room and had led to additional worries on Edwina's mind as she lay awake in bed last night. She felt as if she had been a poor hostess, despite the fact that the point of the evening had been to extract information from a trio of suspects.

Somehow it still felt odd that there was a business aspect in her life that pushed any other considerations into second place. Her mother had raised her to be someone who put the comfort of guests before everything else. She had spent the evening feeling as though she was torn between her priorities and, as a result, had felt groggy and out of sorts when the sun peeped through her window.

It had not helped matters that she had not been able to spend a few hours on her own pottering about the library or amongst the plants out in the garden before anyone else in the household stirred. Beryl had been up early in order to partake in her first typewriting lesson with Geraldine. It was one other reason Edwina felt somewhat out of sorts. She felt obligated to hurry in preparing the breakfast and also in cleaning up afterwards.

Although Geraldine was being hired as a sort of an employee, Edwina did not wish for her to arrive at the Beeches and see any untidiness in the kitchen. Beryl protested that Geraldine would not be likely to make her way into any room other than the morning room, where the typewriter was set up, but Edwina could not bring herself to leave the dishes sitting in the sink.

Simpkins did not offer to help with the washing-up. He drained the dregs from his teacup and then shuffled off towards the potting shed without so much as a by-your-leave. She rolled up her sleeves and set about scrubbing the crockery with a bit more energy than was strictly necessary. Beryl offered to dry the dishes, but Edwina knew better than to take her friend

up on her offer. More than once Edwina had been forced to replace a plate or teacup when Beryl set about the job with her
usual vigor.

Edwina managed to complete the task at hand, sweep the
stone flags on the kitchen floor, and put the kettle on the hob
for a fresh pot of tea before she realized she had not heard
Geraldine arrive at the appointed hour. She untied the strings of
her pinny and hung it on its hook. Crumpet followed her to the
morning room, where Beryl sat behind the typewriting machine, scowling at it as if it had done her a personal affront.

"Hasn't Geraldine turned up yet?" Edwina asked.

Beryl drummed her fingers on the desktop and shook her
head. "No, she hasn't. In fact, she's more than thirty minutes
late."

"Do you suppose she took offense to your questions yesterday at the telephone office?" Edwina said.

Beryl stopped drumming and gave Edwina her full attention.
"She didn't seem offended, but I would have to say she didn't
seem as though she was entirely telling the truth either," Beryl
said.

"Do you think she lied about Alma's alibi?" Edwina asked.

"I really am not sure what was wrong, but I couldn't shake
the impression that she was not sharing everything that she
knew," Beryl said. "Have you ever heard anyone complain that
they thought Geraldine listens in on the telephone lines?"

Edwina was quite surprised by the question. She had never
given such a thing any thought. Her father had been entirely dis-
approving of the newfangled device. In a rare show of strength,
he had refused to allow one at the Beeches during his lifetime.
The one consolation her mother had found in her grief after her
husband's death was in the installation of a telephone in her
home. She had taken to the instrument with zeal, and hardly a
day had gone by when she could not think up a reason to lum-
ber down the hallway, lift the handset, and place a call.

Edwina had felt no such love of the telephone. In fact, she had felt it almost unseemly the speed with which her mother had acquired one after her father's passing. He had barely been tucked into his grave at the Walmsley Parva churchyard before her mother had stopped in to the telephone office and made arrangements to have one installed.

Edwina's mother had encouraged her to share in her enthusiasm, but Edwina had never warmed to the instrument. Now she felt justified in her reluctance to embrace the new technology. She had always felt awkward about speaking into the receiver and waiting for a response. She cast her mind back over the sorts of conversations she had conducted over the telephone in recent weeks. She was relieved to realize nothing more interesting than an order for bonemeal from the seed merchant had transpired in the past few days. However, she thought it unlikely that every resident of Walmsley Barbara could say the same.

"I can't say that I have ever heard anyone suggest that Geraldine abused her position at the telephone office. But that doesn't mean she did not do so. What gave you cause to ask?"

"I happened to pass through the alleyway that runs along the telephone office when I went to visit her there yesterday. There is a window on the side of the building that looks down onto the switchboard, but it is set quite high up in the wall, and I doubt most people would pay it much mind, Geraldine included."

"That still doesn't explain your suspicions," Edwina said.

"I caught sight of her sitting at the switchboard as I passed by, and I took the opportunity to watch her without being observed. A call came in just as I stopped at the window, and rather than removing her headphones, she seemed to be attending to the conversation beyond what the switchboard operator was required to do."

"That's not quite nice, is it?" Edwina said. "Still, that has nothing to do with her failure to arrive today, does it?"

erhaps not. But then again, you never know," Beryl said.

dwina thought it possible that Beryl was simply looking for reasons to dislike Geraldine. She had heard the way that Beryl muttered over the typewriter and had been quite shocked at her friend's vocabulary. She wondered if Beryl was simply annoyed at the necessity of asking for help with the typewriter and thus was inclined to find fault with the young telephone operator.

Edwina did not consider herself a gossip, but people did tend to confide things in her, especially if they pertained to domestic help or uncomfortable social situations. On many occasions, she had been consulted on the character of a parlourmaid or the trustworthiness of a potential childminder. Years spent assisting with the girl guides, the educational services offered by the Women's Institute, and various activities involving the church had put Edwina in a position to evaluate knowledgeably the character of the younger generation.

Geraldine had never struck her as a particularly prepossessing young woman, but neither had she been a glaringly bad apple. Still, Beryl's instincts about such things had rarely been amiss. If anything, Beryl was far too inclined, in Edwina's opinion, to give others the benefit of the doubt.

"How long do you intend to sit here and wait for her to arrive?" Edwina asked.

"I'll give her another quarter of an hour, and then I shall consider our appointment canceled for today," Beryl said.

"I shouldn't consider dismissing her without speaking with her first," Edwina said. "Ever since the war, it's been impossible to find good help. The trouble over domestic servants, even when one has the funds to pay for them, has been quite shocking."

"I doubt very much that Geraldine would consider herself to be a domestic servant," Beryl said.

"The principle is the same, though. Standards in service of any sort have gone entirely downhill ever since the war effort made opportunities available in the armaments factories and other sorts of employment in the cities," Edwina said.

She might come off as an old fuddy-duddy who was longing for times past, but she was not the only one to say so. The war years had exposed many of the cracks in the social structure, and Edwina had been slow to embrace the changes that rippled through the country. Young people seemed to want nothing whatsoever to do with small villages and country life. They all wanted to try their luck in London or other large cities. They seemed eager to shake off the dust of small country villages, even if they had been employed for high wages at grand estates.

When Edwina had broached the subject with Charles one evening, he had taken a rather liberal view. Charles had said that the war had served as a great equalizer for the classes. He'd pointed out that it was not surprising that men who had seen their officers fall apart in the treacherous conditions of mud and disease and vermin no longer felt it their duty to work for long hours, little pay, and even less ability to direct their own lives.

Edwina had conceded that he made a good point.

"You can't expect them to want to molder away in the country, not after all they saw during the war years," Beryl said, pushing her chair back from the desk.

Not for the first time, Edwina wondered what Beryl had spent her time doing during the war. Every time the topic came up, she felt a small gap grow between them. Their usual easy camaraderie felt slightly strained, and Edwina wondered if it was something Beryl was not saying or if Edwina's own sense of guilt at her small contribution to the war effort caused it.

"Nothing is the same since the fighting broke out, is it?" Edwina said.

"You can blame it on the trenches," Beryl said. "Once a workingman has seen those who call themselves his betters panicking under fire or shooting themselves in the feet in order to be sent

/ from the front, he can be forgiven for declining to serve same sort of man once armistice was declared."

"I suppose the classes were thrown together in an unprecedented way," Edwina said. "Still, I can't help but reminisce about the days when it was possible to keep a parlourmaid, a cook, and two gardeners."

"I'm afraid you will have to get used to the idea. Now that the serving class has realized that they need not live under the thumb of those with property, they are unlikely to do so."

"Do you really think it was such a bad system?" Edwina asked.

"Indeed I do. Can you imagine having a curfew from your employer or being required to ask for permission to walk out with a young man?" Beryl asked.

Edwina had not considered it that way. In the past, her parents had always felt it their duty to advise their servants on all matters, including romantic entanglements. It had been her mother's considered opinion that the average serving girl had no better sense than a chicken in a coop or a rabbit in a hutch. She had said as much to Edwina on more than one occasion.

Now that she came to think on it, Edwina realized that her mother had been strict about the sort of men with whom her domestic help was allowed to walk out. She wondered if her grandparents had had any say over Simpkins's connection with his wife, Bess. She thought it unlikely, as men were not so tightly leashed as women, but it might be worth asking, should she find the opportunity presented itself.

"I suppose I can see why the freedom of factory work might have its appeal," Edwina said.

She thought back to her own youth, when her mother had been resistant to any young suitors that turned their attention towards Edwina. It had not seemed strange at the time that Mrs. Davenport had been equally strict with her servants. In fact, Edwina had felt that they had far more freedom than she herself did.

For one thing, they had earned a wage and had been able to do with their money as they saw fit. Edwina had had no such resources and had been entirely dependent upon her parents until they both passed away. By the time she had gotten her hands on the purse strings, the finances were in a sad state of affairs, and it had done her more harm than good to be in charge of her financial destiny.

"I shouldn't think it would be easy to convince anyone to take up domestic service now or in the future," Beryl said. "Perhaps that's why Geraldine decided not to keep her appointment. Maybe she felt that it was beneath her to attend to me here at the Beeches. Perhaps I should have offered to meet her at her own home or even in a common meeting space, like the village hall or the reading room. I may have offended her."

"Or it may just be that you are correct about her withholding some information about the investigation, and she did not want to spend time with you alone. She may have felt that it would prove impossible to keep her secret if she encountered you once more."

"Either way, it seems I shall not have a typing lesson this morning, after all," Beryl said, gazing at the machine before her through narrowed eyes. She stood and tidied away the papers and writing implements scattered across the surface of the small desk.

"Why don't you wait for her by reading the post. I left your letters on the hall table," Edwina said.

With less vigor than she usually displayed, Beryl nodded and exited the room. Edwina thought she seemed unhappy about something, but found the thought passed quickly from her mind as she eyed the typewriter. She waited for a moment to be sure that Beryl was not about to return, then slipped around the desk to the chair and took a seat. There was something quite irresistible about the gleaming machine.

She remembered countless happy hours spent plunking away on the one in her father's office when she was a younger woman.

..ad never had any formal lessons, but she had prided herself
on being rather a good typist, nonetheless. Her father's office
help had occasionally been called away on family emergencies
or on account of illness.

On one such occasion, his secretary, a plain, humorless woman
who lavished her hours away from the office on perfecting a
strain of sweet peas through careful crossbreeding, had been hit
by a passing lorry and had required a lengthy stay at a conva-
lescent home. Edwina's mother had not wished for her husband
to take on a young, attractive secretary, even on a temporary
basis, and had insisted that Edwina fill in until Miss Soames was
well enough to return.

The duties were light, and Edwina found plenty of time for
daily practice on the typewriting machine. In fact, she enjoyed
it so much that she occasionally remained behind after her father left work for the day in order to tap away for a while
longer. She did not mention to him, or to anyone else, for that
matter, what she had been typing.

Beryl was not the only one in the household with an interest
in writing a book. Edwina had made the mistake early on of con-
fiding her cherished desire to become a novelist to her mother,
who had immediately quashed the idea with an unladylike snort.
She had suggested that if Edwina was determined to make a
spectacle of herself, she should confine her efforts to a cookery
book or some improving religious tracts to send along with
missionaries to Africa.

When Beryl had so casually and confidently announced her
intention to pen a book of her own, Edwina had felt perturbed.
While she rarely allowed herself to feel envious of her famous
and far more accomplished friend, she had not been content in
the least to hear that Beryl had decided to turn her attention to
the one arena in which Edwina dearly wished to excel.

It was just like Beryl to give absolutely no thought to her
own lack of qualifications to undertake such a venture. How

anyone who thought that reading was something to engage in only if one was confined to bed with a serious illness could imagine herself qualified to write a book was beyond Edwina's comprehension.

Still, to give Beryl her due, Edwina had benefitted from Beryl's willingness to trod without caution along unfamiliar roads. If it were not for her friend's spirit of adventure, they would never have started the private enquiry agency. As her fingers reached out for the keys on the typewriter, she felt heartily ashamed of herself for imagining that there was not room enough in the literary world for both of them. She told herself that if Geraldine did not turn up to give Beryl her lesson, she would own up to her skill and offer to teach Beryl herself.

Chapter 34

Beryl had spent so much of her life in parts of the world that did not value the ticking of the clock as highly as the British. Still, she found her good humor had taken a bit of a beating by Geraldine's complete failure either to appear for their appointment or to send word that she was unable to honor that commitment.

She left the morning room and headed for the telephone stationed in the hall, intent on giving the errant Geraldine a piece of her mind. She lifted the receiver, but much to her annoyance, no one on the other end of the line picked up. She felt a fiery indignation rise in her chest.

She picked up her mail from the hall table and thumbed through it. She was so aggravated that she couldn't even bring herself to take an interest in any of the letters that had arrived by the morning's post, including those from former husbands. Beryl was surprised at her lack of interest. Generally, she found her spirit soared whenever she read letters from old loves. They so often contained either entreaties for a second chance to win her affections or generous checks.

She felt rather disgusted with herself for wasting the better part of the day by stewing about in a foul mood. She decided to take herself in hand by heading for the telephone office to demand an explanation of Geraldine. She mounted the stairs and strode to her room. She stuffed her post into the drawer of her dressing table and faced the mirror.

Leaning towards the glass, she realized her lipstick was in need of refreshment. She selected a tube from the tray on the dressing table and began to apply it generously to her lips. She spritzed her wrists and the back of her neck with her favourite perfume, then tied a jaunty silk scarf around her neck. She always felt best prepared for confrontations when she knew she cut a dazzling figure.

With little effort, she convinced Edwina to accompany her to the village. Edwina expressed a desire to stop into the bakery. Beryl was not entirely certain if Edwina's errand was a genuine one or if she was inventing something in order to improve Beryl's mood. Either way, the two of them strolled into the village less than half an hour later.

"I hope you do not intend to make a scene," Edwina said. "It simply won't do for Geraldine to take the notion to ignore our line when it lights up on the switchboard from now on."

Beryl had not considered that offending Geraldine might have far-reaching consequences. One of the novelties of village life was how everyday acts impacted the future. Having always lived a footloose lifestyle, she had not needed to concern herself with such small details. It hardly mattered if one spoke one's mind to an aircraft mechanic, a sea captain, or a porter. The relationship would not be a long-lasting one, and Beryl had always found it expeditious to solve any interpersonal difficulties straightaway.

Perhaps Edwina's attitude of placating and smoothing ruffled feathers was not simply an act of timidity, Beryl thought. As she considered the matter, it occurred to her that her friend simply used a completely different way of navigating life's difficulties. Bearing that in mind, Beryl resolved to moderate her tone more than she would were Geraldine an impertinent shopkeeper in a dusty village in a country she would likely never visit again.

"I shall comport myself with dignity and give her every opportunity to explain her absence. For all I know, she's been bumped on the head and developed amnesia," Beryl said. "I am resolved to give her the benefit of the doubt."

She felt slightly disgruntled at Edwina's look of skepticism. She squared her shoulders and turned down the alley that led towards the telephone office. She peered once more through the small window, feeling a flicker of sympathy for her companion, as she realized that Edwina's head did not reach the sill. As she peered inside, she noticed the office seemed empty. That certainly explained the lack of response to her attempt to place a telephone call. The lights in the office were not even switched on.

She hurried ahead and popped out the end of the alley. She mounted the steps to the telephone office and grasped the door handle. She stepped inside and called out, but no one answered.

"Is anyone in?" Edwina asked as she stepped in next to Beryl and looked around.

"Not that I can tell."

"The telephone office is never empty at this time of day," Edwina said. "Something is very wrong. Let's have a look around."

Beryl turned back towards the telephone office door. She stepped onto the stoop and looked up and down the street. She heard voices coming from the general vicinity of the butcher shop. Edwina appeared to have noticed the commotion, too, as she followed her down from the telephone office and made her way towards Sidney Poole's establishment.

As they approached, Beryl realized the noise was not coming from inside the butcher shop or even from in front of it, but rather from somewhere around the back. Beryl had never spent any time behind Sidney's shop. There was no reason to do so, and if she were to be honest, she was not sure that whatever happened behind a butcher shop was something she wanted to see, at least not if she wanted to continue to enjoy a roast chicken or a pork chop from time to time.

Edwina led the way, gathering her skirt closely to her slim frame in order to keep it from brushing the walls of the buildings on either side of the narrow passageway. As they popped out the end of the tight corridor, Beryl was surprised to see the number of people assembled there.

A sort of yard area lay before them. Several shops seemed to abut each other, and behind them was a spot of flat ground. Crates and refuse bins stood stacked behind the greengrocer and the butcher shop. To the right of the butcher shop was a cabinetmaker's shop. A sort of makeshift shed was attached to the back of the cabinetmaker's, and it housed a heaping pile of fragrant sawdust.

A young man whom Beryl recognized from time spent at the Dove and Duck stood to one side of the sawdust pile, a broom in his hand and a shocked look on his face. Constable Gibbs squatted in front of the pile and seemed to be inspecting something carefully. Her back was to Beryl and Edwina, and she took no notice of them. Beryl held a finger to her lips and motioned that they should creep up behind her to see what all the fuss was about.

Sidney Poole and Gareth Scott hovered nearby. Alma appeared out of nowhere to join her husband. As Beryl approached, Constable Gibbs shifted slightly, and the focus of her attention came into view. There on the ground, beneath the pile of sawdust, only her head exposed, lay the motionless body of Geraldine. Her eyes were open, and they bulged slightly from her head. Her tongue protruded grotesquely, and Beryl noted a silk scarf was wrapped tightly around the young woman's neck.

"What are the two of you doing here?" Constable Gibbs said as she straightened up and turned around to face the two sleuths.

"I had an appointment with Geraldine this morning, and she never turned up. I tried to call the telephone office, but there was no answer, so we decided to come into the village to make enquiries," Beryl said. "When we heard all the hullabaloo, we followed the sound, and here we are."

"As you can see, Geraldine had a very good reason for not showing up for her appointment this morning," Constable Gibbs said.

"When was she found?" Edwina asked.

"Not that it's any of your business, but Milton Boyers found her when he went to tidy up behind the shop about an hour ago," Constable Gibbs said, indicating towards the young man holding the broom. "When was she supposed to have met you?"

"At ten o'clock. I had engaged her to give me typing lessons, and we agreed to meet at the Beeches this morning," Beryl said.

Beryl felt her own throat constrict, and she reached up unconsciously to loosen the knot in her own scarf.

"It looks like you're going to need to find somebody else to teach you to type," Constable Gibbs said. "Now please take yourself off somewhere out of the way and leave the police business to me."

"As you wish, Constable," Beryl said. She turned to Edwina and lowered her voice. "While I feel terrible for Geraldine, there is some good news about this."

"What's that?" Edwina said.

"It's hard to believe that two murders in Walmsley Parva in such a short space of time would not be connected," she said.

"I hardly think that two murders in the village constitutes good news," Edwina said.

"Certainly it does not for Hector or for Geraldine. But it may very well be good news for our client," Beryl said.

"You mean because he is still in custody, he can't be blamed for what happened to Geraldine?" Edwina asked.

"Exactly. Let's go find out what people are saying," Beryl said.

Edwina nodded, and without consultation, they headed back out towards the high street.

Chapter 35

Minnie Mumford stood at the confectionery counter of Prudence Rathbone's shop, her head bent towards the proprietress's own, their voices pitched low, as Beryl and Edwina entered. If anyone would have news about what had befallen the unfortunate Geraldine, it would be Prudence. From the look on Minnie Mumford's face, Prudence did in fact have something to share.

Edwina nodded politely to Minnie as she passed on out of the shop. Edwina assumed the tea shop owner was eager to pass on whatever Prudence had shared with her own patrons. Edwina did not hold with gossip herself, but she did understand that it was the lifeblood of such a small village. There was a certain social status to being amongst the first to know about any juicy bit of news, and Prudence and Minnie were always at the forefront of any goings-on.

Having been the focus of a nasty spate of gossip the previous autumn, Edwina found this part of her new career distasteful. She had never been one to revel in the sufferings of others, and having experienced the effects of the village grapevine firsthand, she knew how debilitating such unkindness could be. But needs must, and while gossip could be wounding, being unjustly convicted of murder could easily be said to be more so. Edwina squared her shoulders and made straight for the glass countertop Prudence was making a fuss about buffing with a soft cloth.

She looked up and bestowed one of her toothy smiles on Edwina. Prudence always put Edwina in mind of a meerkat or a prairie dog, with her mousy-colored hair, bulging eyes, and long neck swiveling to and fro as she surveyed the street outside her shop for signs of nefarious activities.

While it could be rightly said that Prudence liked nothing more than to be the carrier of fresh tales, she did like to stretch out the experience and could be quite coy about sharing what she knew. Edwina had found the best way to deal with her was to express no interest whatsoever in what news she clearly wished to share.

"Good afternoon, Prudence. I wondered if you happen to have any typewriter ribbons in stock?" Edwina said.

"Typewriter ribbons?" Prudence asked, tapping the side of her face with a long, knobby finger. "Have you hired yourself out as some sort of secretary?" Edwina could see the wheels in Prudence's mind turning as she considered the possibility that there was something else she could tell the other residents about Edwina. It was always a pleasure to thwart her.

"Actually, the ribbon is for me," Beryl said, stepping forward. "I have hired Geraldine Howarth to teach me to type for a project I'm working on, and I thought it would be sensible to have an extra ribbon waiting in the wings."

Edwina glanced at Beryl out of the corner of her eye. Her friend was so good at laying the groundwork for interviews. She did such a wonderful job of positioning Prudence in exactly the right spot to extract what she knew with the least amount of fuss. Prudence was practically licking her lips in anticipation just at hearing Geraldine's name spoken aloud.

"Geraldine?" Prudence said, leaning across the counter, gripping it tightly. Edwina was pleased to notice that Prudence had left a wide smudge across the freshly polished glass.

"Yes, Geraldine, the telephone switchboard operator. Why? Do you think there's someone who would prove a better typing tutor than she?" Beryl asked, allowing a note of concern to enter her voice. "She seemed very competent to me when I engaged her two days ago."

Beryl turned towards Edwina, who nodded vigorously. "I've never heard a disparaging word spoken about Geraldine. Sensible girl, I've always thought," Edwina said. Edwina could practically feel Prudence's excitement rippling out from her in invisible waves of anticipation.

"I don't suppose she will be available to teach you anything now," Prudence said with a superior look on her face.

"I can't imagine why," Beryl said, turning back towards the postmistress. "Has she gone and got herself into some trouble?"

"I very much doubt that a nice girl like Geraldine could have gotten into any trouble," Edwina said. It was a bit uncomfortable knowing that Prudence would enjoy correcting her, but Edwina reminded herself that the case and Frank Prentice's interests came before her pride.

"That's where you're wrong," Prudence said, crossing her arms across her washboard chest. "Geraldine is in about the worst sort of trouble a person could be in."

"I hope you're not implying that she's gone and gotten herself in the family way. That's the sort of thing that can absolutely ruin a young woman's reputation," Beryl said, drawing herself up to her full height and glowering at Prudence.

For just a heartbeat, Edwina thought Prudence looked slightly disappointed. A dead girl was one thing. A disgraced one, who would be fodder for gossip in the coming months and even the years ahead, would have proved far juicier. She recovered quickly, however, and arched a sparse eyebrow at Beryl, as though she pitied her.

"Far worse than that, I'm afraid. Geraldine has gone and gotten herself murdered," Prudence said. "It's all over the village. I'm surprised you haven't heard about it."

"We can't all be as well informed as you, Prudence," Edwina said. A bit of flattery had been known to go a long way with the shopkeeper. "Although I can't say as I believe the rumor. Why in the world would anyone harm Geraldine?" She turned to face Beryl.

"Nice girls like Geraldine don't go around getting themselves murdered. I'm sure there must be some sort of a misunderstanding. Didn't she live at home with her parents?" Beryl asked.

"Yes, and as far as I know, she didn't have an enemy in the world," Edwina said.

From behind the counter, Prudence cleared her throat. "That just goes to show what you know," she said. "She had a heated argument with Mrs. Kimberly just yesterday evening."

Both Beryl and Edwina turned to face Prudence once more. Edwina could see Prudence practically glow from the attention.

"Mrs. Kimberly, the woman from the condiment company?" Edwina asked.

"The very one. Nasty, it was," Prudence said, as if she was relishing the memory.

"Did you hear this from someone?" Beryl said.

"I saw it with my own eyes. The two of them stood right outside my window, and if they weren't having an argument, I'll eat that roll of stamps," Prudence said, pointing at a spool of postage on the counter beside her.

"I would not have thought they would have known each other," Edwina said. "Did you see something that should have caused an argument between them?"

Edwina knew from personal experience that sometimes even the mildest mannered of women could become aggressive when thwarted during a shopping expedition. She was ashamed to recall it, but there was one humiliating occasion in the Woolery, where she and another customer had nearly come to blows over the purchase of the last two balls of some especially fine periwinkle-blue worsted.

Just the memory of the incident brought heat to her cheeks. She could well imagine a similar thing happening between the unladylike Mrs. Kimberly and an inexperienced young woman like Geraldine. After all, if it could happen to her, it could happen to anyone.

"I shouldn't have thought so. It seemed to me they met right in front of my shop. It did not look as though they had been walking along together from somewhere else."

"Could you hear any of their conversation?" Beryl asked.

"As it happens, there was a customer heading into the shop, heavily laden with packages, and I felt it my duty to offer assistance. While I held the door open, I believe I heard Mrs. Kimberly ordering Geraldine to 'leave him alone,' " Prudence said.

"Is that all you heard of the conversation? It seems like little proof of an argument," Edwina said.

"There was far more information to be gleaned from their demeanors. Mrs. Kimberly went so far as to jab Geraldine in the shoulder several times. I remember watching Geraldine reach up and rub the spot as if it hurt her," Prudence said, with a ring of satisfaction in her voice. "If Geraldine had gone to the constable to swear in a complaint, it would not have surprised me. To think, I would have been a witness."

Edwina almost felt sorry for Prudence when she heard the

note of wistfulness in the postmistress's voice. What sort of a life was she leading that being called as a witness to a minor assault charge seemed like such a pleasurable activity? Edwina was more grateful than ever for Beryl's suggestion that they open the enquiry agency. She would have hated to have turned out to be someone with such a small life. She suddenly found the atmosphere in the shop depressing and oppressive. She gave Beryl a look that she hoped indicated she wished to leave.

"Take heart, Miss Rathbone," Beryl said. "I am quite sure the constable will be eager to hear your statement about the argument you saw. It seems you were a witness, after all, considering Geraldine has turned up dead."

"If I were you, I'd close up shop for a few minutes and head over to let her know what you saw. It could prove invaluable to her investigation," Edwina said.

"Do you really think so?" Prudence asked, stepping out from behind the counter and ushering them towards the door.

"It would be your civic duty," Beryl said.

Prudence nodded and yanked open the door. She flipped the sign hanging upon it to the CLOSED side, waited for Beryl and Edwina to exit, then pulled it firmly shut not even remembering to lock it behind her.

"That serves Constable Gibbs right for being so dismissive, doesn't it?" Edwina asked as she watched Prudence practically break into a trot as she struck off in the direction of the crime scene.

"It also means that the longer the constable is tied up with Prudence, the later it will be before she interviews anyone else. Since we are in the village already, let's take the opportunity to ask a few more questions of our own, with the hope it will help secure Frank's release."

"What did you have in mind?" Edwina asked.

"I want to ask Sidney Poole once more about his story concerning the night of Hector's murder. Why don't you run your errands to the bakery, like you planned, and keep your ears open for anything that might be said about Geraldine," Beryl said.

With that, they parted ways, having agreed to meet back up by teatime at the Beeches.

Chapter 36

When Beryl entered Sidney's butcher shop, he was nowhere to be seen. She opened and closed the door a second time, hoping the jangling of the bell would call him from wherever he had gotten off to. She expected he was still behind the shop, keeping an eye on the activity at the crime scene or simply talking it over with the other shopkeepers if Constable Gibbs had completed her search of the area.

Beryl had no interest in encountering Constable Gibbs for a second time that afternoon. Truth be told, she was not eager to catch sight of the unfortunate Geraldine a second time. While she tried to take a matter-of-fact attitude towards most of life's tragedies, the fact was, like so many others, Beryl had seen far too many dead bodies in the course of her lifetime.

She didn't like to dwell upon the horrors she had witnessed during the war years, but it could be said she had seen more than her fair share of them. Her eagerness to travel the globe had brought her in contact with the war on many fronts, and no matter where she roamed, the consequences had been devastating. From Africa to France and even to the Russian front,

Beryl had memories she wished to block out. Geraldine's lifeless eyes staring up at the sky had reminded her of another young woman, whose body she had stumbled across deep in enemy territory on one of her ventures. She pushed the thought from her mind, strode to the wooden counter, and firmly depressed the service bell.

Sidney appeared a moment later. His round cheeks were flushed, and she thought that for a man who was so used to cutting up carcasses, he looked rattled by a human corpse appearing behind his shop.

"Are you here to do some shopping, Miss Helliwell?" he asked. "I have some smoked ham that's just arrived, and I understand it's very good today." He gestured towards the window where cuts of meat hung from hooks for all the village to see. Beryl politely turned and glanced in the direction he indicated, not wishing to dismiss his offerings so lightly.

"I shall keep that in mind, but it's Edwina who is generally responsible for such decisions. I would not dare to purchase an entire ham without her expressly wishing me to do so. She's rather a stickler about the housekeeping," Beryl said.

"What brings you in, then?" Sidney asked. "I saw you behind the shop, so I know you know about Geraldine. Are you here on the case?" He came out from behind the counter and stood next to her, leaning his considerable bulk against a freestanding shelf holding some dusty tins of smoked tongue.

"I'm afraid I need to ask you again about your whereabouts at the time of Hector's murder. I've spoken with your wife, and she has confirmed that she was not actually at home when you say that the two of you were together," Beryl said.

Sidney's posture improved instantly. He had not been expecting her question. That much was clear.

"The fact that she wasn't home doesn't mean that I wasn't there," Sidney said.

"It's not just your wife's inability to give you an alibi for the time of Hector's murder that brings me in. I've also interviewed a witness who saw you arguing with Hector just in front of the cinema. I seem to remember you telling me you did not see him again after you left the pub."

Sidney swallowed, and Beryl watched his Adam's apple bob slowly in his thick neck. His eyes darted towards the door, as if he wondered at his chances of giving her the slip. While she was not a small woman, she would bet on herself against Sidney in a footrace if it came to that. Besides, she would not be above sticking out her foot and tripping him if he was foolish enough to make a run for it. Fortunately, he decided upon the high road.

"I did speak with Hector. I had had too much to drink at the pub, and the more I thought about his forward behavior towards my wife, the angrier I became," he said.

"Going past the cinema wasn't the fastest route to get home. What made you decide to go that way? Were you following Hector?" Beryl asked. She kept her eyes trained on Sidney's face, hoping to detect a subtle tell if he was lying.

"I decided to take the long way home. I was hoping to sober up a bit before I got there, and I wasn't in any hurry to do so, anyway. I had lost quite a bit of money on the Derby, and I wasn't eager to have to tell that to Alma," he said.

"So you weren't following Hector on purpose?"

"No, not at first, but when I saw him up ahead of me, I quickened my pace in order to confront him."

"Did you threaten him?" Beryl asked.

"I expect that I did. I can't remember for sure. Like I said, I did have quite a lot to drink," Sidney said.

"Did you have so much to drink that you can't actually remember whether or not you harmed him?" Beryl said. "It wouldn't be the first time someone killed another person while in a blind drunken rage."

"I admit to having had too much to drink and to following

Hector out of the pub. I caught up with him in front of the cinema and gave him a whacking great piece of my mind. But I didn't lay a hand on him."

"Is there anyone who can vouch for you about that?" Beryl asked.

"Since Alma wasn't home, I don't suppose there is. You can believe me or not."

"What about Geraldine? Do you have any thoughts about what might've happened to her?" Beryl asked.

"None whatsoever. Geraldine was always a nice girl, and I can't think of a reason anyone would have had to hurt her. It's just a shame, really. I can't imagine what the village is coming to," Sidney said.

"Have you ever heard anyone mention that Geraldine listened in on telephone conversations?" Beryl asked.

"I've never heard something like that, and I don't think it's nice of you to be putting about that sort of a rumor. Like I said, Geraldine was well liked, and I expect that it will turn out to be some sort of a madman who just came upon her, dragged her out behind the shop, and killed her right there," Sidney said.

Beryl thought he seemed to have developed quite a detailed imagining of the crime. Then again, she had to wonder if he had imagined it or if he was, in fact, remembering exactly what had happened.

Chapter 37

Minnie Mumford's tea shop was known for its delicious cakes and scones, but Edwina decided to purchase her baked goods from the bakery up the street. She did not wish to endure any barrage of questions from Minnie that a stop into the Silver Spoon Tearoom was likely to yield. The bakery sat at the far end of the street and was better known for its loaves of wholemeal bread and floury baps than teatime treats, but Edwina felt she had made the right decision.

She was even more convinced when she stepped into the warm, yeasty-smelling shop and spotted Nurse Crenshaw peering into a basket filled with baguettes.

"Hello, Nurse Crenshaw," Edwina said. "Are you enjoying a rare afternoon off?"

"Rare and unexpected," Nurse Crenshaw said. The nurse was a thin greyhound of a woman. Her features were delicate, and her aura was that of a quivering race dog. Edwina had never warmed to her, but as she was the nurse for the only doctor in Walmsley Parva, Edwina made a point of treating her with as much courtesy as she could muster whenever they met.

"Were you not expecting to have the afternoon off, then?" Edwina asked.

"No indeed. The doctor was called away on account of the tragedy with Geraldine, and he asked me to cancel all his afternoon appointments. He said that I was welcome to leave the surgery as soon as I had done so. Of course, I couldn't telephone the patients, so I had to send an errand boy out with messages for them all."

"What a lot of fuss," Edwina said. "I don't envy you the task of getting ahold of everyone. We've come to rely on the telephone so quickly, haven't we?" Edwina said.

"It does make things much more efficient, at least when the switchboard operator is available to attend to her duties," Nurse Crenshaw said, pursing her thin lips. Edwina marveled at the fact that the woman made it sound as though Geraldine was guilty of a dereliction of duty as opposed to being the victim of a violent crime. Still, there was no need to ruffle the nurse's feathers.

"Beryl and I were rather inconvenienced by the inability to use our own telephone today, so I completely understand your difficulty. I hope you didn't have too many appointments you needed to cancel," Edwina said.

"Fortunately, there were only two. I was able to send a messenger to the vicarage and then along to the Smith farmhouse. Old Mr. Smith has not managed to recover completely from his bout with pneumonia over the winter," the nurse said.

"I recommended that a visitor to the village, Mrs. Kimberly, make an appointment with the doctor for today. She was not one of the ones you had to cancel?" Edwina said.

The nurse's face tightened. "Mrs. Kimberly was one of the fortunate patients to visit the surgery this morning. Not that it did her any good, mind you."

"I should've thought the doctor would have been more than capable of addressing her difficulties. He is so well respected in the community," Edwina said. She had not found him to be the most helpful of medical men herself, but there was no reason to put Nurse Crenshaw's back up. It was widely known in Walmsley Parva that the nurse doted on her employer. Any harsh words of criticism were unlikely to endear Edwina to her.

"It's hardly the doctor's fault if the silly woman didn't know he could be of no real use, considering she doesn't actually have a medical problem," Nurse Crenshaw said.

"She's not beyond help, is she?" Edwina said. While Mrs. Kimberly had appeared unwell the evening before, she had not looked like someone wasting away. She had simply looked a bit green about the gills.

"I should think not. She's just a time waster. Women these days seem to have less and less sense all the time," Nurse Crenshaw said, lowering her voice. "After all, what sort of woman does not expect to feel queasy during the first few months she is expecting?"

Chapter 38

One thing Beryl had not counted on when she had proposed the idea of starting a private enquiry agency was how often she would encounter people who felt no compunction at lying to her. When she came to think on it, Beryl realized she had been lied to more frequently in the past few weeks than in the entire rest of her life put together.

At least she knew that she had been lied to more frequently. It was possible that she had been lied to at similar intervals throughout the rest of her life but had not spent sufficient time in any one location to confirm that such a thing had occurred. She did not care for the experience at all. The realization left her in a confrontational state of mind.

Feeling hot under the collar, she left the butcher shop and made straight for Alma's House of Beauty. As she stepped through Alma's doorway, she realized that Edwina had been lied to recently too. Beryl swept her gaze around the room, which was empty save for Alma, who stood behind her chair, sweeping hair off its surface with a small whisk broom. Alma looked up expectantly, but her smile faded as she took in Beryl's expression.

"Were you dissatisfied with your wash and set the other day? Hattie is still learning, so sometimes things go a bit amiss," Alma said.

"I am not here to discuss my hair but rather to discuss yours," Beryl said, closing the gap between them and pointing at Alma's head. "You led Edwina to believe that you had been busy dyeing your hair at the time of Hector's death. She was easily taken in since she is not well versed in the properties of hair coloring."

Alma's eyes widened, and she clutched her small broom defensively in front of her torso, as if to ward off an attack on her vital organs.

"What makes you think that I was not telling the truth?" Alma said. One of her hands snuck up to the side of her head, and she carefully patted her hairdo.

"Your roots," Beryl said, removing one of her gloves and reaching out to point her finger at Alma's center part. "You would not have roots like that if you had colored your hair on Saturday evening. Where were you really?"

Alma's shoulders slumped, and she dropped the broom with a clatter to the floor. She made her way around to the front of the chair and sat in it heavily. Beryl felt her anger evaporate as she looked at Alma's stricken face.

"You mustn't tell Sidney. Please, promise me you won't tell him," Alma said.

"I've had more than my fair share of husbands. Unless what you share with me is necessary to solve the case, I shan't tell anyone save Edwina," Beryl said. "But that's the best that I can promise you. And I shall not stop asking questions until I get to the truth." She sank into the seat next to Alma and pulled off her second glove. She wished for Alma to believe she had all the time in the world to hear her story.

Alma heaved a deep sigh. "I was with Milton Boyers," she said.

Beryl looked at Alma with new respect. While she thought

nothing of peering into cradles and extracting the contents, she knew most women were unlikely to do the same. And truth be told, even if they wished for dalliances with younger men, their interest was infrequently reciprocated.

Beryl did not think Alma likely to be such a woman. With her loose-fitting smock, slightly smeared lipstick, and sensible shoes, Alma was a dark horse indeed. Milton Boyers was no older than twenty-five, and despite her artful use of hair dye, Beryl estimated Alma to be in her fifties. Truly, the longer she thought on that, the more astonished she felt.

"No smoke without fire, then," Beryl said. "Your husband was consumed with jealousy, but he pointed his suspicions in entirely the wrong direction."

"I don't want you to mention it to my husband, because Sidney would be very jealous, but you have taken the entirely wrong impression. I was with Milton, and I was keeping it a secret because of Sidney's jealousy. But I wasn't doing anything wrong," Alma said. "At least not in the way you are implying."

Beryl noted two spots of bright color on Alma's cheeks. If the hairdresser had not been conducting a romantic liaison, she wondered just what she had been up to.

"What were you doing with that young man, then?" Beryl said.

Alma glanced towards the door, as if to be sure no one was about to enter, before answering. "If you must know, I was giving him dancing lessons. The poor lad was entirely smitten with Geraldine, and he had been taking her out dancing in an effort to woo her."

"Where did these so-called dancing lessons take place?" Beryl said, trying to keep the note of disbelief from her voice. Nothing about Alma suggested her middle-aged body contained the soul of a lighthearted dancer.

"Here in the shop, of course." Alma swept her hand out in front of her. "The chairs all push back, and the curtains in the windows provided sufficient privacy. Milton would slip out the back door of the cabinetmaker's shop, and I would let him in the back door here so that no one would see him."

"How long had this been going on?" Beryl asked.

"A couple of months," Alma said.

"And you just felt sorry for him? You were willing to risk trouble in your own marriage to help the boy out?" Beryl asked.

"Not exactly. He paid me for the lessons," Alma said.

"From the looks of things, I should have thought that your shop and Sidney's were both doing quite well. What need would you have had for the money provided by dancing lessons?"

"Sidney is not the only one who likes to place a bet from time to time. Lately, my losses have been outpacing my wins."

For the second time during their interview, Beryl felt absolutely astonished. Edwina had always said that there was a hidden depth to the average village inhabitant, but Beryl had not quite understood how right her friend was until speaking with Alma Poole. Not only was the quite ordinary-looking woman seated next to her an expert dancer, but she also enjoyed gambling, to the point where she needed to keep her hobby from her husband.

"What do you place your bets on?" Beryl asked.

"Anything really. There's a woman in town who runs a betting pool for ladies. We didn't see any reason why the men should have all the fun, and since none of us are all that interested in most sporting events, we decided to place bets on other sorts of things, like how many times the vicar would forget his place in the sermon on Sunday morning. Or what the price of butter would be on the third Tuesday of the month, that sort of thing," Alma said.

"And you've had a losing streak of late?" Beryl said, leaning forward eagerly. "What have you lost on?"

"I lost a packet on the driving lessons," Alma said. "In a way, much of this secrecy is your fault. Yours and Edwina's, that is."

"The driving lessons?" Beryl said.

"Yes, the ones you are giving to Edwina. Someone in the pool suggested that we placed bets on whether or not Edwina would learn to drive your motorcar. The bet then became revised to lay odds as to whether or not she would take lessons at the Blackburns' garage or if you would give them to her yourself."

"And you bet she would take them from the Blackburns?" Beryl said, trying to keep annoyance from her voice.

"No. After seeing the look of terror on her face every time you whip through the village, I put down quite a bit of money betting she would never learn to drive at all," Alma said. "I had to dip into the grocery money to cover my losses."

"I'm very sorry to have contributed to your economic woes, but it seems to me that you are responsible for assuming that Edwina was not made of sterner stuff," Beryl said.

"I know better now than to bet against Edwina no matter how outlandish the proposed bet would be. I don't suppose you'd like to give me a tip on what's next for the pair of you?" Alma asked. She gave Beryl a hopeful smile.

"I don't think that's very sporting of you, and to be fair, I never have the slightest notion what will be next for Edwina and for me. That's part of the fun in life, don't you think?"

"Knowing what is next would help with my financial bottom line. It may sound crass, but I could have come out ahead if I had had any notion to put Geraldine down for the death pool," Alma said, shaking her head.

"You have a pool on who is likely to die next in the village?" Beryl said.

She thought she had never heard of anything so unseemly in all her life. Had the mild-mannered ladies of Walmsley Parva placed bets on who would be next to die at the hands of the enemy during the war or from influenza during the epidemic?

Beryl prided herself on refraining from judging her fellow woman, but it was enough to make her skin crawl.

"Absolutely. We did suspend it during the war years, as we felt it was not quite nice to make light of such sacrifice. But we've been back in full swing with it since January of nineteen twenty," Alma said without turning a hair.

"Geraldine's death has probably put an end to Milton's dance lessons too, hasn't it?" Beryl said.

"Unfortunately, he was in yesterday to let me know he wouldn't need any more lessons," Alma said.

"Yesterday? Did he say why?"

"He said Geraldine had told him that it didn't matter how good a dancer he was, as she was never going to walk out with him again, and that he would be better off saving his money."

"And he took her at her word?" Beryl asked.

"He seemed to do so."

"Was he angry at her?"

"I think he was more hurt and resigned to her refusal. He said she told him she had her heart set on a life that was far better than the one a village cabinetmaker could offer. He simply seemed brokenhearted when he told me," Alma said.

Beryl slid off the chair. She had a few things she wanted to ask Milton. Perhaps his disappointment had turned to rage. Maybe he had decided that if she was determined not to dance with him, he would be sure she didn't dance with anyone else. She also needed to confirm Alma's story about the lessons.

"Remember your promise to keep the dancing lessons to yourself. I would be obliged to you if you would refrain from mentioning the betting pool too."

"I will keep my word about the lessons if the investigation permits. But I will only hold my tongue about the betting if you answer one last question."

"Which is?"

"Who is the current front-runner in the death pool?" Beryl asked.

Alma raised a meticulously plucked eyebrow in surprise. "You are, of course."

"Me?" Beryl asked. She noticed she was clutching her gloves with a straggling hold. She forced herself to relax her grip and resisted the urge to crack her knuckles. "Surely I am not considered old enough to be next on the list."

"The pool isn't based simply on age. There are many other factors to consider, like drinking habits, driving proclivities, and the likelihood of being killed during the course of a normal day's work. You have been the safest bet since you arrived last autumn."

Chapter 39

After selecting a half dozen currant buns and one loaf of whole-meal bread, Edwina exited the bakery with her purchases tucked securely down into her wicker shopping basket. She had every intention of heading straight back to the Beeches to confer with Beryl about the status of the case. Any earlier noise Edwina had noticed on account of the investigation into Geraldine's death seemed to have died down. As she neared the telephone office, she spotted Eva Scott slipping furtively out of the building.

Edwina quickened her pace and hurriedly followed Eva up the street towards the cinema. She could always say that she was there to offer a word of condolence. Eva and Geraldine were known to be good friends since childhood, and surely the young woman was not unaffected by her death.

The truth was, Edwina was surprised at how Eva was behaving. She was usually such a sensible girl and one who was likely to follow the rules. In fact, Edwina had always noted a sort of kinship between herself and Eva Scott. She was rather surprised at the young woman's demeanor as she kept casting a glance over her shoulder as she walked swiftly up the street.

As soon as Edwina saw Eva turn into the cinema, she slowed her pace. She told herself that she was getting slightly soft and that it was high time she made more use of her bicycle than Beryl's motorcar. She checked her hat to be sure it was held firmly in place and dabbed a stray drop of perspiration from her forehead with a lace-trimmed hanky. It would be easier to intimidate Eva into telling the truth if she looked like a well-groomed and upstanding citizen.

Confident that her appearance did her credit, Edwina made her way to the glass and brass door of the Palais and pushed her way inside. Eva jumped when Edwina said her name.

All the more proof the young woman had something weighing heavily on her mind, Edwina thought as she stepped decisively towards the ticket counter and placed her shopping basket upon it.

"I wanted to stop and tell you how sorry I was to hear about your friend Geraldine," Edwina said. "What a shocking loss." Eva's lower lip wobbled, and Edwina noticed tears welling up in her blue eyes.

"She was my best friend," Eva said. "How could something like this have happened to her?"

"I'm sure Constable Gibbs is working very hard to answer that," Edwina said. "Has she been in to interview you yet?"

Eva shook her head, sending a cascade of tears running down her face. Edwina was about to look in her handbag for a clean handkerchief to offer to the young woman, but Eva dashed the tears from her cheeks with the back of her hand.

"I hope she doesn't ever get to me," Eva said.

"Most people find it distasteful to be interviewed by the police. I'm sure you will comport yourself credibly," Edwina said.

"It's just that the truth is horrible, and I don't want it to be a matter of record," Eva said.

Edwina's body tensed from head to toe. Had Eva been involved with the murder?

"Is the truth the reason that you were just sneaking out of
the telephone office?" Edwina asked.

Eva looked at her, a startled expression on her face.

"It's part of it, I suppose. In a roundabout way," Eva said.
Edwina reached across the counter and patted Eva on the back
of the hand. The girl began to sob in earnest. Edwina searched
her handbag for a clean handkerchief, then passed it to the
overwrought young woman.

"I think you had better tell me all about it," Edwina said. She
pointed to a pair of velvet-covered chairs at the far side of the
cinema lobby. Eva followed her like a small child and took a
seat where Edwina indicated.

"We argued the last time we saw each other," Eva said. "I
was envious of her, you see."

Edwina was surprised to hear that Eva had envied her friend.
Both girls were well liked, and each had a respectable job involving decent pay and some measure of responsibility. There
was only one thing that came easily to mind to cause an argument between the pair.

"Did you argue about a young man?" Edwina asked.

"Geraldine was just so much more popular with the young
men than I am. I didn't usually mind, but I hated to see the way
she treated one in particular," Eva said, dabbing her eyes with
Edwina's handkerchief.

"Which young man was that?" Edwina asked.

"Milton Boyers," Eva said. "He was head over heels for her,
and she just strung him along because she could."

"So you rather fancied Milton yourself, then?" Edwina
asked.

"I always had, but he never look twice at me when Geraldine
was around. I didn't mind so much when she seemed to be in-

terested in him, but I was angry with her when she decided he was no longer worth her time," Eva said.

Edwina wondered why Geraldine could have lost interest in young Milton. He was a decent-looking boy with a respectable job and all his limbs. After the war a specimen with so much to recommend him was not easily to be found.

Edwina could well see why Eva would be angry at the way Geraldine treated him if she was interested in a relationship with the young man herself. As much as she disliked considering it, it sounded as though Eva would benefit from Geraldine's death.

"Did she tell you that she was no longer interested in Milton, or did you simply surmise it from her actions?" Edwina asked.

"She told me herself that she was going to ask Milton to stop pestering her. That was the exact word she used. *Pestering*," Eva said.

"When was this?"

"Yesterday. She came to tell me all about it before she planned to tell him. She seemed almost proud of herself," Eva said.

"Did she give a reason why she had decided to speak to him with so much finality?" Edwina asked.

"She told me she had a far more serious suitor and that she was tired of Milton following her around like a big puppy," Eva said.

"Do you know who this new suitor was?"

"She wouldn't tell me anything about him. She just said it was serious," Eva said with a sniff.

"She didn't say anything else that gave you any idea as to his identity?" Edwina said. "It might be important to the police investigation."

"What do you mean?" Eva said.

"From what you have had to say, Milton is a strong suspect

in Geraldine's death. If you could help to offer a different suspect to the police, you might be doing him quite a favor," Edwina said.

Eva shook her head slowly. "I really wish I knew more about him, but all she would say was that she had fallen in love with his voice before she ever laid eyes on him."

"Are you sure there's nothing else you can tell me?" Edwina asked. "Did you argue about anything else?"

"I told Geraldine that she should not have kept Milton dancing attendance on her if she had another man in her life. She said that he would simply have to get over it, because she was planning to elope with the other man," Geraldine said. "She told me I should try to win him for myself, since she no longer wanted him."

Edwina thought about Geraldine's willingness to take Beryl on as a typing student. Beryl had mentioned the young woman was eager to earn a little extra money. Could a wedding have been what she was saving up for? Even an elopement would require funds. She would want a new dress at the very least. Most young women would want a great deal more.

"If that's all that you argued about, what were you doing in the telephone office? Surely you had no business in there."

"I was putting a letter in Geraldine's cubby in the office cloakroom," Eva said.

"Why would you leave her a note if you knew that she was dead?" Edwina asked.

"I wasn't leaving a letter from myself. I was returning one that she had asked me to hang on to for safekeeping. She asked me to hold on to it until she returned from Gretna Green on her husband's arm," Eva said.

"Why would you put it in the cloakroom?" Edwina asked.

"I was hoping that the police would find it and I would not have to get involved. Milton is a rather traditional young man, and I didn't think he would be interested in a girl who had been mixed up in a police investigation," Eva said.

"I'm afraid that no matter what, you are going to be central to this investigation," Edwina said. "If Milton can't see past that, you're better off without him." Edwina stood and smoothed her skirt. She left the young woman sitting alone with much to think about.

Chapter 40

Milton Boyers sat on a tall stool at a workbench with his back towards Beryl. In one hand he held a block of wood; and in the other, a piece of sandpaper. He wasn't making use of either one.

"I wondered if I might have a bit of your time, Mr. Boyers?" Beryl said.

He turned slowly, and from the red rims around his eyes, she could tell he had been crying. But were they tears of grief or tears of concern for himself? He would not be the first young man to kill a woman who had rejected his advances.

"I don't have anything else to say about Geraldine," Milton said. "If you're here to do some investigating, I don't have to talk to you."

"It's not really you I'm interested in," Beryl said. "I am actually here to confirm an alibi for Mrs. Poole. Could you do that for me?"

Milton placed the sandpaper in the woodblock on the bench and got down off the stool. He took a step towards her, and Beryl was struck once more by how desperately unhappy he looked. He seemed nothing like the vivacious young man she had often seen at the pub, laughing and joking with the other men and throwing back pints of beer.

"Did Mrs. Poole send you?" he asked.

"She knows that I'm here and has given her approval for you to speak to me, if that's what you're worried about," Beryl said. "I promised her that if her alibi had nothing to do with Hector Lomax's murder, I would keep what I knew to myself."

"So you want to know if I was with Mrs. Poole at the time of Hector Lomax's death?"

"It would be a great help if you would tell me the truth," Beryl said.

"I was in her hairdressing shop with her. She was giving me dancing lessons I no longer need," Milton said.

Beryl placed a hand on Milton's sagging shoulder. "I know that you are feeling her loss acutely, but I hope you will keep something in mind."

"What's that?" he said, looking at her with sad eyes.

"Learning new skills is never wasted. A good-looking young man like you must have plenty of young women who are eager to dance with him, especially in a small village like this one. Do your grieving and then look around and see if there's somebody who was especially nice to you while you got back on your feet," Beryl said.

With that, she turned and walked out of the workshop. As she heard the bell jangle behind her, she spotted Clifford Hammond in front of the pharmacist's shop. Right before her very eyes, she noticed him tapping out a pipe on top of the stone hitching post mounted at the side of the street.

She waited for him to turn his back and walk away before crossing the street and bending over the pipe ash. She leaned in closely and inhaled deeply. She was absolutely certain it was the same brand of pipe tobacco that had been left in the churchyard, on the headstone. She straightened and hurried to catch up with him.

Mr. Hammond was a spry man, and his long legs carried him

quickly along the street and away from the center of the village. Beryl caught up with him when he paused on a stone bridge spanning a sparkling creek. She thought once again how out of shape she had become and how embarrassed she was by her breathlessness. She would have to undertake an exercise regime immediately. Perhaps she could borrow Edwina's bicycle instead of using the automobile every time she needed to leave the village.

"Good afternoon, Mr. Hammond," Beryl said. "I assume you've heard about what happened to Geraldine Howarth."

"I don't usually go much in for gossip, but I needed to stop into the post office for some stamps, and Prudence Rathbone had to tell me all about it the minute I stepped through the door. I wouldn't have taken you for one who was similarly inclined to gossip, though," Mr. Hammond said.

"I'm not. All my questions have a point," Beryl said.

"Are you asking me if I was involved in that girl's death?" Mr. Hammond said.

"Now that you bring it up, were you?" Beryl asked.

Mr. Hammond threw his head back and roared with laughter. "You are a brazen one, aren't you?" he said. "No, I didn't have anything to do with her death. Is there something about me that makes you think I'm a raving lunatic?"

"I don't think you are raving lunatic, but I do think you know more about Hector's murder than you let on," Beryl said.

"And why is that?"

"Pipe ash. You tapped some out on a hitching post just now," Beryl said. "I watched you do it."

"I am not surprised that business is slow, but I am disappointed to realize that you are reduced to following people for such a small matter as that. Is it a crime to tap out a pipe on a hitching post in America? Because, as far as I know, it isn't here," he said.

"It's not a matter of the tapping being a crime. It's more

about what you might have done before or afterwards. The same sort of pile of ash was left on a headstone within sight of Hector's body. That was you, wasn't it?" Beryl asked.

"What if it was? There's nothing to say that happened during his murder," he said.

"That doesn't sound as though you are denying being there," Beryl said.

"I'm not denying being at the churchyard on the night Hector died. I often cut through the churchyard on my way home from the pub."

"Did you see anything suspicious? Anyone lurking around?"

"Anyone lurking around besides me?" Mr. Hammond said. "No, I had the place all to myself except for an owl who was perched in the tree above my head."

"What about the other day at Hector's house?" Beryl said.

"What about Hector's house?"

"Someone tried to set fire to a pile of clothing in one of the bedrooms at the cottage," Beryl said. "You don't happen to know anything about that, do you?"

"I didn't start a fire at Hector's house, if that's what you're asking." He crossed his arms over his chest and leaned against the bridge railing.

"What were you doing that night?" Beryl said.

"Are you saying you didn't notice me?" Mr. Hammond said, a wide smile stretching across his face. "Because I most assuredly noticed you."

Beryl felt mildly annoyed by his teasing tone.

"I assume you mean that you saw me camped out on Hector's property," she said.

"That's right. I was within sight of you most of the time that I was on his land, but you paid no attention to me whatsoever. If I were a murderer, I could have easily done away with you," Mr. Hammond said.

Beryl suddenly thought of Alma's death pool. Perhaps the

gamblers were right to lay odds on her as the favourite. She really was losing her edge.

"You are assuming I did not notice you, because I did not confront you," Beryl lied.

"I am assuming you did not notice me, because you asked me for an alibi. If you had noticed me, you would know where I had been."

Beryl felt chagrined. She hurried the conversation along to cover her discomfort. "What exactly were you doing on his land if you weren't setting fire to his home?"

"I was unblocking the stream. Like I told you before, I need the water in order to keep my crops alive. Now that Hector was no longer there, I set about taking back what was mine," Mr. Hammond said.

"Are you sure you weren't interested in getting a little more revenge by wiping his possessions off the face of the map?" Beryl said.

"I wouldn't have risked the destruction of my own property by setting fire to Hector's cottage. I never would have been inclined to do so, but certainly not during times of severe drought. Although, if I had noticed the property on fire and Hector had still been inside, I can't say I would've put it out."

"Is there anything else you can tell me about that night?" Beryl asked.

"I can tell you that when I was coming back from the field, I noticed somebody hurrying along the lane, heading away from Hector's place," he said. "I had half a mind to give chase, but since I didn't care what happened to Hector's property, I didn't bother. Maybe whoever I saw is the one who set the fire."

Chapter 41

Edwina hurried to the telephone office once more. Bold as brass, she turned the knob on the door and pushed her way inside. She looked round the small office and noticed a door on a far wall. She entered a small cloakroom and spotted half a dozen cubbies next to some coat hooks. Pushing aside her feelings of squeamishness at snooping through someone else's belongings, she began to rummage through the two occupied cubbies. The first belonged to the telephone office's only other switchboard operator, Sylvia Thorndike.

The second appeared to belong to Geraldine. Not only did it hold a pair of cream cotton gloves with her initials stitched near the cuff, but an envelope addressed to her sat beneath them. With a quivering hand, Edwina slid the envelope from the cubby and carefully eased a letter out from inside it. She unfolded the creamy sheet of paper and gazed down at the message written upon it.

There was something familiar about the handwriting. After a moment Edwina realized that the odd lower loop on the *y* was placed to the right of the stem. It was a match for the envelope addressed to Simpkins that Edwina had found at the cottage, tucked into the reading-room book. Surely there could not be two people in the village with such a peculiar trait in their handwriting, could there?

As she read the note and comprehended its meaning, she felt a wave of sadness for young Geraldine. The girl must have left the telephone office with such high hopes for her future. Hopes that had been dashed by misplaced trust. She still was not entirely sure who had penned the note, but she knew that it was likely whoever had done so had murdered Geraldine and had sent a letter to Simpkins.

She briefly considered stopping in at the police station to show the note to Constable Gibbs but thought better of it almost instantly. She must consult with Beryl before taking such measures. With any luck, her friend would still be somewhere in the village, pursuing her own line of enquiry. She folded the note back into its envelope and tucked it away safely in her shopping basket, beneath the loaf of bread. She gave the pair of forgotten gloves a last sad glance before heading out in search of her friend.

Edwina was steaming towards her like a locomotive. Surely her friend had something important to share. Beryl only hoped it was concerning the investigation. Young Jack Prentice was giving her the eye from the corner where he sold newspapers, and she wished she had a positive report to give him. She knew it was cowardly of her, but she was relieved that Edwina's arrival provided her with a good excuse for putting off speaking with him, at least for the time being.

Edwina took her by the arm and practically dragged her off towards the village green. As they sped towards a bench at the far side of the duck pond, Edwina filled Beryl in on her conversation with Nurse Crenshaw, on Eva Scott, Geraldine's plans to elope, and on the letter she had discovered at the telephone office.

Beryl took the opportunity to inform her friend about her

own progress with Alma, Milton Boyers, and Clifford Hammond. Between the two of them, it had been an eventful afternoon. When they arrived at the bench, Edwina sat down and placed her shopping basket beside her. She extracted from its depths a slightly grubby envelope and handed it to Beryl, who hastily skimmed its contents.

"I think I know who wrote this," Beryl said. "Is Simpkins still planning to have his meeting at the Beeches this afternoon?"

"I believe so," Edwina said. "Is he in any danger?"

"He very well may be. We need to convince Constable Gibbs to accompany us there immediately," Beryl said. "There's no time to waste."

"Are you going to tell me who you think the author of the letter is?" Edwina said.

Beryl told her.

With that, she grabbed Edwina by the arm, and the two of them practically ran across the green in search of the constable.

Chapter 42

It had taken some doing, but Beryl had managed to convince Constable Gibbs to return with them to the Beeches. Beryl thought it was because the constable wanted to save face in her investigations, as she had run out of leads entirely. Besides, she had said, she enjoyed watching Beryl make a fool of herself.

Beryl was inordinately relieved to arrive on the scene and to hear Simpkins's voice rumbling along the hallway. Beryl waited impatiently while Edwina fetched the envelope she had found at the cottage from its place of safekeeping in her bedroom. Then, with the constable and Edwina in her wake, she rushed down the corridor and pushed open the door of the library. Charles Jarvis, in his capacity as Simpkins's solicitor, seemed to be presiding over the meeting. He held a sheaf of papers in his hands, and his wire-rimmed glasses perched on the end of his nose.

Simpkins, Mr. Armitage, Mr. Fanhurst, and Mrs. Kimberly all sat in chairs facing him. As a group, they turned to stare as Edwina, Beryl, and Constable Gibbs rushed into the room.

"Sorry to interrupt your meeting, but I have an important question to ask of Mrs. Kimberly," Beryl said.

"What's this all about, Miss Helliwell?" Mr. Armitage asked. "We are trying to conduct an important matter of business."

"I'm sure if Miss Helliwell has brought the constable, it will be worth our time to listen to her," Charles said. He turned towards the interlopers with an expectant look on his face.

"Mrs. Kimberly, are you expecting a child?" Beryl asked.

"I can't see that that's any of your business," Mrs. Kimberly said. Beryl noticed she protectively placed both hands over her abdomen.

"It does seem rather impertinent to sling indelicate questions at Mrs. Kimberly," Mr. Fanhurst said.

"That's the thing about a murder enquiry. What's indelicate or private no longer matters. Isn't that right, Constable?" Beryl said, stepping aside and allowing Constable Gibbs to show herself more fully to the occupants of the room. Beryl watched their faces and noticed Mrs. Kimberly seemed to shrink backwards into her chair. Mr. Armitage looked amused and Mr. Fanhurst appeared annoyed by the intrusion.

"Unfortunately, privacy is one of the first casualties in any investigation. Mrs. Kimberly, please answer the question. You can consider this an official request," Constable Gibbs said.

"Not that it's anyone's business but my own, but yes, I am expecting a child. As a matter of fact, I intend to contest the will on behalf of my unborn baby. If my husband had lived to hear the news that he was about to become a father, I'm quite certain he would not have left his estate to a stranger," Mrs. Kimberly said, turning to scowl at Simpkins.

"If Colonel Kimberly had heard you were expecting, I am certain he would not have left you the small legacy that he did," Mr. Armitage said. "In fact, if he were not already dead, the shock of the news would've likely killed him."

"Are you suggesting what I think you're suggesting?" Mrs. Kimberly said.

"I'm not *suggesting* anything. I'm full on stating that it beggars belief that Colonel Kimberly could have fathered a child. I happen to know he suffered from mumps as a child, and it left him sadly unable to produce an heir," Mr. Armitage said.

"How dare you sully my character with that kind of an accusation? A woman's reputation is her most valued asset," Mrs. Kimberly said. Her voice had taken on a shrill quality, and her complexion paled.

"I think your most valued asset is your life," Edwina said. "I think you are in grave danger of losing it to the hangman's noose."

"Preposterous," Mrs. Kimberly said. "I have no idea what you're talking about."

"I'm here to arrest you for the murder of Geraldine Howarth," Constable Gibbs said, taking a step towards Mrs. Kimberly. "I hope you will come away quietly for the sake of your child. I would not want you to be injured."

"I have no idea who you are talking about. Why would I want to harm a stranger?"

"You were seen quarreling violently with Geraldine over a man not long before she died," Edwina said.

Mrs. Kimberly's eyes took on a wild look. She began to tremble from head to toe, and every trace of her posh accent faded from her voice. Edwina had been right to guess that Mrs. Kimberly came from far humbler beginnings than her current position would have indicated.

"I didn't have anything to do with the murders. It was all Rupert's idea," she said, her voice breaking. "All I did was tell Rupert about my husband making a new will."

Beryl looked over at Mr. Fanhurst, who sat in his chair as still as a mouse that suddenly realized a snake had it in its sights.

"Do you have anything to say for yourself?" Beryl asked him.

"I don't think I'm going to dignify these outrageous accusations with an answer," he said.

Mrs. Kimberly slid towards the edge of her chair, as if poised for a fight or for flight. She wheeled on her accused accomplice and pointed a finger at him.

"Rupert is the father of my child. My husband said he had discovered that we were having an affair and that was the reason that he changed his will in favor of Mr. Simpkins. When I told Rupert that we had been found out, he said he would take care of the problem," she said.

"How did he propose to take care of it?" Constable Gibbs asked.

"He sent a letter to Mr. Simpkins, asking him to meet with him on the night of the Derby. He said that it would benefit him financially to do so. He asked that Mr. Simpkins telephone him to confirm the appointment, as it was a matter of urgency and he required a quick reply," Mrs. Kimberly said.

"So that explains what had been in the envelope," Edwina said.

"I would've remembered a thing like that," Simpkins said.

"I think it's a good thing for you that you never received it, considering what happened next," Beryl said.

"Rupert told me that a man calling himself Simpkins phoned him and arranged to meet him in the churchyard here in Walmsley Parva. When the fellow showed up, Rupert hit him over the back of the head with a shovel, which he then placed next to a drunkard he found passed out near the lych-gate," Mrs. Kimberly said.

"To think Hector did me a favor, after all," Simpkins said. Beryl thought his skin looked quite grey underneath his sprinkling of stubble.

"Rupert said that if Mr. Simpkins died before my husband, there was no way he would be able to inherit. Rupert was pleased with himself at his cleverness. The next morning, when he returned from his jaunt down to Walmsley Parva, he proceeded to finish off my husband," Mrs. Kimberly said.

"It must have come as quite a shock to the pair of you that

Simpkins was alive and well and that Mr. Fanhurst had murdered the wrong man," Constable Gibbs said.

"Right angry, he was," Mrs. Kimberly said. "As soon as he heard from Mr. Armitage that Mr. Simpkins was going to be in charge of the company from now on, he determined to finish the job."

"Is that why you came to Walmsley Parva?" Edwina asked.

"Yes. Rupert suggested we hurry down here and see what could be done about Mr. Simpkins."

Mr. Fanhurst stretched his long legs out in front of him and leaned back, as though he were completely at ease. Beryl found his performance tedious. He had about him the air of a preposterously privileged young man who thought himself untouchable. The notion that he had disposed of Geraldine, Hector, and Colonel Kimberly so callously disgusted her. Realizing that he had intended to do away with Simpkins made her blood boil.

"How very droll. I never would've thought you had the wit to invent such an entertaining story," Mr. Fanhurst said. "Unfortunately, you have no proof. And everyone knows that an expectant mother is inclined towards an imbalanced mind on account of all the rollicking emotions impending motherhood brings."

"But there *is* proof that you are involved," Edwina said. "You really should have disguised your handwriting. Or at least you should not have used the same sort of handwriting on both notes."

She handed the envelope she had retrieved from Hector's cottage to Constable Gibbs, who compared it with the letter found in Geraldine's cubby.

"I hope you will note the strange formation of the lowercase *y*," Edwina said, tapping on the letter in the constable's hands.

"If you are going to murder a girl, you should not leave her a note asking her to meet you in the same spot where she is killed," Constable Gibbs said.

"Is the letter signed?" he asked. "If not, I can't see how you can connect it to me."

"I'm willing to testify in open court that you used the term *black beauty* to refer to your automobile," Beryl said. "Just like the writer of this note happened to do. Combined with Mrs. Kimberly's testimony, I would say that you would have a hard time avoiding the hangman."

"I expect you're right about that," Constable Gibbs said. "Telling the truth might go a long way to inspiring leniency from the court."

Mr. Fanhurst's shoulders slumped. He seemed to be folding in on himself. Taxed with the proof, Beryl thought it likely he saw no means of escape. She had noticed from their previous cases that oftentimes criminals felt a sense of relief after unburdening themselves, and it appeared that Mr. Fanhurst was cut from the same cloth.

"I couldn't believe it when old Armitage showed up with the news that a grubby old gardener from a rural village was about to become the head of Colonel Kimberly's company. How was I to know that the geezer who contacted me wasn't the real Simpkins?" Mr. Fanhurst said. He looked at Beryl with pleading eyes, as if to ask if she could believe his bad luck.

"Were you the one who tried to set Hector's cottage on fire?" Beryl asked.

"I ransacked the place, looking for the note, but didn't find it. Where was it hidden?"

"I think that Hector already destroyed the letter, but the envelope had been used to bookmark a page in a Zane Grey book he had borrowed from the local reading room," Edwina said. "He had used the back of it to write out a shopping list."

Mr. Fanhurst laughed. Beryl wondered if he was bordering on hysteria, but he managed to collect himself and to continue.

"Caught out by a penchant for Western novels and a tendency towards thrift. Incredible," he said.

"What I don't understand is how Geraldine was involved," Constable Gibbs said.

"I think it was probably her tendency towards eavesdropping on the telephone calls, wasn't it?" Beryl said.

"She never would have ended up the way she did if she hadn't been such a nasty little thing," he said. His face hardened a little as he spoke, and Beryl could see the ruthless monster beneath his suave and genial façade. "She heard me speaking to you outside the telephone office that day we first met Miss Helliwell."

"She recognized your voice, didn't she, from your conversation with Hector confirming the appointment to meet at the churchyard?" Beryl said.

Mr. Fanhurst nodded. "After you pulled away from the curb, she approached me and said I was just as handsome as she imagined I would be when she heard my voice on the telephone that night with Hector. She went on to say that she admired my motorcar and that she had every expectation that I would be happy to drive her away from village life."

"She blackmailed you into eloping with her?" Constable Gibbs said.

"She did. I suppose she thought she could get away with it. After all, Mrs. Kimberly was no higher in station when she married the colonel than Geraldine was. If you hadn't gone and argued with her in a fit of jealousy on a public street, we likely would have been in the clear," he said, facing Mrs. Kimberly.

"You managed to convince Geraldine to keep it a secret from even her closest friend," Edwina said. "I suppose you told her it was more romantic that way. Young girls are so susceptible to that sort of notion."

"She really wasn't very bright. I asked her to meet me behind the telephone office. At first, she was reluctant to abandon her job in the middle of her shift, but I told her no one would blame her when they realized what a fortunate match she had made. She was so gullible that when she arrived and I offered her a gift of a silk scarf as a token of my affection, she asked me to tie it on for her. The girl was practically begging me to strangle her with it."

"Did you ask her to meet you there because you knew about the sawdust pile behind the carpentry shop? Had you planned to bury her underneath it?" Constable Gibbs asked.

"No, that was just convenient. I had thought I might need to run her body farther out into the country somewhere and dispose of it. As it was, I was able to deal with the whole nuisance much more conveniently and with no waste of petrol," he said.

Constable Gibbs let out a snort of disgust. As she read the charges against both Mr. Fanhurst and Mrs. Kimberly before leading them away, she gave Beryl and Edwina a grudging look of respect.

Chapter 43

Edwina noted the marked resemblance between Simpkins and the elderly woman seated in the chair opposite her. Simpkins had asked if it would be possible to invite his aunt to call upon them at the Beeches. When he had asked her if she could shed any light on his sudden good fortune, she had mentioned it would be a story best related in person. As he was certain Beryl and Edwina would wish to hear it firsthand, he had asked Beryl if she would collect his aunt in the motorcar and bring her up to Walmsley Parva.

Clorinda Judd helped herself to a second scone and complimented Edwina on the lightness of her baked goods. Edwina accepted the compliment with good grace but found herself impatient for the older woman to get on with things. She could tell that Beryl was feeling restless too. She kept eyeing the clock and clearing her throat. Simpkins seemed to feel the same and leaned forward to urge his aunt into sharing her story.

"Aunt Clorinda, I wanted to ask you if you could tell me where my mother got this ring," he said, handing Bess's wedding ring to her.

"I wondered if you were ever going to be curious about that," his aunt said with a smile. "It certainly took you long enough."

"It's very valuable, isn't it?" Beryl asked.

"You can say that again. In fact, it was valuable enough to serve time in prison for," she said.

"Does the ring have anything to do with Simpkins inheriting from Colonel Kimberly?" Edwina said.

"In a way, I suppose it does. I expect it will come as a shock to you, Albert, to know that your father, Simpkins, was not your biological father. You are, in fact, the son of a man named William Peel," his aunt said.

Edwina felt her breath catch in her throat. The idea that Simpkins was not Simpkins was deeply startling.

"I guess that explains why no one could say where I got my ears," Simpkins said, reaching up to tug on one of his oversized lobes.

"I think it is why no one bothered to explain where they came from. I knew you were William Peel's child the moment I laid eyes on you in your bassinet."

"How did I come to have a different father than the man who claimed me?" Simpkins said.

"Your mother, Orelia, came up to London to help my mother during one of her many confinements. While she was staying with us, she met a young man who lived in the neighborhood and fell in love with him," Clorinda said.

"William Peel?" Edwina said.

"Precisely. One thing led to another, and she soon found herself in the family way. William, being essentially a man of good character, made her an offer of marriage," Clorinda said.

"So why did they not marry?" Beryl asked.

"He wanted to provide his new family with a fine start in life. Unbeknownst to Orelia, he and a couple of other lads from the neighborhood burgled a jewelry store. Sadly, they were caught, and he was sentenced to twelve years in prison," Clorinda said.

"How dreadful," Edwina said.

"It certainly was. Orelia needed to find a father for her unborn child, so she returned to Walmsley Parva and accepted the
proposal of Alfred Simpkins, who had long fancied her. They
married straightaway, and he believed Albert to be his biological son. When William was released from prison, he went in
search of his young love, but he discovered her to be happily
married to another." Clorinda took a sip of her tea.

"How heartbreaking," Edwina said.

"She was in a right state. She begged him not to ruin her marriage or to tell Simpkins that the boy was not his child. She told
him she was happily married and that her son had a good father. He agreed not to destroy their lives but convinced her to
accept a gift as a token of his affection."

"Is that how she came to have that ring?" Simpkins asked.

"Yes. She accepted it with the understanding that she would
pass it on to you for your own bride one day."

"So William Peel was Colonel Kimberly's business partner.
William must have wanted to make things up to his son, even
though he could not provide for him during his lifetime," Beryl
said.

"Not long before she died, William sent a note to Orelia,
telling her that he had made good, after all. He said he had been
keeping tabs on all of them from afar and knew that her husband had passed on. He promised that he would leave a legacy
for Albert upon his death."

"How did he come to be involved in Colonel Kimberly's
company?" Edwina asked.

"It was his prison sentence that did it, really," Clorinda said.
"The food was so bad, you see, that he smothered everything in
mustard. When he came out, he found he had developed quite a
passion for the stuff and devoted himself to perfecting a recipe."

"How did he team up with Colonel Kimberly?" Beryl asked.

"As far as I know, they just met on a train or in a pub or

some such thing. William needed an upstanding front man for his idea. He couldn't imagine that England was prepared to buy foodstuffs from an ex-convict. They made up a story about the colonel having a secret recipe passed down to him by a revered cook in India. They started the product line with chutney to help make the story seem more plausible."

"My father died many years ago. And so did William Peel. Why didn't my mother ever go to Colonel Kimberly and ask him for what she was owed?" Simpkins said.

"Your mother didn't want you to think less of her. Or to think less of your father. She said the money was simply not worth what it would cost, and she preferred to leave the whole thing well enough alone."

"So Colonel Kimberly decided to keep all of it for himself until he found out his wife was betraying him with his nephew?" Beryl said.

"I suppose so," Clorinda said.

"I hate to say so, but it sounds to me that Colonel Kimberly got what he deserved," Edwina said. "And in the end, so did Simpkins."

"It almost seems as though the money is tainted. I'm not sure that I want anything to do with it," Simpkins said. "Perhaps I would be better off not accepting such ill-gotten gains."

Edwina was aghast to think that Simpkins might not enjoy his unexpected legacy. Although she had been saddened to think that he might leave her employ, she found she was even more distressed to consider that he might not enjoy his due. She looked over at Beryl.

"Having been the recipient of many ill-gotten gains, I can tell you that they are often the nicest sort of winnings. It really doesn't matter the source of your income so long as you use it for a purpose that you can feel good about," Beryl said.

"I agree with Beryl," Edwina said. "There are any number of charitable causes that could use a generous donation. The church roof fund, for instance."

"I shouldn't want to look as though I were getting above myself," Simpkins said. "They might put a plaque up or something in the church, and that would just be embarrassing."

"There's no reason you would have to announce that you are the one to make the donation," Beryl said. "It could be completely anonymous. You could stuff a bunch of notes into an envelope and slip it through the letter box at the vicarage when no one was looking."

Simpkins leaned back in his chair and closed his eyes. Edwina would have thought he had fallen asleep from the excitement, except for the fact that he drummed his fingers on the arms of his wingback chair. When he opened his eyes once more, he had a mischievous grin on his face.

"I think I would like to use the money to follow in my father's footsteps," he said.

"In which way?" Edwina asked.

"Which father?" Beryl said.

"I think I would like to follow William Peel's example and invest my income, at least a portion of it, by becoming a silent partner in a worthwhile company."

"And which company would that be?" Beryl asked.

"Why, your private enquiry agency, of course," he said, with a giant grin spreading across his face.

Edwina felt a wave of disbelief wash over her. It had been one thing to consider that Simpkins might be far wealthier than she could ever hope to be. It had been at least as troubling to think that he might head off in a completely new direction and no longer spend any time at the Beeches. It was even more distressing to consider that he might have an equal say in her adventure.

In her vast experience with Simpkins, she had never known him to be silent about anything. Not about the proper double digging of asparagus beds, the correct manner of overwintering dahlia bulbs, or the need for vigilance when deadheading petunias. She could no more imagine him keeping silent about the day-to-day running of a private enquiry agency than he had been about his gardening duties. It had been difficult enough to adjust to the idea of becoming a businesswoman in the first place. Sharing such duties with her jobbing gardener was unthinkable.

"I think that's an absolutely marvelous idea. Imagine all that we could do with a little bit of capital to really set us up," Beryl said. "What do you say, Ed?"

Edwina felt the eyes of the other three bearing down on her. She did not wish to insult Simpkins, but it was the sort of proposition she felt required much mulling over. He seemed to recognize her hesitancy.

"I can see that you need a little time to think it over. But here's a notion to sweeten the pot. The very first thing I would want to pay for would be driving lessons for Miss Edwina at the Blackburns' driving school. After all, I expect you would like to learn to drive if the lessons weren't quite so harrowing."

Edwina felt her heart give a little leap. Perhaps Simpkins wouldn't be such a terrible partner, after all.

Author's Note

One of the very best parts of my job is the research that leads to the creation of the stories. I begin each of my historical mysteries by researching real events that occurred at the time and in the area in which the story is set. When something tickles my fancy, I dig around until I have satisfied my curiosity. I noodle and stir and tuck away each idea next to the last until I have enough to propel me into the actual writing.

While most of this book was constructed from imagination, there are some parts of it anchored firmly in reality. Sometimes real events inspire large parts of a book, and other times they provide small details and texture concerning life in another era. This book owes more to the daily life details than it does to major trends or happenings. I hope you will have enjoyed reading about them as much as I enjoyed sharing them with you.

June 1, 1921, was the first time the results of the Derby Stakes were broadcast live over the wireless. It opened a whole new era of possibilities for both those who placed wagers and those who ran the books. A British thoroughbred named Humorist was the second favourite for the race but came in first to win. Sadly, despite his string of early successes and his future filled with bright promise, he died of tuberculosis later that same month.

The drought mentioned in the story was sadly real and caused much grief. This book begins on June 1, and as a result, takes place during the hundred-day drought that ended on June 25, 1921. Walmsley Parva is located in Kent, a thriving small-fruits region of England. As an avid gardener myself, I found my mind wandering easily to murder when considering the ways a lack of water would damage my own trees, shrubs, and flowering plants.

Fortunately for Edwina, as of 1919, Beryl's beloved automobile, a Rolls-Royce Silver Ghost, came equipped with an automatic starter. I am quite certain Beryl would not have convinced Edwina to try driving if something as unseemly as a crank starter was involved.

Edwina was unusually fortunate to have access to a hairdresser well versed in the art of cutting hair. In 1921 many women who wished to lop off their long locks were forced to take their trade to a barbershop, where there was no assurance their business would be welcome. Men were known to gather around and jeer at women who made so bold as to ask for such services.

The social ramifications for women who took the plunge and cut their hair could also be daunting. Friends and family were not always supportive of what was widely believed to be an unfeminine spectacle. Still many women, like Edwina, braved extraordinary criticism, and before the decade was out, had helped to normalize the unthinkable. I, for one, am extremely grateful!

Acknowledgments

I consider myself very fortunate to have so many people in my life who help make my books possible. It is always such a pleasure to be able to thank them.

I am always grateful for the support and enthusiasm shown for Beryl and Edwina by my editor, John Scognamiglio. I also want to express my thanks to all the other supportive people at Kensington who do so much to send the books out into the world in the best possible light.

Thanks go out to my agent, John Talbot, who was the first champion of the series. I would also like to mention my cherished blog mates, The Wicked Authors, Sherry Harris, Julie Hennrikus, Edith Maxwell, Liz Mugavero and Barb Ross. I don't think I would have made it here without all of you. If by some miracle I had, it would not have been nearly as much fun.

I want to thank Susan Van Kirk for generously sharing her knowledge of bridge. I also wanted to thank my friend and neighbor Linda Richards for her willingness to humor me by answering my impertinent questions about all things British.

I am privileged to have such a supportive and accommodating family. My sisters, Barb Shaffer and Larissa Crockett know just when to call to ask how things are going. They also are kind enough not to take offense when I forget to answer the phone. My mother is willing to wade through knotty questions of grammar with me at the last minute. My children, Will, Max, Theo, and Ari provide encouragement, good humor and patience, especially when deadlines draw near.

And finally, I owe a lasting debt of gratitude to my husband, Elias Estevao, who cheerfully slays all the dragons.